# IT WAS ALL THE CAT'S FAULT

A ROMANTIC COMEDY

ELIZABETH SAFLEUR

This book is a work of fiction. Names, characters, places, and incidents are the product of the author's imagination or are used fictitiously. Any resemblance to actual events, locales, or persons, living or dead, is coincidental.



Elizabeth SaFleur LLC
PO Box 6395
Charlottesville, VA 22906
Elizabeth@ElizabethSaFleur.com
www.ElizabethSaFleur.com

Edited by Trenda Lundin, Chas Patrick
Proofed by Claire Milto
Cover design by Cosmic Letterz

**ISBN:** 978-1-949076-44-8

# FOREWORD

This book is dedicated to our animal, bird and, yes, even our reptile friends who have given us more joy than we probably deserve.

Dear Readers,
Please forgive my editorial liberty in the following pages. For instance, if anyone actually finds bandages graced with Thor's image, let me know?

*Callum*, I love you. I'm sorry I featured a feline friend before you. You'll forgive me, right?*

**See the Westie (who owns me) on my social channels. He believes you only follow me there for him.*

# 1

Thor howled like it was Eve's fault he found himself lost inside the wall of the laundry room.

"It's okay, baby. I'm getting help. Promise." She pressed her hand against the wall and shifted the phone to her other ear. *Oh, someone, please, answer.* "Pick uuuup."

Her cat, who she loved more than life, screeched yet another profanity at her. Who could blame him? The words that would come out of her mouth if she ended up behind some icky old house wall would shock Lucifer.

"Thor, listen to the song." She pressed the phone against the place where he might have settled. The elevator-music rendition of *Bridge Over Troubled Waters,* which must have been plumbing humor or something, drifted out of the earpiece. "See? You're gonna be all right."

Thor mewled behind the drywall.

Tomorrow, she was leaving a scathing review of that YouTube tutorial on how to hook up her dryer vent. They said a little space between the hose thing and the wall was perfectly fine. *Fine my behind.*

She brought the phone back to her ear, leapt up from her

crouch, and began to pace. Did no one honor their "call us anytime, day or night" promises anymore? "I swear, if someone doesn't answer—"

"Flow 'n Go Guys emergency line." A gruff voice replaced the music.

*Thank God.* The two handymen she knew weren't answering because who would at three a.m.? So a plumber could help, right? "Hi, uh, I know it's late and I'm not sure you can do anything—"

"What's the trouble, ma'am?"

"It's my cat. He got behind the dryer and he won't budge. I even brought out the good treats and still…"

The man laughed in her ear. "He's in the machine or the wall?"

Funny, huh? "The wall." Her hand went straight to her hip. For an organization that made her listen to *Bridge Over Troubled Water* eight times in a row, he had a bit of nerve for his response.

"Is he hurt?" The male voice sobered.

Thor, her great explorer, growled low. "I don't think so. I think he's just… lost." She sat down next to the place where he was scratching inside the wall. "It's okay, Thor. Mama's right here, and the nice Mr. Flow 'n Go guy is going to get you out." She cupped her hand around the phone. "You can get him out, right?"

"Address?"

All the air flew out of her chest in relief as she recited her name and location.

"I'll be there in about twenty minutes. You got any tuna fish? Open a can. That would lure my dog from six blocks away in a heartbeat."

"Huh. Smart. Thank you. And thank you much for coming over so late."

"No problem, ma'am."

She jumped to her feet and killed the call.

In her pantry, she moved boxes of Minute Rice and dusty cans of beans around the shelf. "Tuna. Who doesn't have tuna?" Obviously, she didn't.

A red, flat box toward the back caught her eye. "Sardines in oil." Where had that come from? A sticky note was affixed to the top. *"The new superfood,"* it read in her mother's handwriting.

She'd rather die of old age, thank you very much.

But a quick check of the expiration date revealed it was still good. Maybe it could work to lure her baby out for a late-night snack. Or early morning. *Whatever.*

To think thirty minutes ago she'd been enjoying *The Avengers* on her laptop like any civilized single girl who couldn't sleep and needed some dream material. The next thing she knew, her cat was crying out downstairs like they were under home invasion by the trickster god Loki.

She brought the *superfood* over to the kitchen counter, popped the tab top, and her head jutted back immediately from the smell. "Oh, God. You owe me, Thor," she called toward her laundry room.

Breathing through her mouth, she dumped a few of the little fish into a cereal bowl. Thor's mewling started anew, and she picked up the pace. She whirled, and the open tin tipped over the edge of the counter.

"Gah." Stinky oil and the rest of the fish splashed down her robe, sweatpants, and slippers to finally land on her brand-new daisy rug in front of the sink and the cheap vinyl flooring she would replace as soon as she could find someone to do it, which may be never given how her house renovations were evolving.

Thor howled again—much louder.

"I'm coming! With deconstructed fish pieces." She kicked

off her slippers only to land her feet in slippery oil, because why not make things worse all around?

Rug and slippers would need to be hauled outside first or she'd faint from the smell alone.

She grabbed some paper towels to mop up the disgusting goo from the floor and the bottom of her feet but paused. Silence blanketed the house. *Crap.*

Holding the bowl as far away from her face as possible, she rushed the dish to the laundry room—more like a "nook" that really should have been a second bathroom in this tiny bungalow.

She set the bowl down and started doing that stupid *"here, kitty kitty"* call that Thor had never responded to in his life. "Sardines. And you can have whatever is left on the floor, too."

No scratching, no mewling, no purring, no sound at all came from behind the wall. His palate was offended? Wait until he got a whiff of the kitchen.

She sat down on the floor and knocked on the wall. "You in there, baby? Thor? Answer Mama." A furtive scratching sound along with a long howl responded.

Her eyes stung. Screw waiting for the plumber guy. She had an ax somewhere, and that wall was coming down if needed.

As she sprang up from her crouch, blood rushed to her head. The room shifted, tilted. She grabbed the door jamb but the fish smell pressed in on her. No time to faint. Who eats sardines anyway? Her stomach rolled with nausea and she swallowed hard. She didn't have time to throw up.

She sucked in a long breath—through her mouth. She was *going in.*

She darted to the sink, dropped to her knees which instantly slid on fish oil, and opened the cabinet door. Something had to be in here to breach drywall or plaster or whatever it was made of, but *noooo.* Finding nothing of value, she'd have to run to the icky, unfinished basement where surely, there was something that would help. Of course, the entrance to said basement was outside.

A quick glance at her bare feet made her resolve to keep shoes by the back door from now on. Right now, she could either waste time running upstairs for her tennies or accept she might break her foot or perhaps die from blood poisoning because she'd step on a rusty nail.

A low growl sounded from the laundry area. On second thought, how hard would it be to punch a hole in the wall? Before she could try a swift kick to test its strength, her doorbell rang.

Thank the plumber gods.

When she opened her front door, a tall mountain of a man topped with blond hair, shining green eyes, and a scruffed-up, chiseled jaw greeted her. This guy couldn't be a Flow 'n Go Guy. Plumbers weren't this handsome. Or she'd been lied to by every sitcom she'd ever seen.

He frowned and peered around the doorframe to check the door number. "Do I have the right address for an Eve Chatham?"

It was almost four a.m. This guy could be a male mirage, a hallucination from lack of sleep and fish fumes.

"I'm Brent Shadwell? Flow 'n Go Guys?" He lifted a big box with a long, coiled line in his hand.

"Yes, of course. Come in." She gestured him in. "Thanks for coming." Her hand shot out, an automatic reaction. He set down the big box and accepted her handshake, which was a little slippery thanks to the oil coating her palm.

He glanced down at their joined hands, let go fast, and wiped his palm on his jeans.

"Oh, sorry. No tuna, so I had a sardine incident." What a way to make a first impression, but at least they'd both reek.

Kind of like both people ordering food with garlic in a restaurant. Thou shall not have bad breath without the other having it, too.

She swiped her hand on her robe and gestured for him to follow her. "He's this way. He's alternating between silence and total freak-out."

"Sounds like a cat. Let me guess. Through the dryer vent?"

"This has happened before?"

"You wouldn't believe it."

It took all of five seconds to get to the laundry area. She pointed to the washer. "He's behind there."

The guy sniffed and glanced around. Probably looking for a safe spot to set his equipment down because the whole place smelled like a fishery—and not a good one that might pass inspection, either.

"I took your advice." She toed the bowl. "Didn't work."

"Guess his palate is more sophisticated than my lab." His smile was entirely too bright —and awake—for almost four a.m.

"I don't understand it. Thor usually eats anything."

"If they get really scared, it doesn't always work." He set his stuff down closest to the far wall.

*Great.* Fish destruction for nothing. "You been pulling cats out of walls long?"

"You're my second this month."

"Seriously?" That relieved her for some reason—like maybe these things didn't just happen to her. "Yeah, well, it's been one thing after another here."

Brent yanked the dryer and washer away from the wall in a loud screech. "You were smart to call us. The old pipes in these structures require a delicate touch."

Thor growled his displeasure, probably at the scraping sounds Brent made with the washer—or maybe from hearing a male voice in his territory.

Brent chuckled. "Yeah, he's back there all right."

"It's okay, baby," she called toward the wall.

"It will be." Brent straightened and looked down at her. His eyes softened. "Before we get started, you need to know something. I have never lost an animal like this, and I promise you he'll be fine."

Her heart squeezed at the kindness in his voice, and she took in a long breath. "Thanks. You can probably tell I'm a little freaked."

Brent nodded once. "Quite understandable." He stared back at the dryer. "You might have mice. He could have followed one in."

"What?" She glanced around her feet, her gaze darting to the corners of the space. If anything furry peeked out at her… That would be the icing on the house's to-do cake.

He peered around the dryer at the big tube going through the wall. "Wow, that's some shoddy work." He clucked and shook his head, a mop of blond hair falling in his eyes.

"Thanks a lot." Weeks & Sons Renovations wanted $600 to basically stick a big plastic tube in the wall, which was akin to highway robbery. Trying it herself was smart financial management.

He swung his gaze to her. "YouTube?"

"I'll have you know they have a lot of good tutorials there." She had to at least try even if it did end up with Thor's great wall exploration.

He got down on his knees and opened a strange, computer-like box. It didn't take long for him to insert a camera snake into the wall. "You're lucky this wall isn't plaster and lathe. Must have been replaced at some point."

She probably should have checked that before thinking she could kick her way in.

"So, Thor, huh?" He tapped on a monitor. "You a fan?"

"Uh, sure. Thor is big and hunky like…" Jesus, she was an

idiot, describing her cat like that. Well, it was ridiculous-o'clock in the morning. No one could expect her to be articulate.

He peered at his screen and tsked. "I'll be damned. Copper pipes. That's amazing." His T-shirt rose up as he fed more of the snake into the wall. Tanned skin on his back, which she had no business noticing. But then his forearms flexed. Oh, *those* were worth noticing.

She curled her lips between her teeth to keep her mouth from gaping because seriously, this guy turned the cliché plumber on its head gasket.

*Stop.* She'd made a deal, and she was sticking with it—no getting googly-eyed over anyone until her Bachelor of Arts graduation certificate was framed and hung on the wall.

So what if getting her degree happened a few years later than anticipated. She'd have it at the end of the year at the ripe old age of twenty-nine. But if she kept up her studying habits, she'd graduate with a 4.0 perfect average, summa cum laude, like she had in high school. She wouldn't break her winning streak for anything or anyone.

Brent's gaze swung her way. "Two yellow eyes? You sure about the Thor resemblance because your guy looks a little short." There went his snicker again.

Please, spare her the plumber humor. She still did that stupid snort-laugh thing she'd been trying to break—another goal of hers. "Wait until you see him. You'll revise…"

As if on cue, Thor let out a series of chirps.

One side of Brent's lips lifted in a smirk. He then eased back and lifted a small drywall saw—something she never, ever thought she'd recognize but, again, YouTube. She was now quite familiar with power equipment.

"This is going to sound scary and it's going to mess up your drywall, but I can put it back in, patch it up. You'll need to paint it."

"Please. Whatever it takes." If he had to rip all the walls down to get to her fur baby, she'd help him do it. She'd also double her donation to the Catopia rescue organization in Thor's name after tonight.

She grasped the guy's arm—his very firm forearm. "But you're not going to hurt him, are you?" A flash of that traumatizing magician show she'd been dragged to at age eight flashed in her mind. To this day, the fake screams as the girl was sawed in half rang in her ears.

"Not intending to hurt him. He's up against a beam about six inches away from where I'll be cutting. Trust me." He'd softened his voice once more, probably a learned habit due to years of working with distressed women who'd tried to do their own home repairs and lost their furry children behind walls.

She nodded and covered her ears. She shrank back as drywall dust flew in all directions as the saw did its work.

Once a small square was punched out of the wall, Brent reached in and extracted a mass of fur and rigid limbs. That's when the screeching truly started.

"Wow. A Maine Coon." He winced but lifted Thor high and placed him in her arms.

Thor began to struggle immediately. She brought the bowl of sardines to his face. His freak-out morphed into a full attack on the contents. "Thor, you and I are having a talk about this later."

"That work?"

Brent had a warm smile, and she found her own cheeks lifting in response. "Not in the last ten years. Oh, you're bleeding!" Red dots had bubbled up on his arm.

"Comes with the job. He probably smelled my dog on me." He rose from his crouch. "It's no big deal."

Blood ran in rivulets and dripped onto his jeans.

"I have bandages. Stay." She put Thor down, and he went

straight for the bowl. It scraped along the floor toward the corner with his enthusiastic food raid. Maybe now the place would smell a bit better.

"Yes, ma'am." Brent grinned.

Her cheeks rose—again. This guy had one of those smiles that demanded a returned one. She scooted off to find bandages in the bathroom down the hall.

She only found her Avengers-themed band-aids in the medicine cabinet—an impulse purchase the day she'd moved in and got her first renovation battle wound. *Just great.* But a girl had to have a reward when she attempted her own house repairs and injuries happened—like how the screwdriver had slipped as she'd attempted to put in a new back door door-knob and she stabbed herself. She'd needed two Thor bandages over her thumb to stop the bleeding.

How mortifying was it going to be to hand Brent a Hulk or Iron Man band-aid? She could pretend she didn't find any, but who didn't have basic first aid on hand?

She pulled out more items from the cabinet. Three measly regular band-aids were all she needed—and didn't find. All right, which one of the Avengers would be the least humiliating?

Why was she caring what he thought at all?

She grabbed three Hulks and a tube of Neosporin. If Brent asked about them, she'd pretend she had a nephew who loved The Hulk the best. She was not parting with her last Thor band-aid. They were a rare find, and she was saving it for a special injury, which was appropriate. Thor displayed the greatest loyalty of them all and, therefore, deserved the most love and special circumstances.

When she returned to Brent, he was cranking off the water. He wiped his hands on a towel. "Your guy there seems to have recovered. He's helping with clean up."

Thor's little tongue lapped at the oily floorboards in front of the sink. "It's the least he can do."

Chuckling, he sat down at her kitchen table, took out a pen from his pocket, and began to write on a yellow receipt pad.

"Thank you so much again for coming out at this hour." She handed him the three bandages, which he took, but he waved off the Neosporin offering like a typical male.

He glanced down at them. "I prefer Iron Man, myself." He leaned back in his chair and his grin returned. "But let me guess your fave. It's the long flowing hair, isn't it?"

The back of her neck prickled and heat filled every inch of her body. "That's not the *only* reason."

She plopped down in the seat across from him. A weird emotion snuck up on her. The sickening smell of sardines mixed with lack of sleep the last few days caught up to her in a rush. Her eyes misted—out of nowhere.

"Hey, you. Thor's going to be fine." Brent touched her arm. Ooo, calloused fingers that sent a zing up her spine.

She pulled her arm away or she really would have cracked. "I know. Thanks to you. And I'm fine." He was being so nice, and it would be such poor manners to dissolve into a weepy puddle in front of him.

"You sure? You look—"

"I'm all good. Here." She plucked the band-aids from the table and gestured for him to put his arm on the table. Having a job would stem the stupid tears that she could shed later when she was alone. Just her and her cat and fish remnants on the floor…

He placed his huge forearm—and seriously, it was huge—on the surface, and she stretched the Hulk over the scratches on his skin. Let the record show his muscles barely moved. Guess plumbing repairs were hard work.

She wadded up the wrappers and tossed them in the little trash can behind her. "How much do I owe you?"

"Nothing. We do pet rescue for free." He handed her the yellow receipt which, sure enough, had nothing but zeroes listed.

"Seriously?" A thrill ran straight through her at all the big, curly zeroes. "I might have to frame this." Tonight was the first free thing she'd got when it came to this house. "Please. Let me give you something."

He slapped the lid shut on his monitor thing by his feet. "Let me fix the wall and your vent for you. I can do it for, say, seventy-five bucks."

"You're kidding. Nothing related to this house has cost anything under five hundred dollars." Of course, all her renovations were going to be worth the hassle someday.

The second she'd stepped inside 331 Magnolia Street, she'd known this was her home. First, being able to say "I live on *Mag-noh-leeya*" sounded too cool. Like she lived in a *Gilmore Girls* episode or something.

Plus, the first time she'd entered the house, her dad going along for support, it had welcomed them.

The wood floors had creaked a hello as she strode through the empty space, and light had streamed in, warming the wood floors to a yellow glow. The leaded glass in many of the windows, all the nooks and crannies, and built-in shelves and drawers, however, had sealed her decision. No one paid attention to those kinds of details anymore, and the house needed her. It was so run down her heart hurt for it. She'd hate for this place—and its history—to be bulldozed for yet another McMansion that could blow over in a strong enough wind.

He glanced around. "These Arts and Crafts bungalows are nice. How long have you had the place?"

"Three weeks." Her first big purchase of her life—a fantastic investment, her father had said.

"Not many of these left. You scored a find. Like people, it just needs a little love."

At the word "love," a strange warmth spiraled inside her. She felt exactly the same way.

He cast his eyes down on her. "I gotta say, I'm impressed you tried to do some things here…" he glanced around, "for yourself first."

His take on her was unusual—for sure. Most people who learned she worked, went to school, and was trying a home renovation called her straight-up crazy. "Most people say I've lost my marbles." She made circles near her temples.

"So, I shouldn't turn my back on you and my drywall saw."

*Snort.* "I wouldn't know how to work it."

"Ah, saved." He moved toward the hallway to leave. "I can come back, say, Saturday? Keep the door closed until then. And sorry, fixing the wall isn't free."

"I wouldn't expect it to be. Saturday is perfect." She miraculously had the day off from her two jobs *and* school, which was starting a new semester tomorrow. It didn't matter how she showed up. Day one of any class was always the easiest, and she could sleepwalk through all the welcome lectures.

He paused at the front door. "I'll give you my private cell phone number. If he gets back in the wall before I can patch it, call me." He set his stuff down and patted his shirt. "I don't have a business card with my direct number on it."

She pulled out her cell phone from her robe pocket. "I'll put it right in."

He recited his number and she added him as "HFGG" for Hot Flow 'n Go Guy because why not? A) it was true, and B) it was fun to have a secret. If anyone would ask but who would see?— she could say the "H" stood for handy. Kind of like Iron Man.

She tapped the number. "I'll call it. Make sure I got it right."

The Scorpions' "Rock You Like a Hurricane" sounded from his jeans pocket. More plumbing humor, probably. He pulled his phone out and glanced at it. "Number obtained."

After re-pocketing it, he lifted his things, and they stood there for an awkward minute, staring at one another. He had those eyelashes that were completely wasted on a man— thick and dark, framing his eyes. The green color stood out even more.

One of his eyebrows lifted. "You sure you're okay?"

"Fine. Peachy."

He sucked in a long breath and glanced down at Thor, who sat at his feet. He had one paw up to his face, delicately licking the pad, his tail twitching behind him. "How about you? You good?"

A snuffle left her nose, and she slapped her hand to her mouth. Had she always been this awkward around men? Maybe. *Yes.*

She picked up Thor, and Brent ran his hand down his head, his fingertips coming dangerously close to touching her. Thor, amazingly, tolerated being manhandled. "Big guy, take care of Eve here. See you this weekend." Brent then winked and strode out.

As soon as she closed the door on him, Thor darted straight upstairs, probably to bury himself under the covers on her bed as if nothing had happened.

She peered out the side window. Brent hauled his equipment into a large white truck.

A tug formed in her belly. Who was she kidding? It was more of a lurch. Plenty of guys at school chatted her up, even a few asked her out. She didn't bat an eyelash at any of them. But this guy… had something.

*Tools, Eve. He has tools.*

She laughed at herself and turned away from the window. She should sleep, but her body thrummed like a nest of hummingbirds had taken residence inside her.

A few hours was all she needed before getting to the Peppermint Sweet shop by noon. Perhaps she'd scrub the kitchen floor, see if that wore her out. There also, as always, was a pile of laundry to do—and her robe and sweatpants could use some bleach.

Instead, after she scrubbed her hands of any fish oil, she abandoned her stinky clothes in the washer to deal with tomorrow and snuggled up with Thor and her laptop in bed. Together, they re-watched her favorite scene from *Rush*—the most underrated Chris Hemsworth movie of all time.

"Look, Thor." She pointed to the screen.

He purred loudly, eyes closed, not appreciating the nude chest scene *at all*.

"Can you see the resemblance?" Her mind hadn't been playing tricks on her. Hottie Flow 'n Go Guy Brent did look like Hottie Hemsworth a bit. *A lot.*

"Remember, we might have noticed him, but we have our hands full with two jobs, school, and a house that needs a little attention, right?" That's what Brent had said—it just needed love. There was no time for noticing men, for shallow flirtations.

"But we like his power tools, don't we?"

Thor stretched in answer.

Had it come down to this—confiding in her cat about men and power tools? Why, yes, it had. And tonight's encounter was simply going to be an interesting story she'd tell someone someday. How her cat got stuck in the wall.

How a man who resembled an action hero swooped in and… *Scratch those thoughts right now.*

She had a deal to uphold—one struck long ago, and it was unbreakable.

But now she'd move to a bigger question. Was her vibrator charged?

# 2

Scarlett cranked the filter handle of the espresso machine. "You look like death. Pull another all-nighter?"

Eve stifled her third yawn since arriving at Peppermint Sweet two minutes ago. "Good day to you, too."

"Want me to ruin this espresso so you can have it?" Scarlett inclined her chin down at the cup.

"You know me so well."

"Oops." She batted her eyelashes toward Greta who was pushing open the kitchen door with her butt. "I need to make it again."

Greta smiled and snapped her with a towel. "You make my customer mad, I'll charge you both."

Thank the gods—both real and mystical—for the owner of Peppermint Sweet. She let them swipe muffins from the long glass counter and never charged them. She never grumbled if Eve was a few minutes late running between her place and Horace's Dry Cleaning, her other job. And she often let her bolt from her shift a few minutes early if she had a test to study for.

She downed the espresso and threw on her work

uniform. The red and white stripes of the baker's apron were so clichéd. At least she got to wear black jeans and a T-shirt underneath.

"Up all night studying?" Scarlett placed two espressos on a tray. "Table six, by the way. Let's give them two cookies for free since they had to wait an extra sixty seconds." She rolled her eyes. "This one-click culture is killing me."

"No studying. New classes start tonight. But I was up all night. Thor went exploring and ended up in the wall in the laundry room. Had to call Flow 'n Go Guys to get him out. And guess what?" She slipped two cookies into one of the waxed paper envelopes. "The guy was kind of hot and I have his number. I'm seeing him Saturday for—"

Scarlett's mouth dropped open in a loud gasp. "You're going to get naked with the Flow 'n Go man? Girl. *Friend.* Is this wise? Are you falling off the wagon?" Her hand flew to her mouth. "Don't tell me. He's..." she dropped her voice and glanced around, "worthy of breaking your self-imposed sexual exile?"

"I'm not in exile. I have my priorities straight." Scarlett wasn't wrong about her sexual Siberia, and oh, how Eve wished she was, but she was struggling to keep up with working, school, and a house that had too many issues, all hidden from—or overlooked by—the home inspector. She was so close to finally getting her bachelor's degree, the first step to following her father's business footsteps negotiating big merger deals.

Scarlett waggled her eyebrows but then straightened and snapped her fingers. "Spill. I need more info on him if you're going to get *nekkid* with him."

Oh, come on. "Who said anything about getting naked? He saved my cat and now has to patch the wall. But..." she hushed her tone to a whisper, "he looks like Chris Hemsworth."

Scarlet's eyes flew open. "He *is* worthy. What's his butt like? Did he show crack? Never mind. Number, please." Rating men's body parts was Scarlett's favorite hobby.

"At least a twelve." It could have been higher because one should never underestimate the beauty of a stellar butt—even if she wasn't getting near said butt. Because, no, he wasn't worthy of breaking her focus. Not when she was this close to fulfilling her promise to herself—and her dad.

Scarlett waggled her finger at Eve. "Shut. Up. Show me his picture." When Eve didn't move fast enough, Scarlett stuffed her hand inside Eve's apron and started fishing for her phone.

"Hey, quit trying to cop a feel." She laughed and spun away. "I didn't get a picture."

Instead, dreams of Thor wielding power tools filled the entire four hours of sleep she'd managed to catch. It was a warning: keep your eye on the Bachelor of Business Administration ball, the only *singular* ball she should be watching. That, and keeping the roof standing over her head at home.

Scarlett placed her hands on her hips. "Have I taught you nothing? You didn't pretend to take a selfie and capture a snap? Or start shooting away with your phone in your hand? You gotta do this. I mean, what if he turned out to be a serial killer and we found your dead body clutching your phone? Then we could identify him."

She dipped her chin. "Been reading too many murder mysteries lately? He's not a serial killer. He was… nice."

Greta cleared her throat. "Ladies. Before the coffee is cold, please."

Eve lifted her tray and turned. Her phone buzzed in her pocket, but it would have to wait.

Maybe she should have tried to get a picture of HFGG, but then that would make her as bad as men judging women by their looks. It was fine to do that to celebrities—came with the territory—but a real person like Brent?

Yeah, she could have tried anyway. Maybe he'd even be flattered. He had to have tons of women fainting at the sight of him. Brent surely had been the most popular guy in his school. Then, later, he was the guy everyone wanted to hang out with at happy hour after work, too. He oozed all the prerequisites—kind, good-looking, competent, funny. In other words, cool. The X-factor. The Thor superhero vibe.

The kind of guy that always went for girls like her sister, Persephone. In fact, he likely was returning to a woman like that right now—all long, glossy hair, with a perky smile. He couldn't be single.

After delivering the espressos, she dropped the empty tray on the counter and yawned—loudly.

"Eve, doll." Greta snapped her fingers in front of her. "You pull an all-nighter or something? You're looking a little dreamy."

Perhaps she did look like death after all. "Sort of. House stuff again." And little shut-eye.

"Down another espresso, and once you deliver this pie to that cute couple in the window seat, help me with the muffins in the back?"

She did what Greta said, but the extra activity didn't help one bit. She still yawned every few minutes, and she didn't have the energy to look at her phone when it buzzed with yet another call. The spate of robocalls lately were killing her.

The day dragged, with spurts of customers and then nothing—her least favorite coffee shop rhythm. Hours ticked by like years.

Scarlett pulled herself up onto the counter and flounced her long paisley skirt around her. "Man, it's like a funeral parlor in here today."

Eve chuffed. "If Greta finds you up there…"

"She ran to the bank." Scarlett swung her feet and twisted her mane of curly hair into a big ponytail. "What's your new semester going to bring? Learning anything totally useless that you'll be rewarded for in the corporate world?"

Eve's fingers shook as she took another sip of her fourth espresso. "Lots of things. But I'm doing something really cool this semester. Taking a home remodeling and repair course for construction management."

Scarlett arched an eyebrow. "That's cool?"

"It's going to be super fun." Her cup rattled when she lowered it to the countertop. She was practically mainlining caffeine at this point. "It covers all the basics of different power tools. Generators, chainsaws, circular and drywall saws." She ticked each one off with a finger. "And other basic do-it-yourself repairs so I'd at least know what to look for if I have to hire someone."

Lordy, let them get to plumbing at some point. The next time Thor decided to take a detour into another wall in her house, she would get him out herself—and fast.

Scarlett scrunched up her face. "Only you would be excited about construction. Except, if the guys are as hot as your plumber guy last night, maybe I'll go home and break something. Or go into that line of work instead of writing."

"How's the Great American Smut Novel coming? Any closer to leaving the glamorous world of Peppermint Sweet?" Eve had yet to see any of the pages, but she had to give Scarlett two big thumbs up for following her dream.

Scarlett waggled her eyebrows. "Still trying to convince my heroine to jump my hero's bones already. But it'll come. I shall not be deterred." She slapped her lap with both hands.

"Good for you." Her friend's focus was probably why they were besties—neither would be shaken from their goals even though a great ass often turned Scarlett's head.

Eve was more of a butt window-shopper—sometimes

she'd buy into its promises but most often not because nothing looked as good at home as it did out in the wild. She'd rather have something that couldn't walk out the door —like real skills, her own bank account, *real estate*.

Scarlett tapped her lips with a finger. "You sure I can't convince you to jump the plumber? I need some inspiration."

Like Eve would tell her anything if she had. Think again. "I'd rather go to renovation class."

Scarlett slowly shook her head. "Only you, Eve. *Only* you."

Eve shrugged. "If I'm going to own a fixer-upper, I need to learn how to do some things."

"Like find a house that doesn't require so much work?"

True, her house had its share of problems.

It was only seven rooms—a living room, a dining area, the washer and dryer alcove off the kitchen, a downstairs guest bedroom-slash-office and bathroom, and a giant loft-space upstairs she used as her bedroom since it also had a small bathroom.

But it also had doors that didn't close right, two windows that didn't open at all, and a furnace that clanged like a bad garage band.

Eve's phone buzzed again, and heaving a sigh, she pulled it out. "These robocalls are driving me bonkers." They were mostly calls for upgrading her car service plan and updating her Google listing. Only she didn't *have* a Google listing.

**<Hey, forgot to ask. What time on Saturday?>** HFFG flashed at the top. It was *him*—the great butt with power tools.

Her heart thumped hard in her chest.

Scarlett frowned. "What's wrong? You look like you've seen an announcement they're never making another Avengers movie."

"It's from my Flow 'n Go guy. He's wondering what time to come by this weekend."

"It's a sign. You must take it. Put him on…" she lifted her chin toward Eve's phone, "speed dial. Then you can have a booty call at the same time. You multi-task well."

"No. Way."

"Why not?" Scarlett's eyes got dreamy. "Then I can write you into my book. Wouldn't that be fun?"

"No time." She tapped out a message to Brent. Something simple, direct.

**<<Noon?>>**

"Yeah, yeah, I know. The deal you have with your dad. But any deals you made at age twelve should be littered with loopholes. Like, *you were only twelve*."

Eve pursed her lips. "This one is iron-clad."

"Because some kid—also twelve, mind you—turned you down for a Sadie Hawkins dance?"

"No." That was a blessing in disguise. Sure, remembering him saying instead, "Introduce me to your hot sister. I'd go with her," even now made her want to track him down and scald his balls under the espresso machine. In the end, she got something better than a stupid date. But really? As if Persephone, age sixteen, would deign to go out with a thirteen-year-old?

When her father had found her afterward in their backyard on their old swing set, eyes swollen and her cheeks tear-stained, and heard the story, he'd offered her something even better than going to a dance.

He'd given her a future.

Eve leveled her gaze at Scarlett to have this conversation for the umpteenth time. "Not everything can be about men, ya know. We can't have everything but—"

"We can have anything. I *know*." She sent her eyes heavenward. "Still going to try, though," she added lightly.

Eve wouldn't. Her father had departed that bit of wisdom to her, and it'd been her guiding principle her whole life. The day of The Grand Humiliation, he'd settled himself in the swing next to her and twisted the chains to square himself to her. "Eve-bee, not everything is about boys. There's a whole world out there where you can have anything. Just get focused on it." Then he struck her a deal: save for half her college education, get a business degree, and he'd hire her on the spot.

College. Work. None of that had even flitted through her mind before. Then again, she was twelve years old.

"With your beautiful brains," he'd said, "everyone will clamor to be in the same room as you. I swear it." Something had flipped upside down in her. She would be more than pretty. She would be *a beautiful brain*.

He'd held out his hand. "Deal?"

She'd shaken her dad's hand, swearing she'd save the money and earn her degree—and she had. More than enough, in fact, to make her own (albeit small) down payment on her (also small) house.

Eve's phone pinged. Brent had tagged her message with a thumbs-up. The fact that it made her ridiculously happy he'd acknowledged her text meant nothing. Not. One. Thing.

She sighed and turned the screen over so she wouldn't be tempted to type more. "I mean, look at what focusing on men, and only men, did to my sister."

Her dreams of becoming a physical therapist had slipped away as fast as the limousine had pulled away from the church on her wedding day. Now she couldn't buy a pair of jeans without handing over a debit card that pulled from her husband-funded checking account.

Scarlett rolled her eyes but then graced her with a smile. "I still love hearing that story about you charging your sister interest on a micro-loan, however. Age sixteen and already a loan shark." She bumped Eve's shoulder with her own.

"I was fifteen, and she was desperate." For Chanel boots.

Her father's eyes had glowed with pride when he'd learned she'd even made Persephone sign an agreement for $300 with five percent interest, calculated monthly. Still took her sister a year to pay it off.

Scarlett sent her eyes heavenward. "And from that moment forward, you've done nothing but work, work, work." She leveled her gaze on Eve. "You're due for a totally shallow, up-against-the-wall nailing that will wake the neighbors."

The woman had nothing but sex on the brain. Eve rinsed her cup in the sink as she turned on the water. "I don't need that."

Scarlett groaned. "*Everyone* needs that. No one is that autonomous even if you are going for some kind of female independence record."

"I know how I sound and look to you, but I am so close, I won't have my life deterred."

"Who said anything about life? I'm talking one night of using his glorious body."

Eve flicked her hand in dismissal even though Scarlett's words conjured up the memory of Brent's incredible arms. And kindness. He was a good guy. She could tell.

Maybe she could ask HFGG to show her how to use some equipment when he came by this weekend. Watching his arms flex as he worked his tools would be a bonus. Looking wasn't touching. Observing him would be good homework, like a practicum. Like a self-declared *internship*.

Eve set her cup in the small dishwasher. "Anyway, he's probably married." The fact that she honestly kept thinking about his marital status was enough to turn her insides over.

Was she so brainwashed as a female that because she was single, every man she met was sized up as a potential romantic interest, then boyfriend, then marriage material or not?

Or worse, maybe it was her family's female DNA igniting —trying to take over her life. Kill her now.

"You didn't check out the guy's ring finger?" Scarlett sighed. "You are hopeless when it comes to men. You're too out of practice." She hopped down from the counter. "Here. I won't let you be single forever." She snatched Eve's phone and spun away while tapping furiously.

Eve darted forward and made mad clawing motions. "Don't you dare. Scarlett, I mean it."

Scarlett held out her phone, which Eve snatched. "Just give me the details for my writing inspiration." A huge grin plastered on her face.

Eve stared down at the phone and every blood vessel in her body rose up like a blushing tsunami. "Scarlett, I'm going to kill you."

# 3

Eve was dead on her feet by the time she got home after her night classes, and she only had the energy to throw in a load of laundry before she fell face-first into bed. Thor purred loudly by her head as he commandeered his favorite spot—her pillow.

She rolled to her back, picked up her phone, and read Scarlett's texting handiwork for the hundredth time.

**<See you tomorrow. Can't wait to see your power tools!>**

Brent would think she was crazy. Actually, he'd think she was *Scarlett*. All flirty and aggressive and *interested* in him. The woman had even added an exclamation point, something Eve never used.

Brent had answered with a thumbs-up emoji. He thought she was trying to get into his tool belt, didn't he?

Dammit, Scarlett. She was officially her ex-bestie.

She let the phone plop to the bed. "Wipe it from your mind," she said to her ceiling.

Thor's paw reached out. She already had one needy male in her life, and he was palming her face with a chirp.

She dragged him off her pillow, earning a loud, meowing complaint.

She closed her eyes and told herself to fall asleep—fast. *Sleep.* Blackness soon flitted on the edge of her mind.

*Whoosh, clink.*

Her consciousness raised, but she quickly fell back into that dark void, instinctively knowing the sound was merely the washer working.

*Whoosh. Clink. Clink. Clink.*

The sound would stop soon enough. She rolled over and pulled her pillow half over her head.

*Plink. Whoosh. Clink. Plink. Plink. Hisssssss. Flap. Flap. Flap.*

She sat up and listened… hard. A sustained trickle of water sounded under her bed. She flopped backward to her pillow. The sounds of her appliances were new to her, that was all. But then the soothing run of water turned into an unmistakable rush as if class five rapids had unleashed downstairs under her bedroom.

*For all that is holy and chocolate...* She pushed her covers off her and sat up. Maybe she was in over her head a teeny bit with this house.

She followed the whooshing gurgling sounds all the way to the gush of water loud and clear behind the washing machine.

"You had to wait until night to burst?" she yelled at the wall. "Thor, if you did something in there…" Of course, he was still upstairs in her bed, which was where she should be. Or, perhaps HFGG wasn't as skilled as YouTube. All looks and no real talent?

She grabbed towels from the dryer she'd planned to use the next day and every rag she could find and dropped them to the floor to sop up some of the water, though it appeared most of it was cascading down the inside of the wall.

"Seriously, people?" she asked to no one. Where in the

ever-loving hell was the shut-off valve? "Don't tell me…" It had to be in the basement.

The renovation gods hated her, didn't they?

She trudged to the backdoor, unlocked it, and headed outside to the cellar door in the back in bare feet. Adding a water shut-off inside the house was a must to be added to her renovation list. Also, shoes might need to be strategically placed in every room for these types of things—or sleep in her tennies, just in case.

She yanked on the rusty old cellar door, nearly dislocating her shoulder. She felt around for the light switch quickly. A shudder racked her whole body as sticky spider webs coated her fingers.

As soon as pale yellow light dawned at the bottom of the short stairs, she took one step down. *This is how women get killed in horror films. Someone sabotages the place—though usually the electricity—and the stupid woman goes into the dark basement by herself.*

She stomped down the rickety stairs anyway. It's what Carol Danvers, a.k.a. Captain Marvel, would have done—though with more flair. However, scaring off any spiders that might be close by with loud noises seemed more important than style.

The basement was nothing but exposed earth under half of the house with half-high concrete walls, cobwebs draped over exposed beams, and the deep, dank smell of old soil. It was disgusting in the daytime, but late at night, shadows in the beams overhead bore down on her as if daring her to enter.

Two bare light bulbs cast a golden glow over the contents: a few boxes of Christmas decorations and a rolled-up sleeping bag.

She nearly jumped a foot at the chirp of a lone cricket. Maybe she needed to channel the Black Widow.

She quickly moved to where the water shut-off valve might be by the looks of the bare pipe layout. The floor was gritty and cold, and she hoped any bugs in the area had run for cover. If she stepped on anything squishy… A tremble ran through her chest.

Time to call up that superhero courage even if she was alone. She didn't think the cricket would be much help should anything leap out at her.

Following the wall, damp seeped into her bones, and her limbs began to shake with cold.

By the grace of some goddess, she found the rusty handle of the shut-off valve and cranked it until the whooshing upstairs stopped. She high-tailed it back up the stairs. The cricket was on his own.

As soon as her feet hit the dewy grass outdoors, she paused. Oh, no. No more leak, but that also meant no more water and no morning shower. Could she wait to call someone in the morning? She had to be at work at the dry cleaners at nine a.m., and Horace was a true cranky-pants about being late.

*Crap. Crap. Double crap.*

Eve at least had the good sense to quietly close the cellar door behind her. She wouldn't wake the neighbors next door. She prided herself on being an asset to Magnolia Street. She'd be living here a long time. They *had* to like her.

Once back inside, she yanked the sheets from the dryer and stuffed them around the machines, praying they'd absorb some of the water.

After mentally adding *"buy bleach"* to later rescue her towels and sheets that were sacrificed to the job at hand, she retrieved her phone.

Surely, there was a YouTube video on how to repair pipes. Yeah, probably with a trip to the Home and Hearth store that was *not* open. She should call someone.

Brent did say to reach out with anything, and perhaps it was his fault there was a leak?

She couldn't bother the HFGG at home at eleven at night. He already thought she might be after him—which she was *not*—and calling might make him think she was pretending to have a crisis when she really wanted to see what was under his tool belt, which again, she did *not*.

Her father would come over, except he was probably out of town.

Nope. She could handle this little blip on her own. Muster her inner bravado. Call Brent's *main company* number. They probably had lots of people on staff, and not just Brent.

"Emergency Flow 'n Go line."

Oh, my God, it was *him*. "Hi, it's Eve Chatham again."

"Hello, Eve Chatham." His voice was gravely and warm. Did she not notice that yesterday? No matter, he had access to power tools, which, if you'd have asked her if that was a turn-on five years ago, she'd have laughed. Not anymore.

A shaky titter released from her throat. "I hate to ask this but, well... The good news is it's not about Thor in a wall this time."

# 4

Eve stared into her closet. If she changed before he got there it wouldn't be bad, would it? Jeans and a T-shirt would be ideal. Casual, they stated, like she was up watching TV. And certainly wouldn't send any signals that she was trying to crawl into his toolbox.

The baby wipes she usually used to clean Thor's paws worked well to clean the bottoms of her feet. She also mentally added *"pour concrete over the dirt basement floor"* to her ever-growing to-do list. She then pulled her hair up into a ponytail and pushed her mother's voice from her head that said, "Eve, put on some mascara and blush *at least*."

Whatever HFGG thought of her, so be it. With any luck, there would be no mention of Scarlett's text message.

Thor rubbed himself along her legs and purred.

"Now you're awake, too, huh? Don't get any more exploring ideas. Remember. We're focusing on keeping this place going."

When Brent arrived, she answered the door with a smile —to be polite, not because he looked even hotter the second time around with his scruff and chiseled jaw. It was that compassionate smile that couldn't be faked that pushed him into pure Hotsville.

He lifted a toolbox. "We have to stop meeting like this."

Ignoring his cornball remark, she gestured him inside. "Thanks for coming. Really. You pulling a second all-nighter?"

"Yeah, my dad's still not feeling well. I'm covering for him."

"Oh, I'm sorry he's ill."

Brent shrugged. "Trying to get him to retire." Thor was rubbing himself all over Brent's leg. "Guess he remembers me."

She scooped him up. "Don't want you to go home with fur all over you."

"I don't mind. But my dog will think I've been cheating on him."

"We can't have that. Cheating is a deal-breaker." That did *not* come out of her mouth, except it had. She wanted to slap her own face.

"For me, too. Now, where's that leak?"

Smooth transition back to business. Excellent. Her legs and arms were heavy with fatigue, and he had dark circles under his eyes, too.

"I shut off the water." She led him back to the laundry room.

"Good thing the hole wasn't patched yet. With any luck, the leak or burst pipe is close by where Thor decided to hide."

She paused in the alcove's entranceway and pulled the soaked sheets and towels away. They dripped a little as she hauled them into her plastic laundry bin to deal with later. He didn't seem to notice the slick floor and went to work. He yanked the washer and dryer from the wall in seconds.

With those arms of his, she had no doubt he could move a lot of things, unfazed and unruffled.

"This is easy." He nodded. "Burst water hose. I've got a bunch of hoses in my van. Maybe one will fit."

When he left to retrieve whatever he needed to get, she set Thor down on the floor and she sat at her kitchen table. Thor simply jumped up on the chair next to her, eyeing her like it was her fault he was up for the second time in the middle of the night.

Within minutes, Brent returned, all kinds of black and steel hoses slung over his shoulder like climbing ropes. They landed with a thunk-slap in the laundry room. "You going into construction?"

She curled her feet up under her on the kitchen chair. "What?" Her mind was groggy.

"The textbooks." Through the doorway, he pointed at her small kitchen table. "I recognized them."

She thumbed the pages of the book sitting on top, *100 Things Every Homeowner Should Know*. "No, just electives. I'm a business major." It sounded much better than a part-time barista and cashier for a dry cleaner. She was a student who was going somewhere, the first female Chatham to hang a diploma on a wall—and a wall she owned, to boot.

He yanked out the washer further into the space. "You go to A.U.?"

"I do. I'm going to be the first woman in my family to complete college. And own my own house." That was TMI, wasn't it? Bragging wasn't her style, but it still felt good to say it aloud, like reaffirming her priorities.

His green eyes glanced her way, followed by a wide grin. "Good on you. Wonder why I never saw you there. I'm in my last year."

He looked so much older than someone she'd normally see on campus. "You're a student, and you're moonlighting?"

"Yeah, helping out my dad." When he leaned over her washer, his lower abs were bared, and muscle cuts disappeared into his jeans. She dropped her gaze to her textbook again. It didn't compare visual interest-wise. She glanced up at Brent again when he grunted as he screwed the end of a silver hose to the back of the washer.

"He owns the place. I'm going back for my master's. Turns out having the architectural degree wasn't as much fun as I thought."

"You went into architecture?" That was a super-hard degree to get, which meant he was smart *and* good-looking. "That has to be fun."

"Building is fun. Drawing? Not so much. Standing in front of a drafting table all day, staring out over the Chicago skyline, never getting your hands dirty? Not really for me. I decided to come back here. Be near family, especially with my dad being sick."

Oh, he must be really ill then. "You're close to them?"

"Very."

Not wanting to get overly personal, she dropped her questions and tried—rather unsuccessfully—to not fixate on the way his muscles moved in his forearms.

Thor jumped to her lap, his tail swiping across her face. She spat cat fur out of her mouth and settled him so they both watched Brent *get his hands dirty.*

Even if he was taken (he had to be, right?) and she wasn't interested, admiring him was harmless. Maybe she'd report the physical details to Scarlett—let her use him for character inspiration after all.

She could totally see him do it. Brent's physique wasn't earned at a gym but rather through good, old-fashioned hard work, which was way better on the hotness scale. And she'd bet this was a guy who moved a girl around and grabbed handfuls of his woman's butt. In fact, he most definitely had a woman. Not a girlfriend. Not a wife. This guy said to his buddies, "I gotta go pick up my woman." Because he'd also be super protective.

She squirmed a little in her seat, both a little turned-on at the idea and a little disturbed. Gah, shallow much? Did her body not get the memo that Brent's masterly hands did not fit into her strategic life plan right now?

He'd still make a fabulous character for Scarlett. He could be the architect who left the big city and built his own house in the woods with a wrap-around porch. He'd have rocking chairs on the front porch. Two of them, only he hasn't found the person to take the second one yet. Yeah, that would be a nice, heart-warming story.

Only no way was this guy single.

"Please tell your wife I'm sorry I keep dragging you out in the middle of the night," she said. "You can tell her I'm a crazy cat lady with a falling-down house."

He laughed. "You're not crazy. And I like cats."

"You have any?"

"Nope." He cranked some small tool in his hand as he continued to practically dry-hump her washer with his movements. He paused and glanced over at her, eyes twinkling. "No wife or girlfriend, either." He then winked.

She swallowed. Not from the fact he was single but the way his green eyes sparkled. He wanted her to know he wasn't taken.

It was that stupid text from Scarlett, wasn't it? Her mind didn't get to play around with those thoughts for long, however. He straightened, scrubbed his hands on the sides of his jeans, and dropped his tool into a bag. He swung it over his shoulder like a backpack and leaned against the door opening.

She rose quickly. Thor's paws made a delicate plop onto the linoleum as he was unseated.

Brent's green eyes bore down on her. "Saturday still?"

"Yes." Wow, she'd said that fast. "I mean, if it still works for you."

A half-smile played on his lips. "For you? Anything." He leaned down and grabbed armfuls of leftover hoses and slung them over his other shoulder.

"Then mind painting my house?" Shit, that snort thing happened again. Deep breaths, that's what she needed right now.

"What color do you want it?"

"Kidding, Brent." She had to swallow down the weird feeling of using his first name. It was like they'd been friends or something forever, probably because he was easy to talk to. Maybe this was what happened with plumbers who visited you twice in twenty-four hours. You bonded. You'd share house war stories later, like, "Remember that time Thor forgot which side of the wall he was supposed to live in?" and "Remember how we never saw each other in the daylight because everything happened after midnight?"

He moved toward the hallway. "I'd choose a dark forest green if it were me."

"Why?" Like a little puppy, she scooted after him. Talking about her house was safe territory.

"Then, if you paint the trim white, it'll set off the architectural features. But no white indoors. It dulls the wood details." He spun at the doorway, the hoses swaying along his side.

Her hand shot up and did that stupid finger-point move at him. "You seem to really like Arts and Crafts houses."

"You could say that. I also admire people who appreciate them." His lips brushed her hair as he leaned down toward her and whispered. "And yes, I do have a lot of power tools."

She'd felt his breath move over her neck. Her blood raced, her ears filled with its whooshing. "About that... uh..." She massaged her palm with her thumb. She had to broach the whole text thing with him. Set him straight.

He straightened, but his eyes slanted downward at her, appearing quite comfortable at her squirming. "Any in particular you're interested in?"

His gaze lazily drifted up and down her. It was a blatant check-out, that eyeing thing that men do to women. But guys didn't do that to her. His assessment was... unexpected. But then, what had she been doing for the last forty-five minutes? Blatant objectification. And her text, or rather Scarlett's, most definitely gave him the wrong idea.

Time to reveal her priorities. She crossed her arms. "I watched a video the other day about how I can get my own sander and sand down my own floors and—"

"Whoa. Whoa. Whoa." The extra hoses on his shoulder waggled every which way like limp octopus tentacles as he raised his hands. "Do not get seduced by YouTube. What kind of sander? You going to use a radiator/heater extension edger or a floor edger as well because that millwork..." his flapping hoses bounced in the direction of her tiny living area, "is original."

"I haven't decided."

"You got the delicate touch?"

"For wood?" So much for turning the conversational table. Everything that came out of her mouth now made her want to slap her own face. "I mean..."

He shifted a few of the hoses. They sent off a sizzle as they rubbed against one another and freed one of his hands. He held it out, palm up, and curled his fingers. "Let me see."

When she didn't immediately take his hand, he reached over and took it himself. The nerve, but, *oooo*, callouses. Little zings went off in her chest. "What are you doing?"

"It's a tiring machine to work. I'm checking your strength."

"Checking out my muscles?"

"Yes. So when I bring my sander by—"

"You'll show me?" To show her how to actually do something? That was her kind of catnip.

"Like I said." He dropped his hand but leaned down closer to her again. "I've got whatever tool you need."

She chewed on her lip, and her thighs squeezed together. Her physical reactions were merely because he stood too close. He brought all his manly scent into her sphere—something, along with his arms, she should not be noting.

"I'm a fast learner," she said.

His grin bore down on her. "That's because you're going to cheat and watch how on YouTube tonight, aren't you?"

"Of course, I am… because I don't want to mess up your stuff." She twisted her hands together, the one he'd clasped still warm from his hold.

"You're the girl who studies every night in case there's a surprise quiz, aren't you?"

"Being prepared is important."

"Ah, but surprises are fun."

Another snort threatened in her nose but she managed to tamp it down. "Not in the middle of the night."

"Well, some are." Oh, another wink.

The man was an unconscionable flirt. But he dangled something in front of her she was helpless to resist—learning something useful. "How mad will you be if I do? Mess up, I mean?"

He cocked his head. "Maybe a four."

"That's generous."

"Tools are fixable. Don't ask for my number on the chainsaw, though." He winced a little. "Gretel is special."

"You named your chainsaw."

He shrugged one shoulder, sending the hoses dancing again. "She's a hard worker. She deserved it."

"Which tool is Hansel?"

"When I get to know you better, I'll let you know. And it's Hans." He gave her another wink.

A swirl of warmth moved in her belly at his wink. The man *was* an unconscionable flirt, but her reaction wasn't because a good-looking, talented, nice guy was flirting with her. Okay, maybe a little. It was more because these feelings were happening out of the blue. Normally, her mind and body were on board with each other. The last few days, however, certain parts of her were going rogue at the oddest times.

It had to be from sleep deprivation, and maybe a little bit about how she'd finally met a guy who actually appeared to be listening to her, offering to help her. How was a girl to resist that? Especially when it was wrapped up in a package like him? She was human, after all.

He cocked his head. "You interested?"

"Thanks, I am. In your tools, that is. Power tools. I mean, your sander." With every word, she grew more flushed—from the inside out.

"Great." He waggled an eyebrow. "Consider it done. I gotta say, it's refreshing to finally meet someone who wants to learn." He finally stepped outside with a muffled clank of tools and swish of hoses.

"I do. But hey, wait." She hadn't meant to shout. "I have to pay you. For tonight."

"Saturday, Eve. We'll handle everything then."

As soon as she had the door shut, she leaned against it. Her ten-year-old cousin was smoother around boys. Only Brent wasn't a boy—there wasn't a hint of juvenile in him even if he was a big tool tease. Except he seemed to like that she wanted to know more about his, um… equipment. And she liked that *he* liked that about her.

Thor brushed across her leg. She lifted him in her arms and settled in the chair by the front window.

Through the curtains, she made sure Brent got to his truck, mildly mesmerized by his casual swagger. It'd been forever since anyone piqued her interest, and there was nothing that lured her faster than capability. Capability he was willing to *share* with her. Total Swoonville.

It was pathetic, but she was who she was. It didn't stop her from studying his Thor backside as he hauled himself up —with an arm on the truck roof flexing like the god he resembled—into his ginormous truck.

She might have to watch *Thor: Ragnarök*, the best one of the series in her mind, to be absolutely sure she wasn't imagining the resemblance. Details mattered.

She slunk down in her chair under the window.

Oh, God. Something was awakening in her.

Why couldn't Brent be happily married with six kids? Drunk in love? Besotted and entranced? It'd make things much easier. She didn't want to have to resist her attraction to him. It took energy. She wanted him to be wholly unavailable, off the menu altogether.

After all, he could easily turn out like every other guy she'd known. They started out really liking your ambitions and plans, applauding you all the way—until it got in their way or meant you weren't available for them. Most men, in her experience, wanted to be the center of attention and didn't like to play second fiddle to anything. It had happened to Persy, after all.

Plus, Brent was too good to be true. Surely, he had a fatal flaw that she'd yet to discover. She didn't have time to invest in things that wouldn't pan out. Saturday had to be *all* business, and she knew how to ensure it.

# 5

Eve waited until a civilized eight a.m. before calling Scarlett. She started this flirt-a-thon. She could end it. "What are you doing?"

"Writing the most fabulously filthy scenes ever seen by mankind. My sister would faint. I might send it to her. What's up?"

"Want to meet a hot plumber on Saturday?"

Scarlett gasped. "You did the deed with him. I knew you'd cave." The sound of typing filled her earpiece. "Details. I got a new file open and ready."

"Noooo. I want to introduce him to you. He'll give you lots of sexy fodder for your book. He's got incredible arms." Being all business with Brent might be impossible. It would be better to fix him up right away with someone. A girl had limits. A man dangling power equipment with Thor-like arms, as sad as that sounded, was her kind of crack. But standards dictated a man's tool belt was off-limits if he was involved with another. He could still show her how the sander worked, and she'd ensure his romantic availability wasn't even a possibility.

"I think he could be good for you," she said.

The snick of a laptop closing went off like gunfire. "What's wrong with him?"

Eve laughed. "Nothing. He's super-hot and you need to meet him."

"You are out of your mind or…" A long sigh emitted. "He's defective. Bad breath? Criminal record?" A finger snap sounded next. "Bragged about his boy band record collection…"

"Would I set you up with someone bad?" Thor's tail rubbed under her chin.

"Truth. So this has nothing to do with your daddy deal. It's worse. You're scared. You never did trust men. No, wait. This is an 'I will not be my mother or sister' thing, isn't it? They both started college, met super fabu guys—and yes, your dad is one hella' silver fox that I will write about someday—they got knocked up, dropped out, and got married, and now they have this incredibly glamorous, cushy life that any other woman on the planet would kill for. Except you, of course. So you're trying to push a gorgeous guy who looks like the god Thor—who you also adore—on your long-suffering friend so you couldn't possibly fall for him. Did I miss anything?"

She hadn't, and Eve's throat nearly squeezed shut. "I want to be able to pay for my own life. Not have to ask anyone for it." Her voice was small and weak, dammit.

"Yep, I nailed it."

"You swore over the Peppermint Sweet espresso machine…" a sacred and hallowed invention by mankind, "to help me not fall into the life of my sister or my mother. You know how strong those genes are. I mean, once ignited—"

"My God, this guy interests you. Like really."

"Trust me, you're doing your kindred sister here a solid. Meet Brent."

"No."

"Scarlett!" She would not, *could* not follow the footsteps of the women in her family.

Easily-seduced. Drop-outs. Trophy wives. Helpless. Eventually *ignored*.

A scoff left Eve's throat at the very vision of her mother scurrying around, making sure the flowers were in order, the food was perfect, and her lipstick touched up right before her father came home with some business associate who proceeded to ignore her through the whole meal designed to impress him. She would *be* the business associate people brought home, and she would acknowledge every person she encountered at every event.

If she would follow anyone's footsteps, it would be her father's Tom Ford loafers into a board room. In fact, she had several times when she'd interned for him. It was only when the whispers about Eve "not being all that" and "only the boss's daughter, the happy recipient of nepotism" reached her ears did she stop, vowing only to return with a degree in hand and under a real interview scenario.

A wine cork being opened sounded. "You know, plenty of people who go to college are married…" A loud splash came over the line. "Or at least have midnight booty calls."

"That's what every woman in my family said—once. I mean, look at Persy. Got pregnant while in school and dropped everything else."

"The woman's got some skills."

Eve threw her head back on the chair. "Yeah, she does. She wears a two-carat Tiffany solitaire like nobody's business."

"Do I detect a hint of jealousy?"

"Swearing on Thor's hammer, no." Eve loved her family, but she could be different and love them just the same. Eve would never put herself in a position to worry about funds being suddenly cut off like Persephone's first husband had done to her—after she'd caught *him* bare-assed on his desk at work with a colleague.

It was the first time she'd ever seen Persy cry—standing in Macy's with a useless credit card like it was the end of the world. The second was when the lout had the house locks changed and she couldn't get back inside. The memory alone boiled Eve's blood. She'd offered to fetch a hatchet and they'd take down the front door together, but her sister wouldn't do it. Instead, Persy slunk away with her vintage Kelly bag slung over her arm and moved back in with their parents.

That's what you get when someone else pays for the welcome mat—that sucker can be yanked right out from under you. Better to have your own.

Of course, her sister had married her first husband's colleague less than a year later. After all, to her sister, being single for longer than four months was akin to spinsterhood or "like living on Tristan da Cunha"—her exact words. Eve was impressed her sister even knew what the remotest place on earth was.

Persy never did tap into all her potential. She knew it. Their father knew it.

Their dad had pulled Eve aside at her sister's second wedding—vows spoken on a beach in Hawaii because why not drop a hundred grand for a ten-minute ceremony where everyone could wear white flower crowns? He'd told her how proud he was that Eve had stuck to their deal. "Eve-bee, don't walk in your sister's shoes," he'd said. As if. She'd kill herself in those four-inch stilettos.

Thor yowled from the kitchen.

"Please, Scarlett? Hormones make people do stupid things." Like watch Chris Hemsworth movies at ridiculous-o'clock in the morning after a plumber who looks like him shows up with promises of hands-on demonstrations when, if anything, she could have caught up on school reading. He *had* to be more than looks, didn't he? Like truly similar to Thor.

Scarlett huffed. "Okay, the Victorian age is calling on the other line. I'm sure they want their thinking back. But because I swore on the holy java bean to always help, I shall endeavor to cockblock you. I cannot believe those words came out of my mouth, but there you have it."

"You're the best friend ever."

"Why, yes, I am. I need hunkalicious inspiration anyway. Hmmm, a hot plumber named… what's his name again?"

Scarlett and Eve may be the same age, but her friend's brain was a sieve, forgetting even her niece's name sometimes. "Brent."

"Do you mind if I call him HFGG instead?"

She remembered that? "Don't you dare." Showing Scarlett what she'd labeled him in her phone had been a mistake. Eve was changing his name in her contacts. With any luck, maybe Brent and Scarlett would hit it off. That would be a nice thing for Eve to do. "You're going to fall hard for him, Scarlett. I know it."

No matter how much Eve liked him herself, she couldn't afford to grow infatuated with him or worse, fall into him. He was too tempting, though no one could be that perfect.

But he could share his tools with Eve. She needed those.

# 6

The best way to clear one's head was to clean—at least, Eve had discovered that when she picked up odd jobs in high school as a Saturday maid-for-a-day. It was therapeutic, in a way.

She needed therapy, too. Last night in her dreams, Thor the god came to visit with rainbow-colored washer hoses that, for some reason, had to be brought to her bedroom. She'd woken up with her legs squirming and a keen desire to drain the charge dry in her vibrator. In fact, she had.

Even though Scarlett had promised to come by today when Brent arrived, Eve was slipping.

It was happening. "It" being the famous Chatham female DNA that ensured once you let yourself be interested in a guy, he became your world.

She was losing her mind. Or her mind—and body—were attempting to get her *lost*.

So, she cleaned the house from top to bottom, including the precious baseboards—her *wood*, and yes, she still couldn't believe that had come out of her mouth. She also swiped a wet rag over the ledges over every door frame. For a small house, it sure had a lot of places for dust to settle.

A faint smell of sardines sickened her every time she walked into the kitchen. Thor kept scratching at the floor—some oil must have gotten into the cracks of the linoleum. He looked up at her with his big, begging eyes like she was withholding fish treats from him.

"Trust me, if anything was there, you could have it all." She scratched his head and moved him over as she sprayed as much air freshening spray as she could over the crack.

Brent rang her doorbell at exactly twelve noon, looking far more rested than the last time they'd seen one another. Scarlett, of course, was nowhere to be found. Eve hoped she would not be a no-show because his beard scruff had grown out even more, which moved him from merely being good-looking to dreamy steamy.

Maybe it was time for Eve to give her vibrator a frickin' rest. Her libido still jumped to attention because it was a backstabbing demanding sucker.

But he and Scarlett would be perfect together—her bohemian vibe with his hot handyman vibe. They would live in a yurt on some plot of land on the outskirts of town. He'd build fences by hand and she'd figure out a way to get an espresso machine to work inside their trendy tent.

Then they'd all be friends.

After promising to show her the sander later, Brent immediately went to work, patching up the hole in the wall of the laundry room. He even had brought a new dryer vent system. She would have to dip into her savings to pay him more than seventy-five dollars, especially now that she knew he was a student, too. Surely, he needed the money.

Thor continued to claw and scratch at the floorboards with his big fluffy paws. Every time she tried to get him away, he'd slink his way back, eying her like she was keeping him from a secret feeding trough.

He needed a distraction, and so did she. She was far too close to Brent's arms and winks.

She paused in the laundry room doorway. "Let me know if you need anything. I'm going to take Thor outside for a bit." Leaving him alone outside wasn't an option even with a harness and leash—don't judge. If he broke free, wandered away, and lost his way, she'd die.

Brent lifted his chin. "Sure thing." His brow furrowed as he returned to his work. Maybe it was a good thing Scarlett didn't turn up right away. The man had focus—yet another thing she appreciated.

Outside, Thor immediately crouched down low, eying the birds as if they were about to descend on his territory. "You don't like them, baby?" She scratched his head and he let off a purr.

She settled on the last step of the back stoop and gazed over the old garden. An overwhelming peace had come over her when she had first stepped into this yard—and it calmed her now.

Mammoth hydrangeas and azalea bushes lined the rickety fence that surrounded the long, narrow backyard. A huge apple tree graced the corner, its branches stretched out, shading half the yard. The former owners had loved this land. She could feel it.

In fact, if she was going to be interested in anything or anyone, it would be this place.

Once the inside of the house was fixed up, she'd continue to love on the outside. The tiny yard was so overgrown, and it deserved better. She hadn't even thought of what she'd do to the landscape, except she'd definitely put in a pollinator garden for the wildlife and a bunch of bird feeders. Because she didn't have enough to do already, right?

Her nose tickled with a musky and rank scent growing stronger in the air. Whatever that horrible smell was, it had to be coming from one of the flowering bushes. She'd replace it with something else. Maybe roses…

Fixing up the rickety old one-car garage filled with junk left by the previous owner would be last. For now, pulling her car up next to the house on the cracked concrete drive was good enough.

Thor stared intently at the bushes swaying in the breeze. "It's just the wind." She ran her hand along his back to try to calm him. His hair stuck out like a mohawk, not his best look.

He let out a menacing growl and his tail fluffed full like a brush. "What is it, Thor? See a neighborhood dog? Defending your territory?"

The bushes at the far end rustled, and was that a tail she saw? Something most definitely waddled underneath. Thor suddenly went nuts, hissing and growling and slinking low to the ground.

An acrid, rotting smell was next, and most definitely not from a bush. No, there was no mistaking that scent. *Skunk*.

"Thor, no!" She tried to pull him closer, but he went all cat-snake on her and slipped between her hands. Then, the breakaway leash snapped. "Thor, oh, no, no," she screamed as he disappeared into the shrub.

He darted back out—fast.

The smell, God, the *smell*. It hung in the air so thickly she could almost see a black cloud. Her sinuses immediately clogged because they were smart as if signaling, "Save yourself. Run."

A big, bushy black tail swayed along the fence line like his work here was done and he had better places to be. Then, the skunk was gone—through a hole in the fence, no doubt off to torture another unsuspecting pet.

Brent appeared at the archway. He rubbed his hands on a rag. "What's wrong?" His hand clapped over his mouth and nose. "Oh, man. Was it a direct hit?" His voice was muffled behind his palm.

She moved to grab her skunky cat.

His big frame pounded down the steps. "No! Don't go any closer."

"I got this. Don't worry." She raised her hands and then bent low to try to grab Thor, but he turned into a feline corkscrew, and she kept losing her grip on him. "I don't want you to take your life in your hands while I try to bathe him."

Thor's eyes grew wide like he understood the word "bathe," and that was her biggest mistake to date as he slipped free and she had nothing but a breakaway harness in her hand. He made a beeline for the scene of the skunk crime.

"Thor. Back here now." He darted to the left, and she tripped a little. Her shoelace had come undone.

"Wait. Eve. You shouldn't touch him," Brent called.

Crouched low, Thor moved toward the fence once more, and she raced after him. He might try to follow his skunk buddy through the hole. She tossed the harness—because that thing was getting pitched—and got her hand on his back, but once again, he slipped right out of her hand. He let out a howl, which was rich given she was trying to save one of his lives here.

She had to make a dive for him, her knees falling into the grass, and *wow,* the ground was hard, but she managed to get her arms around Thor, who immediately decided touching was highly overrated, and out came the claws.

"Yow. Thor!" As if he'd retract them. "Remember who pays for your kibble, please."

Brent's shadow fell over her body, his hand still over his mouth and nose. "I'm researching here. There are steps for de-skunking. Bathing him isn't good." He held up his phone, and as if on cue, Scarlett's bright blue Civic lurched into Eve's driveway.

She rose with Brent's help and kept a hold on her cat. "What steps?" She spat hair out of her face.

His eyes were watering. "It's been a while, but I remember there's an order."

Scarlett pulled herself from the driver's side and squinted toward them. "Whatcha doing? Oh. Hellooo." She wrinkled her nose and fanned her face. "Never mind." She started to laugh.

"This is not funny, Scar," Eve's stomach began to roil. "Don't come any closer. You might get sprayed, too."

Scarlett slammed her car door and drew closer. "I grew up on a farm. Nothing scares me anymore. Besides, the skunk's only got one spray in it every twenty-four hours, poor guy."

Poor skunk? How about Thor, who did not want to be held—at all.

"Okay." Brent lifted his phone up. "First off. Do not touch the animal," he read and looked up at her. "Step one violated." His shoulders shook a little as if holding in a laugh.

She glared at him. "I'll take him inside and wash him." She turned away.

"Step two says to keep the animal outside and *don't* wash him." He waved his cell at her. "No water."

"Do we just pray over him and it magically disappears? Leave Thor smelling like rotten eggs?"

"My lab tussled with a skunk a while ago, and I remember this special shampoo or solution they have. Let me look it up. I'll get a friend to bring some by." He began to type on his phone.

Scarlett strode up to them. "My, aren't you the knight with a shining toolbox." She held out her hand. "I'm Scarlett."

He pocketed his phone. "Hi, Brent, fixing some things in the house. And guest de-skunking help."

"Yes, I hear you're quite handy." She didn't let go of his hand.

He flushed.

Eve set Thor down, her hand firmly on his back. He was a little too close to her nose at the moment. Maybe she could use the hose on him? Yeah, and have him hate her forever.

He lay down in the grass and turned onto his back as if begging for a belly scratch. Now he was grassy and stinky. Maybe the scent would dissipate a little if they spent a few minutes outside before the bath he was *so* getting.

Scarlett finally let go of Brent's hand. "So, Thor got nailed by Pepe Le Pew. Interesting development." She swung her gaze to Eve. "I popped by to make sure our Eve here wasn't lonely. New house and all." She turned back to Brent. "Eve tells me you're in school. Architectural engineering, I think?"

Now her memory was working?

"I am." He gave her his signature grin.

"Hoping to go into commercial or residential?"

They stood in a cloud of skunk scent and Scarlett carried on like nothing had happened. She was doing exactly what Eve had wanted her to do—be interested. Only now, irritation nibbled at her spine as the two of them ignored her. She rose.

"Anything that gets me out and about. Or..." he looked up at Eve's house, "renovating old houses. Eve made quite a find with this one." His gaze flickered to her and his elbow nudged her as if to say *atta girl*.

Her insides beamed—like seriously lit up like stadium lights. And for one brief second, she forgot her house was breaking down left and right and her cat had nearly lost one of his nine lives.

"I'd say she's excellent at unearthing hidden treasures," Scarlett cooed. "Like where have you been hiding?"

He let out a half-laugh but then frowned. "Where did Thor go?"

Eve's brain veered back to the crisis at hand. She scanned the yard. "Oh, no." She should have been paying attention to Thor.

She frantically glanced around the backyard. Her annoyance quickly turned to panic. "Thor! Here, Thor. Where are you, baby?"

"Unlikely he ran away, but..." Brent glanced at the open back door and then back at her. "What are the odds?"

Oh, Jesus. Her mouth opened and a new wave of skunk smell invaded. She could practically taste it.

"That wouldn't be good." Scarlett shook her head. "Once that skunk oil gets on something, you know, like the furniture and..." she glanced down at Eve's hands, "your skin, it's impossible to get out."

Eve let out a groan and rushed into the house, and for the second time that week, started that stupid *"here, kitty kitty"* song.

Brent's laughter rang out behind her. "Hey, there are more instructions you should know, too..."

She ignored his words and darted down her hallway. Thor was pretty easy to find by following the smell—to her bedroom. He'd gone straight for her bed and buried himself under the covers—*because of course, he did.*

Fish oil downstairs. Skunk oil upstairs. Eve's ever-growing to-do list now had a new item on it: call an odor-removal specialist.

She gathered a pungent Thor in her arms and headed to the bathroom. Like it or not, he was getting a bath with or without this special shampoo Brent talked about or she'd die of skunky asphyxiation.

Thor didn't like being placed in the bathtub—at all—but tough. She grabbed the shower nozzle, and with one hand she held him and with the other cranked on the water. As expected, Thor's growly displeasure turned to alien-level, blow-a-gasket, scramble-for-your-life flip-out. She could barely hang on to him as she wet his fur.

"Ow, hey, come on... You're going to live."

"Hey," Brent's voice rumbled behind her. "I said don't use water." He pressed his lips together as if swallowing down a smile and lifted his phone. "It's the worst thing you can do."

"What? Ow. *Thor*. I thought you liked playing with water." His claws sunk into her forearm. She finally got him to still, his howl lowering to a pissed-off keening. "That's ridiculous. You said there was this shampoo."

He slapped his arm over his belly and let out a horse laugh. "Water..." *Snort*. "Activates... the skunk oil." He took in a huge breath. "But don't worry, I got this covered."

The man had lost his mind. "Don't worry? *Don't worry?"*

He swiped under his eyes. "My buddy Mark's on his way with the de-skunking agent."

She let her butt slide to the floor, and Thor's paws slipped. The shower nozzle slipped in her hand and water doused her from chin to waist. She spluttered as the spray arced in the air. Thor tried to make one more escape, and she managed to grab a hold of his back before he leapt out.

"Man, he's pissed." Brent's voice shook with laughter.

"Are you laughing at me?" she growled.

"Of course, I am." He leaned against the door jamb. "I'll tell Mark to bring two bottles. Ya know, one for you, too." His chuckling didn't die down—not one bit.

# 7

"Ooo, presents." Scarlett cooed the words and took one of the three bottles of de-skunking agent that Mark, Brent's friend, cradled in his arms. "I love a man who knows animals."

"Grew up on a farm." He shrugged one shoulder. One by one, he handed over the other two to Brent, his gaze never once leaving Scarlett.

"Oh? Me, too." The length of time she let the "too" hang in the air sealed the deal. She'd come to flirt, all right—it was just with the wrong man.

"Thanks, man." Brent waved the two bottles at his friend and turned to Eve. The cloud of skunk smell they were standing in was completely overpowering.

"Your guy's got some lungs there." He glanced up at the second floor of her house. Thor's growl hung in the air, coming through the open bathroom window on the second floor where they'd secured him, a.k.a. *prison* if Thor's noises were any indication.

"Maine Coons are vocal. It's going to get worse."

Brent let out a long, breathy snicker, handed her one of

the bottles, and followed her into the house. They stopped in the kitchen to retrieve rubber gloves, of which she had many. Hand protection had become super-important to her over the last few weeks.

As they made their way upstairs, he read the label on the bottle he held, outlining the de-skunking steps. "So, we start with dousing Thor with this—"

"Magical enzymatic solution?" She read the back label of her bottle as she took the steps slowly. She turned and held it up to him. "They even use the word magic."

At the top, she paused with her hand on the bathroom doorknob. "I can do this, ya know. You've already shed enough blood in my house."

"Nah. You're going to need help." He cocked his head toward the door. "I can hear the murder plans forming in his mind already. You hold him, I'll pour."

He reached for the handle, but she tightened her grip on it. "We need a plan." This guy didn't know cats if he thought he could waltz in and start wetting fur again.

"It's best to just do it." He gently pried her hand from the handle and pushed open the door.

An indignant scoff left her throat at his all-knowingness. Just do it? Out of instinct, she crouched down to grab Thor. He did not jet out like a cheetah as expected. Instead, they found him huddled behind the toilet, his eyes big and scared.

She dropped to her knees on the little daisy carpet she was now going to have to throw out. "Oh, baby. I'm sorry." His eyes were wide—and pitiful. He was never going to forgive her for this debacle, even if it was his own fault for trying to make nature friends.

"You got an old T-shirt? It'll help keep the solution on him because it needs to sit for 20 minutes."

"Watch him?" She lifted Thor up and got him into the

bathtub. He'd wilted but growled with a low cry that made her heart nearly split into a million pieces.

Scarlett's muffled giggling drifted through the open window. Once long ago, Eve had a life like that. Just a girl. Standing by a car in a driveway with a friend, talking about nothing. That girl didn't have a cursed house with cursed landscaping that attracted cursed, attacking wildlife.

Brent sat down and placed his hand on Thor's back. A purr rose up despite the rubber glove squeaking as he petted him.

"That's unexpected." Thor leaned and arched his back toward the man's touch.

"Animals like me." He grabbed one of the bottles and opened the top. He poured it over Thor's back. That was the end of his wilted state. Thor might have liked Brent, but his affinity took a turn with that affront. An indignant hiss rose up, and she had no choice but to throw both her hands back onto her stinky cat.

"Hey, you're moving too fast," she said.

"It'll be over before you know it. That T-shirt?"

She huffed again and ran to her room. Her old, gray, ratty Iron Man T-shirt she was going to paint in—she could sacrifice Iron Man—could work. She jogged back to the bathroom with it. In the doorway, her heart flipped anew. Thor's fur was matted down and his head looked three times its normal size. He kept lifting one paw as if wanting to shake it.

She held out the T-shirt. "Here you go."

He took it with a smile.

"What?" She crossed her arms. "Thor's a fan of Iron Man, too." She clicked on the exhaust fan, hoping it'd dissipate the lingering *eau de skunk*.

With some skill, Brent managed to get the t-shirt over Thor. He plopped his butt down on the floor, his big beefy hand wrapped around the image of Iron Man's suit to hold Thor in place. "There. Now, we wait."

"Hey, mind if I abandon you for a bit and go change?" Thor's screeching had at least reduced to a resigned grumble, and her spoiled clothes needed washing—or perhaps burning.

"We'll be right here having a chat about what we learned about skunks today. Right, Thor?" He grinned up at her. "It'll be at least twenty minutes."

She nodded once and then went off to strip the bed—and herself.

It took something to get her clothes off while wearing rubber gloves because no way was she taking them off. She wiggled out of her top and pulled it over her head, which meant she got quite a nose full of skunk smell. She clutched her belly. She would not throw up. She *would not* throw up.

After pulling on a sweatshirt and sweatpants—not her finest look, but at this point, she'd be happy with not smelling like a wildlife preserve—she moved to the bedding. Damn, she'd really loved her new sheet set before it had been defiled. She quickly flipped the comforter and sheets back and a waft of... God, she was going to lose it.

She ran to the open window and sucked in a long breath. She needed to get a grip.

After her belly settled, she managed to get the bedding and her clothes in a big pile. Now what? Even with rubber gloves, they'd end up touching her arms and torso. Could she get them to the washer without touching them? Why, yes, she could.

She kicked them all the way down the stairs, down the short hallway, and to the laundry nook. Using her broom as a shovel, she got the sheets and her clothes into the washer with the rest of the de-skunking agent. She then stuffed her comforter into a big trash bag to wait its turn for the washing machine. No need to let it sit out, scenting the air any more than it needed to.

"There. Iron Man-level ingenuity. No suit required." She and Thor would not be defeated by a mammal the size of a cantaloupe.

She returned to the bathroom with a few plastic grocery bags to collect anything else that would need to be pitched or put in quarantine.

Brent crouched by the tub. "Good thing the washing machine works, huh?" His huge hands engulfed Thor's rigid body. "And Thor and I had a chat. He's sorry you missed your sander lesson and said he's not going to do this anymore." His hair across his forehead was sticking up as if he'd pushed it back with his arm to get it out of his eyes. This man couldn't be anything less than adorable, could he?

"Let's hope he listens to you more than me." She sat down next to Brent, and their knees collided. A simple bump, actually. It was expected. Her one bathroom was the size of a small closet. But they locked eyes for one brief second, and something passed between them—a little zing of familiarity and comfort. A non-verbal *can you believe this?* It felt nice.

She broke eye contact. "I can't thank you enough. I mean, for not running for the hills… after I violated every rule under the sun about de-skunking."

"Sure thing. Like burst pipes, animal encounters never happen at convenient times."

"This week hasn't turned out at all like I expected."

Like Thor getting in the wall, and her washer breaking, and now, a skunk encounter. It hadn't been all bad, of course. Work hadn't been overly busy, her businesses classes were fun, and her home remodeling night class was going to be super helpful—even more, if they added animal roadblocks to home renovation. And when things did go south, Brent had shown up to help—three times now.

Brent's leg straightened more, sidling up alongside her as if he was trying to stretch it. "I think Thor has learned his lesson. When Homer, my lab, was hit, it was in his mouth. Six months of breath that could knock out a grown man. But that's what I get for living in the country."

"Where in the country?"

"Over on Stone Hill Road. I have a house there."

Seriously? Those were estate lots that overlooked horse country. Ancient stone fences hemmed in the old farms, and historic buildings dotted every quarter mile. "You have a farm?"

"I renovated an old carriage house."

"Oh, you are handy." A shaky half-laugh followed. At least she didn't snort.

"These hands have done a lot." He peeled the T-shirt off a frozen Thor, who'd finally given in to the inevitable and relaxed. She tried hard not to stare at Brent's hands—his very large, powerful-looking hands. This man was most definitely more than a pretty face.

She took the T-shirt from him and dropped it into a plastic bag. "This thing is toast, and I owe you way more than seventy-five for today."

"Nah, how about I take you to dinner instead?" He cranked on the water—because apparently, now Thor could be washed?

She swallowed, and heat crept up her cheeks. "You don't need to do that." She dropped to her knees and grabbed the pet shampoo that Mark had also brought. "And I should be the one taking you out to dinner." She tossed in a light tone to her words. It's what a friend would do.

Brent held out his palm. She squeezed some of the gel into it.

"No way. You need something nice to happen to you today. I know it's the modern thing, this women paying for stuff, but I can't do it." With his big hands, he lathered up Thor, now limp but with murderous thoughts shining in his eyes. "It's on me."

"Well..." She shouldn't. First, it signaled *date*. Second, she had one night a week to do laundry and clean, though both seemed done for the day. She should rest and get ready for the week. Then, there was getting some advanced reading in for her classes so she wasn't cramming it in at midnight every night.

She'd be terribly rude if she said no, right? He was being so gracious. Saying "*yes*" would mean she was interested. The problem was she wasn't *not* interested. Resisting someone who was honestly trying to help her would be nonsensical.

"Help me out, Thor." Brent cocked his head toward him. "Should Eve and I go to dinner?" He peered into Thor's eyes, who blinked up at him. Yep, homicide was on his mind. "Yes? I knew you were a smart cat."

By the sound of Scarlett's giggling outside, she wasn't interested in Brent. Her friend's chortle was the one she used when trying to make a guy feel like he was the funniest thing ever but wasn't. That meant Mark would be her literary inspiration, not Brent.

Brent cranked the water on, picked up the hose, and began to wash off Thor. "You have to eat, right?"

She did. Eve reached for a towel. "I might smell like skunk." Who could tell anymore?

"I do, too. Besides, where I'm taking you, it won't matter. You like crabs?"

"My favorite." The whole ceremony of the shell cracking, eating with your fingers, and drinking cheap beer was fun. "You mean Dick's Crab Shack?"

"The only place in town to have them."

He was genuinely a normal, nice guy, someone she could

be friends with. She could handle that. "Okay, yes. But only if I pay for my half."

Brent rose with a thoroughly washed Thor and put him into her arms and the waiting towel. "Then that means you're not paying for the drywall."

Yes, she was—even if she had to stuff money into his jeans pocket. She could reach around and slip it into his front pocket. No, wait, his *back pocket*. The mere thought made her flush. "Brent, this isn't a date. So we're clear. I'm not on the market, as they say." Did *they* even use that phrase anymore? "I mean, I'm hardly ever home except to do homework, and I barely have enough time for Thor. I'm really focused on getting through school. It's really important to me because I want to be more than…"

"A pretty face?"

"Exactly. I mean, not that I think I'm all that or anything…" Jeez, use words much? Why was she telling him all the details anyway?

His eyebrows arched upward. "A *beautiful* face?"

"Oh, I'm not," she spluttered. "And..."

He rubbed Thor's head with a corner of the towel, letting out a half-laugh. "Just say yes, Eve."

"Yes." His ease around being told she wasn't interested was admirable. If laid-back was a person, he'd be it. "You're a nice person, Brent."

"So are you." He leaned closer and dropped his voice to a whisper. "And sorry, I disagree. You are beautiful."

Her skin prickled. He was really good at this flirting thing. She was out of practice in the man department, even ones who were just friends. Had she ever had a male friend? She couldn't recall.

He peered down at Thor. "You, however, are a lot of trouble."

Thor definitely was because, thanks to him, she had a *friends* date with the Hot Flow 'n Go Guy.

She could do this, prove to herself that she was her own woman. It'd be her own little test—and she was very good at getting high exam marks.

Yet she had a feeling she *would* have to stuff money down his jeans to keep things on the straight and narrow. She'd probably make a mess out of that, too, like totally miss and end up stuffing them down his butt crack.

And now, all she could think about was his very fine ass…

# 8

"You have good taste and you're brave. I can tell." Brent sucked on the end of a crab leg.

She cracked open a claw. "You think?" It was amazing how quickly she told this man things—stuff like how she'd chosen 331 Magnolia Street, where she worked, and how she loved her renovation class.

"You chose a fixer-upper. Doesn't get any more courageous than that."

"I'm not sure that's been a good thing given the last few weeks of repairs." All totally unexpected, too.

"Nah. You saw an opportunity and grabbed it. I'd have bought more myself if I had the time." He took a long swig of beer.

*Did he say more?* "You've renovated houses?"

"A few." He shrugged. "I joined a construction crew in high school and soon was doing a bit of everything. It's how I paid for college. Then I started doing it myself."

"Wow." He was handsome *and* compassionate *and* skilled *and* funny *and* smart. He was literally the pentagon of hotness. Scarlett *had* to write about this man.

Brent chugged more beer. "The benefits of growing up with a man who didn't call repair people. He fixed it himself or we didn't get to use it. Makes you resourceful fast."

"Must have been nice to have had competent parents teaching you stuff." Her mother was stellar at making appointments to have *other* people do things.

"I paid attention. Now, my mom… she's the one who is really handy." He pointed a crab leg at her. "She decided she wanted this fancy chandelier she found in an antique store. Rewired and hung it in our dining room by herself."

"Let me guess. YouTube." She laughed.

"The library. No such thing as YouTube back then."

"Even with it, I have a lot to learn around this renovation thing. But it's cool. I enjoy learning." Another sip of beer instantly cooled her lips from the Old Bay spice. Was he staring at her lips? She picked up another crab. "One more."

"You can never have too many crabs. They're like potato chips. Can't have just…" he glanced at her pile of discarded crab pieces, "ten. No, twelve." He nodded up and down. "Impressive consumption there." He pulled a horrified face.

She playfully slapped his arm. "There's hardly anything in them."

Brent was fun. When was the last time she'd had fun? Fifth grade? Perhaps this was his shtick. Make everyone around him feel better, lighten things up, distract people from whatever weighed them down. He was going to be a good friend.

"True statement. Besides, I like a girl who eats." He picked up a claw that was immediately dwarfed in his large hands. "Makes you hot."

"Yeah, crab breath is smoking hot."

His green eyes flickered. "Ah, but I like crabs."

"Well then." She lifted a crab leg and sucked on it hard.

"Now you're turning me on on purpose." He winked.

"You're too easy." She waved her hand.

"For you, I would be." He leveled his gaze on her, a little serious, a little *not* by the way his mouth tilted up.

She licked some spice from her bottom lip, unsure what to say. They were getting too close to a sexual edge, and her Chatham female DNA might be listening, waiting for an opportunity to push her over, make her fail the test. Eve didn't fail tests.

When she set her beer down, it caught on a crab shell and tipped, sending a river of cheap beer down the table. "Dammit." She jumped up. See? Nothing alluring to see here.

He caught her arm, and she sat her butt back down. "Don't worry about it. The newspaper will catch most of it. Beer goes well with crab anyway." He signaled the waitress, who sported the tiniest shorts anyone has ever worn—like Dallas Cowboys cheerleader short, which she did not recall being part of the Dick's uniforms. "Hey, Susan, can we get another pitcher?"

Susan gave him a provocative smile followed by a, "*Sure thing, Brent,*" in a soft whisper that would have most men falling to their knees. She would know. Her sister—and her mother—had pulled that one a million times. How Brent thought Eve was hot when someone like Susan bopped around was a mystery. Brent appeared oblivious to her come-hither face, however. He didn't even glance her way, just reached over and grabbed more napkins from a nearby table and returned to mopping up her spilled drink.

"I don't need any more beer," she said. Her mind had fogged under its influence. It had nothing to do with the fact that her friends-dinner-out had taken a sudden turn. Or that she even noticed Susan flirting with Brent, which should not have bothered her at all.

Except it kind of did.

*Jesus.* Her DNA could be awakening. Red alert.

She rubbed her forehead and immediately regretted it because her fingers were coated in Old Bay seasoning. She grabbed a towelette. "I shouldn't drink anymore."

"Never mind," he called out to Susan.

The too-short-shorted girl winked his way.

Eve's hand fell to his arm. "I could use a walk, actually."

"Perfect. I want to show you something." He took a last swig of beer and rose. "Let's go for a stroll."

He paid at the cash register, refusing to let her contribute, and left a huge tip on the table for the waitstaff. Despite the fact that she really wanted to pay her share, his generosity was nice. She could always stuff money down his jeans later —when her genes weren't listening.

Before they left, she ducked into the restroom to wash the crab smudge out from under her fingernails. This man had smelled enough funky stuff where she was concerned.

They strolled down a few blocks, chatting about nothing in particular. The streets in this part of town had sidewalks, unusual in this day and age, and the air was warm but not too humid.

He moved a low-hanging branch so she could duck under it.

She stopped short. "Where are we?" The twilight made the sky overhead shine purple, changing the way the streets looked, and she hadn't been paying attention to where they were going.

Instead, she'd been aimlessly chatting about her work at Peppermint Sweet and Horace's as well as school—all silly small talk that he seemed super interested in, asking her follow-up questions about Greta's special coffee drinks and what she'd been learning in renovation class with a promise to still give her that lesson in using a floor sander.

He arched his arm in the air. "I give you your sister street. Poplar Avenue. This section of town also has a long row of

Arts and Crafts houses. Thought you could get some inspiration."

She glanced around, really looked. The homes were much nicer than her run-down one—and much larger than her tiny bungalow. "They look amazing." She must have been down this street before sometime but clearly had missed its charm.

Clean, painted in various colors, the homes had elaborate stained-glass windows and large porches and were surrounded by trimmed and neat yards with perfectly manicured bushes and tall, mature oak and maple trees.

He slowed his walk. "Now, see that door with the green shutters along the side? That's one idea. I prefer the stained-glass on either side, but both work for Arts and Crafts."

"I bought my house because of its stained-glass window." The second she'd seen it, she'd known the house belonged with her.

"I didn't see that. Where is it?"

"Upstairs facing out back." Over her bed. At the time, she'd thought the small window was romantic with its rosy tulip pattern.

He moved her to the opposite side of the sidewalk so she wasn't on the street side. "Huh. Wondered why I didn't notice it. I'd like to see it. See if it's original."

Her belly somersaulted, and not because he was proving to be so gentlemanly. He'd have to go to her bedroom to see her window properly. "Sure." Someday. Just thinking about him standing next to her bed made her skin flush.

Needing to rid herself of the nervous energy beginning to thrum inside her, she kicked a little pebble on the sidewalk. "What else can you show me?"

He pointed at a large two-story home. "See that one? Filled with Stickley furniture."

"How do you know?"

"Frozen pipes last winter. One a.m. call."

"So, I'm not the only one." Thank God. Her house was like all the others—old and needing "a little love," as Brent said. "So, things break as if crying out for attention?"

"Now you're getting it. Like I said, plumbing emergencies rarely come at a decent hour."

"You work the night shift a lot? For your dad?"

He grunted a yes. "He gets sick. Chemo."

Her heart gave off a dull thud. "I'm sorry."

"Thanks." His gaze fell to his feet and his shoulders drooped. More pangs thumped through her chest.

Her dad was the only reason Eve ever felt normal—how he was proud of her being focused on school and work. She couldn't imagine him not being around, and the thought of losing him?

"He sounds like a wonderful guy." Not that she knew much about him, but his son had certainly turned out well. She rested her hand on Brent's arm in a comfort move, like a friend would. His forearm flexed. *Whoa.* This man most definitely worked with his hands for a living by the way his muscle had glided under his skin. "After all, look at how you turned out."

He glanced down at her touch, and his eyes cleared. He thought she was copping a feel, didn't he?

"I mean, you make him proud. I'm sure." More house talk—that's what they needed. "I'm glad you brought me here, Brent. It's… helpful. Can you show me more?" He seemed to be the kind of guy who liked to help people.

"Sure."

As they made their way down the sidewalk, he pointed out the materials used in each house, like river rock, clinker brick, quarried stone, and examples of artistic exaggeration in columns, posts, eaves brackets, lintels, and rafters.

He got so excited over the stained-glass windows in

prairie grass designs and other abstracts, he'd surely be sorely disappointed in her small stained-glass window that overlooked the garden in back.

Her foot caught in a crack in the old concrete—because who watches where they're going when one is being shown house porn? His arms grabbed hers, his large hands wrapping around her biceps. Her feet found their way again—and somehow, her hands had made their way to his chest at the same time.

"Oh, strong." The words came out, stuttered and breathless. Their gazes locked for a few seconds. Okay, longer than seconds.

She now *was* copping a feel. But *come on*. Plumbing must be akin to training for an NFL defensive lineman position or perhaps a heavyweight bodybuilder contest because this man was packing some serious strength under those clothes. In fact, her mind went to him standing up on stage, tan, with muscle cuts creating shadows all over his body.

She gave herself a mental slap, like *get ahold of yourself already. Think*. Letting her hormones make decisions for her was not on tonight's docket.

He cast a warm smile her way.

Still, the possibility of a little fling danced on the edge of her mind. More than his amazing biceps, everything about him drew her to him.

She shouldn't be deterred from her plans, not after all she'd gone through to be so close to getting her dream, but it'd been an eternity since she'd felt a man's skin against hers. Like, not even a handshake.

Nope. Not going there.

Pure pheromone chemistry—that's all her imaginings were. He was a good-looking guy, and her body reacted like any hot-blooded girl—especially one who carried a certain

DNA pattern. However, her inherited traits underestimated her internal strength.

She threw her hands back to her sides.

His brows knit together. "You all right, Eve?"

"Fine. Great. No problems." Just doing her usual over-thinking thing over here.

He let go of her arms and continued walking up the side-walk. "Arts and Crafts is not really one style." He raised both hands as if painting in the air. "More like an intellectual approach to many styles, marrying indoors and outdoors, making the best use of space..." Their progress stopped. "Am I boring you?"

"Not at all." On the contrary, his exuberance bled into her. She should have taken out her phone and taken notes. It would have given her hands something useful to do. "You know a lot about these particular homes."

He colored an adorable shade of peach and looked down at his feet. "I might have done a few of these."

Oh, for Pete's sake. She now would have to add humility to his list of amazing qualities.

"Seriously? You should have told me." She mock-punched him and peered up the neighborhood. They'd made a full loop of the street, going up one side and down the other, and were now back where they started. "Which ones? Can you point one out?"

"There's one." He lifted his chin toward the smallest one that was visible. It was two houses up—brown with yellow trim and warm timber columns. The rich wood door was framed by glass. Three small panes of glass graced the top, and two long panes with a prairie grass design in yellow and green wreathed the sides.

It mirrored the outside—like it was a portal between the natural world outdoors and the man-made rooms inside.

Almost magical. She took a few steps closer. "That's my favorite."

He murmured under his breath. "You don't have to say that."

"I mean it. It's… perfect." For one brief second, she pictured herself in that house. Her gorgeous husband and herself walking together up the sidewalk after work. Maybe he'd carry her stuff in. She didn't know what "stuff" it would be, but it would definitely be from the office—*her* office.

"You think?"

His question smacked her back to reality. She wasn't quite there yet in her dreams, but she was feeling pretty positive about life at that moment. Like she could actually have it. Not everything—she knew that wasn't possible—but maybe something more.

A brilliant plan surfaced. Scarlett was right. She really liked this guy and enjoyed getting to know him. Maybe her libido and her brain could work together. She was so close to finally launching a career that didn't rely on "just being the boss's daughter." Why *not* mix in a little something more?

She pivoted to face him. "Hey. I have an idea. Would you be willing to let me hire you?"

What better way to get to know a guy slowly, stay on track, help him out with some work, and get her house renovations done sooner rather than later? She would put some business boundaries around her and Brent because, while they barely knew one another, the chemistry was tripping her up.

She'd put exploring their attraction on a timetable. After her final summer semester. Then her filthy imagining could go to town. And honestly, who knew if he really was into her? He might be like this with everyone.

He cocked his head. "Hire me?"

"I need someone who really knows what they're doing, and I thought—"

"Yes."

She bumped him with her shoulder. "You're easy." Her insides still did a little jig that she might get help.

"Ya think?" He arched one eyebrow. "I don't work for just anyone."

Ah, a bargainer. "I don't have a ton of money, though."

"Don't worry about money. I don't." He shrugged. "There always seems to be enough."

A honk rocketed out of her so loudly she was shocked the windows of the nearby house didn't rattle. "Don't let my family hear you say that. They live and die by their bank balances."

"I'll try to remember that if I ever get to meet them." A smug satisfaction crossed his face.

Oh, no. There would be no meet-the-parents moment. They'd pounce on him like fresh meat ready for grilling. Not to mention it'd send all the wrong signals—like they weren't friends-getting-to-know-one-another, not business-partners-with-a-maybe-fling-possible.

"They don't come by often. Small spaces make them uncomfortable." And he had nothing in common with them. He was dead opposite of the Chathams—and all their friends. They had certain skills but wouldn't know an electric screwdriver from a hairdryer.

His lopsided smile beamed down at her. "No Arts and Crafts for them, then. We'll keep it to ourselves."

"But this will be strictly business, right? For now?" Her last two words just slipped out. "I mean—"

"Of course." He nodded once. "But know renovations are a partnership..." he wagged a finger between them, "between us, and it can get intimate."

"How intimate?" She might as well start drawing boundaries right now—her own personal Great Wall of China.

He hooked his fingers in his belt loops and rocked back on his heels. "I'll have to see what's under your floorboards." His eyes glanced down her body—once. Her two words—*for now*—and already things were escalating.

She could handle it, though. "You won't like what you find under my floorboards." She'd know, having visited her basement more than once and being scared witless by all the insect critters—the little squatters.

He waggled his eyebrows. "How do you know?"

"Spiders and crickets."

"I can take care of them for you. I'm good at catching things."

She could see it. Brent pounding down the cellar's rickety stairs, a bug net in hand like Thor's hammer, then emerging, victorious, the cricket caught and released because he'd be that way—catch and release. Then Brent's hands reaching out, seizing her around the waist to pull her into him to celebrate the victory.

She crossed her arms. "We'd have a business contract." Solid lines around what they would do and not do. She needed to control this situation because her imagination was no help whatsoever. It clearly did not read her internal strategic plan—yet.

"Tell me where to sign."

Her arms fell to her sides. "Don't you want to read it first?" Firm arms and cricket-catching abilities or not, she would not go into anything blindly, and he shouldn't either.

"I trust you."

"Do you always move this fast?" This man was channeling Quicksilver—the one and only superhero she didn't understand *at all*. Like, where did he come from, *really*?

"Life's short, Eve. If I learned anything about my dad's illness, it's you never know what the future has in store."

She swallowed thickly and nodded. "I hope he's going to be okay." There wasn't anything else she could say. His father's health troubles had to weigh heavy on his mind, and she understood the need to stay busy to distract from less-pleasant thoughts. She took his hand and squeezed it once. "All right then. You're hired." And he would *read* and *sign* a business agreement.

"Thanks for trusting me."

"I do." Even if he moved fast and flirted like crazy.

His green eyes shone on her, and something unspoken passed between them. Like they were both in on some secret. Like they knew something more could happen later.

Yep, her hormones were going to be the villain in this story, weren't they?

But the next few months were settled. In fact, their arrangement would be a chance to prove she could handle more than she knew. "Hey, my stained-glass window, want to see it now? It's the only thing in the house that doesn't need help."

"Whatever you want, Eve." His slow wink her way heated her insides anew. She liked the way he said her name, too.

She hooked her arm in his and let him lead her back to his truck.

Of course, when they got to her bedroom, things took a wrong turn—and it was all Thor's fault.

# 9

"Wow, this has been here a while. That's leaded glass." He peered up at the small window in her bedroom space—more like a converted attic with pitched ceilings on either side.

"The realtor said it was put in when the house was built." She reached over to try to get Thor to come out from under the covers. He was digging, which was not like him.

"I can tell." His fingers played along the ledge. His knee pressed into her mattress, which was under the window, and he leaned forward to get a closer look.

The stained-glass design was simple. Three pale pink tulip buds spread out from one long green leaf in the center of the thick, translucent surface. Strips of gold glass framed the design.

"I thought it was pretty. When the light streams in the right way, spots of rose light show up on my bedspread." Or what used to be on her bed before the skunk incident. Now, an old beige blanket was a stand-in until she could buy a new comforter. "Thor, what are you doing?"

Brent's gaze landed on her bed and a wiggling Thor who was oddly clawing around.

He glanced around. "Nice space. Want to do anything up here?"

"Maybe some insulation in the rafters? It can get chilly, even in April."

"Keeping Eve warm added to the list." He stared back down at her bed where Thor was now growling—at something.

Brent stared at her bed, his brows kitting together as if thinking. In fact, he stared for so long, tingles crawled up her chest.

Was he measuring in his mind if he'd fit? If they lay sideways or she was on top of him, or... *Stop it.* Certain parts of her needed a chaperone—or a jailor.

Brent straightened, his knee indent remaining on the mattress. "Besides the stained-glass window, what else drew you to your house?"

Yes, let's talk house, not if he'd be a perfect fit. "It felt grounded in a way. The minute I walked in, it felt real. Solid. I thought it only needed a few cosmetic fixes. Boy, was I wrong."

"Something you should know. Rule number one of house renovation: expect fifty percent more work than you thought. And then double that."

Sounded like what it took to get her college degree. "So, basically, it's unpredictable and you'll spend your life doing it?"

"There will be an end. In about thirty years."

"Great." Thor tunneled his way to the other side of the bed. A low growl came through. She reached out and placed her hand on his back to settle him. "I have other things in mind for my next thirty years."

"You said you wanted a career. But what about family?" He glanced around. "You could expand the space."

"Family? Uh, maybe."

He slowly nodded. "Well, it's good to have something for yourself." He eyed her. "You're unusual, Eve. You're driven and interested in things."

"Thanks. I try." His appreciation for her drive continued to catch her off guard. None of her previous boyfriends—as short-lived as they were—ever understood why she didn't drop everything for them or follow them around like a lost kitten. Most men wanted women like Persephone—gorgeous and willing to follow their wishes at every turn like little poufed-up poodles prancing alongside them.

Thor let out another huge growl. "Baby, what are you doing under there?"

"Looks like he's playing with something. Maybe he caught a mouse?"

She gasped. "He would *never*."

Brent's eyebrow cocked. "He doesn't bring you presents?"

"Ewwww."

He chuckled. "Want me to check for you?"

Her head bobbed up and down because no way was she going to stay composed if Thor gifted her with a rodent. *In her bed.*

He reached over and yanked the covers back.

Her mouth dropped open. *Oh, shit.* Thor had his great big paw draped over something, all right. Her vibrator. Bright pink against white sheets. He yawned and blinked up at her, like, *"What? You left it here."*

She jerked the covers back up toward her pillows, covering both it and Thor, who let out a huge meow. She'd cleaned up her electric boyfriend and threw it there as she was hurrying out that morning. Now, the thing lay there like a good soldier awaiting orders.

And Brent *saw*.

"Not a mouse." Brent snickered. "Thor seems fine. Comfortable."

Fire couldn't be hotter than her cheeks right now. "It's warm under there. That's all." And could she sound like any more of an idiot?

Then again, when was the last time she'd been out with a guy, even on a friends basis, let alone had a man *touching* where she slept, where she dreamt of Thor and his great big hammer?

Where a vibrator was displayed?

At least Brent didn't recoil. His green eyes sparkled at her. "I'll bet it gets quite warm under there."

She turned her face back to the stained-glass window. "You really think my window is original?" Her voice squeaked a little.

"Yes, I do." He was withholding a laugh, wasn't he? At least he didn't say anything else, probably in the mutual understanding that one does not acknowledge that a sex toy had made an appearance. The smile on his face didn't dim, however.

Thor wiggled himself up to her pillow and began licking his paws. She grabbed him, pulled him up into her arms. "Hey, let's talk downstairs." Away from the most humiliating experience of her life.

She didn't wait for him to answer, just turned and headed downstairs.

Thor didn't seem to want to be held, but tough. He owed her. He was officially her support animal for the most embarrassing moment of her entire existence to date—and that was saying something.

Brent followed her down, and at the bottom of the stairs, she paused at the doorway. "Uh, thanks again for tonight." *Please go so I can hang my head in shame—alone.*

Brent eyed her furry child and sighed. "Thor gets all the girls. Thanks for showing me your window. For taking the time. I know you've got things to do." His eyes glanced up the stairs.

Oh, my God. He thought…

"Yeah," she said quickly. "I'll get to work on that contract." Or do anything other than go over every single second of the last ten minutes.

Brent gripped the door handle. "Let me know when it's ready. I'll get started right away. I like moving on projects."

"Okay." No moss grew under this guy's feet. "Maybe this weekend?"

He nodded once and cracked open the door. "And, Thor…" He looked into Thor's yellow eyes. "Stick with the mice. Pink's not your color."

She, herself, pinked from head to toe. "Holding that one in long?"

"Good night, Eve." He turned on his megawatt smile, pivoted, and sauntered down the walkway toward his truck.

*Yep, his butt most definitely was a twelve.* But more than that, he was a wonderful guy. Like, really wonderful.

And—click—her Chatham female brain wandered into "what if" territory just like that, assuming they might *fit*. Even if she may never live tonight down.

# 10

Eve's limbs twitched under the influence of her second espresso that morning.

"What's got you so jittery?" Scarlett tidied a bunch of Danish pastries in a neat row on the tray.

She lifted her little cup. "Didn't get much sleep last night." Not even after waking up her little electric soldier. After all, it was there.

But it had only kept her on edge because a certain green-eyed, power-tool-wielding guy kept interrupting her usual fantasies of a certain movie star because he looked like *said movie star* who was a really genuine guy on the inside. Plus, there was that little fact the thing had humiliated her last night.

"Did you try the valerian I told you about?"

Eve let out a long heavy sigh. "Yes. And the melatonin and the Sleepytime tea. I swear, I'm going to have to start taking sleeping pills."

"Don't you dare. Let me see what else I can come up with." Scarlett slipped the tray into the shelf under the glass countertop. "Hey, wait." She snapped her fingers. "You had a date last night with Brent. It's just us. Spill. You slept with him, didn't you? Was he amazing? Was he huge? I think he was probably like… romance novel-huge." Scarlett widened her hands. "Like, OMG, how is he ever going to fit? And then he fits and—"

"I did not sleep with him." Because, yeah, she already knew his fit would likely be perfect, too.

Scarlett gasped. "That's why you're tired. You got no sleep, you were doing the…" she circled her hips, "horizontal po-wah drill."

Eve threw a towel at her. "We did no such thing. I've hired him to help me around the house. It's all business." For now. Her breath hitched at the memory of his amused eyes as he declared pink was not Thor's color. But she decided she needed to get over it, be a grown-up. In fact… She turned to her friend. "But if I tell you something, promise not to laugh?"

"Absolutely not. What happened?"

"Last night, well… here's something for your book." She glanced around to double-check no one was in earshot but lowered her voice to barely a whisper just in case. "My vibrator was out, and Brent came upstairs to see my stained-glass window and Thor was playing with it so…"

Scarlett's huge guffaw bounced off the walls. She slapped her hands to her chest. "Oh, my God, I can't breathe. He saw it." Her laughter died. "What did he think of it? Was it the rabbit or the little one?"

The only reason Scarlett knew about either was she'd dragged Eve to a sex toy party once and made her buy two. "*In case one dies on you,"* was her logic.

Scarlett wiped under her eyes. "I gotta say, Eve. Your life is a tad accident-prone. I mean, seriously?" She was reduced to a fit of giggles again.

The bells jingled over the door, and they both glanced up.

Green eyes. A mop of blond hair. A huge frame. "Oh, shit," she muttered under her breath. The cups she'd been placing on saucers jangled under her fingertips.

Scarlett sniffed and finally stopped laughing. "Look at what the cat dragged in. It's a live, no-batteries-required man. A handy, hunky… oh, swoon." She slapped her breastbone and fake-gasped. "Whatever will we do?"

"Don't embarrass me," Eve said between gritted teeth, enough humiliation under her belt—and Scarlett's mouth had no governor.

Scarlett's eyes widened. "I think you got that angle covered already."

"He's probably here to talk about my house."

Brent's face broke into a huge grin at seeing her. Eve smoothed down her apron and went to the section of the long counter where the "Order Here" sign hung.

In five long strides, he stood before her, a flat, square package under one arm. "Came by to check out this best new coffee."

She'd said that, hadn't she? Absentmindedly, how Greta had begun to only sell coffee that was shade-grown? And he'd listened to her as they'd strolled down Poplar Avenue.

"Large?"

He lifted one eyebrow. "Is there any other size?"

"Not where coffee is concerned. Take anything with it? To go?"

"Nope. Black. And for here. That is if you can take a break so I can give you your house-warming present." He lifted the square package under his arm.

Her hand slapped to her chest. "Oh, you didn't have to do that."

He shrugged. "I know. But this…" he placed it on both palms and held it like a tray, "belongs with you."

She leaned closer to the package, studying the wrapping's perfectly folded corner. It wasn't the right shape for a new hammer—or a vibrator, thank God. One never knows. She wasn't sure how far his sense of humor extended. "You need a muffin on the house. To go with the coffee."

She busied herself pouring his coffee into the cup and tried hard not to study him from her periphery. She failed miserably at any self-discipline there. He leaned casually against the tall counter, the package under his arm, his gaze focused on the Danishes, muffins, and tarts in the glass case.

Fire seared her fingers. "Ah." She shook coffee off her hand. She'd overfilled the cup.

"You okay?" he asked.

"Fine, fine. Or would you rather have a piece of pie? They're made by a local elementary teacher, Chloe Hart, and they're fantastic." She set his coffee before him.

"Sounds great. So, break?"

She glanced around. It wasn't busy. Being four p.m. on a Sunday, everyone was already heading out, and they would close in a few hours anyway.

Scarlett pushed her toward the end of the counter. "Yes, she can. She hasn't sat down all day."

While Brent commandeered a small table in the corner, Scarlett grabbed her elbow and lowered her voice. "Give him the cherry. Chloe says it's special."

Eve plated a large piece of cherry pie and brought it over to him. She didn't believe in the rumors that the baker had special magical powers with her pies—like having people fall in love.

Once seated, he placed the package before her. "I was thinking about your house project. I know you haven't formally hired me, the business agreement and all, but—"

"Oh, I meant it." The faster they moved their time

together into renovations and she got her house in order, the better she'd feel overall. Somewhere between the vibrator incident and this morning, she decided she'd view Brent as a gift—like the Universe was saying, *"Here, we think you're doing the right thing with your house."*

"Good. Now, open that." He nodded down at the package.

She lifted it. "Oh, heavy." Once the brown paper fell away, she found a small window of stained glass, a design of three tulips growing out of a long green blade of grass like her larger one at home. "Wow."

"When I saw your window, I knew I recognized it. It's been sitting in my attic with a bunch of other odds and ends. It belongs in your house."

"Oh, I can't just take this." This was a real find—an antique. "I'll pay for it."

His brow furrowed. "You do like to pay for things, don't you?"

"It's only right." They were in business, after all.

He placed his hand on her wrist. "It's a gift."

Warmth, like bathwater, spiraled in all directions inside her. "Thank you." She pulled her arm away and bumped his coffee. Some of the java spilled. "Oh, I'm sorry." She yanked some napkins out of the napkin holder and began sopping it up.

He helped her by lifting the window.

"Nothing got on it, did it?" God, if her clumsiness had stained the wood…

"It's fine. I'm glad to see you like it."

She wadded up the wet napkins into a ball to take away later. "I love it. Thank you. It will look amazing in my bathroom. Then two windows upstairs would match."

The bells rang, and what looked like an entire softball team of teenage boys poured in. Dang it, she'd wanted to talk to him more about where to put the window, like could he install it?

"Duty calls." She placed her hand on his arm, which earned one of his beautiful smiles. "Thank you again."

"Sure. I've got to go anyway. I'm also on duty."

She stood there, peering into his face. "Your dad? Any news?"

He shrugged. "They don't know. I'm trying to make it easier on him. Ya know, to be there." He dropped his gaze.

"You are a very good person, Brent."

"Trying to be." The lines across his forehead softened, and he leaned close. "Though, sometimes, I'm pretty bad. In certain ways." He winked.

Oh, the things his wink did to her insides. "As long as you're a badass with your power tools." She needed his professional skills more.

"I'm good with all kinds of tools. Even the pink ones."

Her cheeks flamed. Still, even with her dignity from the Big Vibrator Incident burned to ashes, so many ideas cascaded all around her as spangles ran up and down her legs. Like how his large hand would dwarf *the pink one,* and Thor would be kicked out of her bedroom to sleep downstairs in his favorite chair because the bed's occupancy load would be breached.

Greta called her name. The teenage boys had descended on her counter and they needed all hands on deck. Saved by work—again.

He inclined his head toward the gaggle. "Don't let the Woodstone Prep schoolboys intimidate you. Or they'll have to answer to me."

Oh, man. "You didn't—"

"Go there? Sure did. Scholarship kid." He turned to them. "Men. *Ostensum est respectu meruit viderint vereburtur.*" His spine was flagpole straight and his voice had dropped an octave.

The din settled down, and they slowly lined up as if they suddenly realized they needed to go one at a time. Greta and Scarlett stilled and joined her in staring at Brent.

"Wow," Eve said under her breath. Commanding a room really was an under-appreciated skill.

Brent cocked his head. "They'll behave now that they realize an alumnus was in the room. I might have let it leak to their teacher this was the best coffee in town, too. They go on a lot of field trips."

"What was that phrase you used?"

"Respect shown is respect earned. Our motto. Text you later about a good time to meet?"

She nodded vigorously—a little speechless because he *was* perfect.

*Shit.*

Scarlett sidled up to her and whispered in her ear. "I swear to God, if you don't at least consider him—because he was clearly here for you, not a house—I will marry him and have ten of his babies that you'll be forced to babysit."

"I shouldn't sleep with someone so soon, someone I've *hired*." Plus, she'd told herself she would wait until after graduation. "He probably leaves his underwear on the floor and globs of toothpaste in the sink."

Scarlett threw the long towel in the pile of laundry and emitted a long exasperated sigh. "Of course, he does. You're just trying to be the opposite of your sister. She's running your life and you don't even know it."

*Ouch.*

Scarlett grasped her shoulder. "Sorry. That was a below-the-vagina hit, even for me. But really, Eve. What if Brent's got the *hammer* you need?' She waggled her eyebrows. "Last night was a sign. You're going to have to go for the live drilling." She nodded her head knowingly.

"You've been writing too many sex scenes."

"No such thing. And challenge accepted. Wait until you see what I'm going to write about you."

# 11

Brent stared down at his notebook. "I've got the kitchen floor, snaking the drains, patching the tile in the bathroom, the cellar door. In that order?"

Her teeth finally let go of her bottom lip. "I'd like it all done yesterday, but whatever order you think will work."

He'd texted her that morning at eight a.m., announcing he was "swinging by," which had her bristling. They'd discussed the weekend, not a drive-by on Thursday. It shouldn't bother her that he'd adjusted plans on her quickly, but it did. It made her scramble.

After hiding both vibrators she owned under a pile of PJs in her bureau, she had quickly printed out the contract she'd drawn up, and when he arrived, she shoved it under his nose. He simply skimmed it, then took the pen from her outstretched hand and signed it. She spluttered some protest at his cavalier attitude, but he shrugged and returned to his truck to retrieve tools.

"We'll start with the kitchen floor. That way, you'll feel like you're progressing. Plus, it's going to rain like crazy in the next few days. Doing stuff inside is best."

She gripped the edge of the counter and pressed her fingers into the hard edge, an attempt to send the tension mounting in her somewhere. "I'd rather wait until the weekend, though."

"Why wait? You don't need to be here." He didn't even look up at her.

Irritation nibbled at her insides. "Yes, I do."

Brent peered up from his writing. A long second passed. "Okay. Saturday, it is." His gaze landed on the stained-glass window he'd gifted her. "It looks good in here."

"I like seeing it when I make my morning coffee." She'd placed the small pane on the ledge of her kitchen window. It helped block out the house next door, and the rose light steamed across the linoleum, instantly cheering up the place.

He tapped the side of her cheek. "The pink light looks good on your face."

Her blush must match the light, then. He flipped from business to flirtatious and back again at Quicksilver speed, and it did nothing to tamp down the little nest of bees in her belly.

"Thanks." She stepped backward and moved to the front door. She had things to do, after all, like get to her one and only morning class.

He followed but stopped in the archway. "Where's the big guy?"

Her gaze darted around, too. "I don't know." She moved to the living room. "That's strange. Thor usually sleeps on that chair all day. He likes the sun." A beam of sunlight shone in from the side window despite recent weather reports. It didn't look like storms were moving in anytime soon, but the air smelled fresh—like something was blowing in.

"I'm sure he's around." Brent tapped his notebook with his pen.

She took her stairs two at a time. He wasn't in the

bedroom. Maybe Brent's presence caused him to hide. Oh, man, the laundry room again? She jogged down to the kitchen and found the back door was ajar.

"Oh, no. He got out." She pushed it open and stepped onto the back stoop. "Thor! Where are you?" She sniffed—hard. No strange critter smell hung in the air at least.

"I'm sure he didn't go far."

She startled at Brent's voice and nearly toppled off the stoop. He had sidled up behind her, and his hand grasped her bicep before she tumbled.

"I don't know." Her whine drifted into the air, and her lungs couldn't get enough air inside. She pulled her arm free. "He doesn't yet know this is his house. I don't like him being outside alone. Plus, the skunks."

Had she left the door cracked open this morning when taking out the trash? That meant he'd been outside by himself, probably scared and thinking she'd abandoned him. Somedays she felt like the *worst* cat mom on the planet.

She jogged down the steps and immediately began to swat bush and plant limbs aside. "Thor. Thor!"

Brent, still on the stoop, arched an eyebrow and pursed his lips like he was swallowing down some thought. "Take a breath, Eve. We'll find him." His voice had adopted an annoyingly soothing tone like she was one second away from a meltdown, which she kind of was. Thor had been her constant companion for the last ten years.

"Thor," she called again. He usually stuck close to her and came sauntering along when she called.

No mewls, no pitter-patter of little cat feet, no sign of him anywhere.

Her phone buzzed in her hand. She'd missed four calls from her mother in the last two days but did not have time for her latest gossip. She was going to miss her advanced economics class, which she never did, and Thor...

Eve stilled and took in a few deep breaths and stretched her fingers, palms down to the ground. "It's going to be okay. He'll come back," she said to no one. Cold dread still rushed in. Her eyes pricked. What if he didn't?

She flashed to the far end of the yard and proceeded to scream his name—like the lunatic she swore she'd never be.

As many times as she'd called Thor's name, she might have bothered her neighbors. But not a single one came out of their houses to investigate, to help. So much for Magnolia Street's charm. Five minutes into her scream-a-thon, she had half a mind to bang the shit out of her cellar door for the hell of it.

At least Brent started helping—he'd gone up the street to see if he could see Thor.

She jogged back inside to double-check the house. After peering under every piece of furniture, knocking on every wall, risking an excursion back to the icky basement, and a more thorough search through the bushes, truth set in.

Thor was just… gone.

Her phone rang again. *Jesus*. "I can't talk now, Mom. Thor is missing."

"Who?" Her sing-song voice rang out. Eve could hear traffic sounds in the background. Her mom was calling her from the car.

"Mom. My cat. Remember? You lived with him for three years."

"Oh, well, if he's missing, I'm sure he'll show up. He is a cat, after all." The disgust dripping off her voice irritated. She'd not enjoyed having a cat in the house, worried the cat hair might show up on her outfit. "Now, I need to talk to you about—"

"Mom. Stop. Thor is *missing*."

A long sigh assaulted her ear. "Call animal control. Isn't that what they do?"

That idea made her stomach curl inward even more. "Listen, talk tomorrow?"

"Wait. Evangeline..."

Gah, her mother's use of her whole name instantly stiffened her spine. Something big was coming.

"About your birthday soiree."

"What birthday soiree?"

"Oh, wonderful. I got to you first. I thought for sure Persephone had spilled the beans. Now, it was supposed to be a surprise, but your father has this conference out of town and I think I should go with him. That means next week is—"

"Mom, what are you talking about? Start at the beginning, please." Her mother often started conversations in the middle as if Eve had been privy to the thoughts in her mother's head and she could pick up wherever.

"Your sister and I planned a small family gathering. A surprise. For next week. She was to invite you shopping and then drop by here—"

"Shopping? We never go shopping." Her discretionary income was going toward her house—and cat rescue because it was groups like them who made sure wanderers like Thor didn't live on the street.

A cry sat at the back of her throat. She slapped her hand to her forehead as if that would stop the tears. "Thor?" She jogged up the back steps to retrieve a flashlight from inside. Maybe Thor was in the garage.

"Eve!" Her mother made an annoyed sound as if Eve had hurt her ears. "Your father and I need to head out of town next week. I want to move your birthday party to this weekend."

After getting the flashlight from the junk drawer, Eve jogged back down the back steps. "Mom, I have work."

A long sigh emitted from the other end of the phone. "You can take one afternoon off. *Surely.*"

"I don't have time for this right now. Tomorrow." She killed the call. Later, she'd apologize about hanging up abruptly. Right now, finding Thor was more important than her mother's social calendar.

The sun was climbing in the sky and the temperatures were rising. Eve grunted when she tried to lift the garage door, and a bead of sweat ran down her back. The old thing complained loudly, but her effort only raised it one inch.

"Dammit." Her growl echoed against the cheap tin. "Open."

She set the flashlight down and yanked with both hands. The door crawled up another six inches. She'd make do. Lying belly-first on the concrete, she shined the flashlight into the space.

Shapes of boxes and old rusted equipment—like a weed whacker that probably didn't work and a chair with no seat —rose in the gloom, but nothing moved.

The door suddenly flew up in a loud clang. "I need to add this door to the list," Brent said.

She spat a strand of hair from her face. "How about contracting a bulldozer." She darted up to standing. Dust clogged her throat as she moved a large box out of the way to peer deeper inside. "Who leaves all this junk sitting here?"

She'd shouted. She *was* one second from losing it. She couldn't control her breath, her arms and fingers stung from little scratches from the bushes, and her eyesight wavered because stupid tears that would not recede threatened.

"You never know when you might need a... unicycle." Brent pulled one out, its tire flat, and blew the dust off the seat.

Why was he being so calm? She swiped under her eye. "Leaving it all here to rot? The previous owners should have cleaned it out, donated it all." She didn't have time for this idle chit-chat. "I'm going back up the street to see if I can find him."

"Hold on." Brent set the unicycle against the cobwebbed wall and moved into her space. "Is Thor microchipped?"

"Of course."

"Then if someone picks him up, they'll either take him to a shelter—"

"A shelter!" That's where she'd found him. No one had asked her to the prom, so her father had said she could finally get a kitten. Thor had looked so pitiful in that tiny concrete cage, a little furball all alone, shivering in the corner. They were like kindred spirits.

Eve sniffed. She *would not fall apart.*

Brent's brows furrowed. "Or a vet or animal control. They'll all scan him and call you."

She slapped her hands along her side. This was not how things were supposed to go—at all. She and Thor always stuck together. He didn't like being away from her and she him.

Brent pulled her into him and she snuffled into his shirt. His broad chest was like a wall against her forehead. A clean-cotton-and-fresh-air-manly wall.

"Would you be this calm if it was your dog?" She cried into his T-shirt, which immediately dampened because tears had escaped from her eyes.

"Homer regularly goes on field trips. Trust me, they return to where the regular food is."

"Sometimes. And sometimes they get hit by a car or eaten by a coyote or adopted by another family and never let outside to find his way home ever again." She was crying for real now, which only royally pissed her off.

Brent pulled back and smiled down at her with irritatingly calm, beautiful eyes that appeared greener in the bright sunlight pouring through the open garage door. "Let's go inside and wait for him."

She pushed at his chest, freeing herself completely of his embrace. "No."

"I promise you." He held up both hands. "He'll make his way back."

"Are you patronizing me?"

"Never. Listen..." He stepped forward. "I'm sure he's not going to go far away from his sardine-scented kitchen and skunk friends."

That made her laugh a little. "The half-a-bottle of bleach on the floor didn't work, huh? I can't smell anymore. A sacrifice to the renovation gods."

"Got you covered. I'll add sanding the wood floor underneath when replacing the linoleum. Then you'll finally get your lesson, and if we get lucky, there will be an old floor to restore."

He was trying to distract her. "I'm not lucky." She rubbed her forehead. She had to get a grip and stop taking her frustration out on this man. "But thanks for being here and helping."

"I'll always help you." He cocked his head as if studying her.

"What? Oh, I've got dirt all over my face?" She swiped at her cheeks as if that would help.

"It's your eyes. They're all golden-brown in this light."

Oh, wow. Add poet to the list now?

"If I kissed you, would it make you feel better or worse?"

She swallowed. It did little to change the tension in the air between Brent and her. It was like an invisible cord was trying to pull them together. "What do you mean... kiss me?" He stepped forward, and she didn't. Why couldn't she move? Her blood raced, and the air crackled all around them with an unnamed anticipation. "Would that help find Thor?" she asked quickly.

"I don't know. Is he possessive?"

A half-snort came out of her mouth. "I guess not. You've been here a few times."

His hands cupped her shoulders and slid down her arms, leaving a trail of desire and unspoken possibilities. "Want to test it out? See if he grows jealous? I know I would."

*Oh, my.* She kind of did want to see—and she should not feel this eager.

A small mewl followed by the brush of fur on her bare ankle indicated Thor had arrived.

"Oh, my baby." She scooped him up. "Where were you?" He complained as she smushed him to her.

Brent nodded his head. "Told you."

She rolled her eyes at him, all talk and thoughts of kissing vanishing like mist in the air.

"Yoo-hoo. Evangeline? Are you back there?"

"Oh, no." Battle stations, everyone.

She turned to face the driveway. Her mother stood there, her hands clasped together, a Chanel bag hanging off her shoulder.

Eve glanced up at Brent. "I want you to know I'm sorry. In advance."

# 12

Her mother's eyes immediately focused past her and landed on Brent. Her smile widened.

Eve knew what lay behind that enthusiastic grin. Her mother was taking in every single detail about Brent.

Were his jeans stained?

Were they an acceptable, known brand and not some bargain-bin castoff?

Was his T-shirt neck stretched out or smartly pressed?

Was his beard the casual scruff that screamed "male model" or that of a man who had just rolled out of bed?

Did his haircut look professionally cut or done by someone who merely snipped here and there?

These were the kinds of details her mother would ferret out in an instant because to her mother, these details were life and death.

And if she found out Brent had offered to kiss her?

"Why, hello. I'm Katherine Chatham, Evangeline's mother." She extended her hand, which Brent took.

"Brent Shadwell."

She took one long second to shake his hand and then turned to Eve. Her mother's gaze ran more slowly over her.

Eve pulled down the hem of her shirt. Her outfit of cut-off shorts and a Maroon 5 T-shirt were not on Katherine Chatham's approved clothing list.

"Mom. This is a surprise."

"Well, when I heard the distress in your voice, I had to come by and see if you were all right. See if there was anything I could do."

Sure, she did. She came by because she hadn't sorted out the schedule that would suit her best.

"I see that Thor has been found." She gestured her pink manicured fingers toward Thor, who was purring loudly in Eve's arms. "Evangeline, aren't you going to invite me inside?"

It was time to get this over with. Once her mother decided something, it happened. Brent, strangely, followed them back into the house. The man had no idea what he was in for.

"I'll start taking some measurements," Brent said. "Mrs. Chatham." He nodded toward her and wisely stayed in the kitchen as Eve led her mother by the arm into the living room.

"Mom." Her shoulders sagged and her stomach clenched. As much as she loved her mother, she didn't have time or energy for this little motherly drive-by. She had a class to get to. "What are you doing here?"

Her mother drew her arm free, her smile dropping in dismay, but then her gaze softened. "So, Brent," she whispered, craning her neck to peer toward the back of the house. "He's handsome. Nice smile."

"*Mooom.* He's helping me fix up the house." Thor jumped into his favorite chair, circled twice, and then molded to the seat.

Her mother heaved a sigh and glanced around. "You know, Evangeline, if you bought in Shipland Hills, you wouldn't have to fix anything." She sniffed toward the couch Eve had scored from her favorite second-hand store, Circa.

All those cookie-cutter townhomes with perfect landscaping and an architectural review board that only allowed white curtains to show from the outside? *No thanks.*

"Now." Her mother clasped her hands together. "About Saturday."

"I can't. Work."

"It's one day, and it's your birthday." She twirled her hand and continued her inspection of the room.

"My birthday is next week, and we don't need to do anything. I'm fine with—"

"Nonsense. We must celebrate." Her flat tone wasn't very celebratory. "Just family… and a few close friends. Be sure to invite your friend, Scarlett."

"How many close friends?" Her mother, in addition to never having worked, had never learned to count properly. A few could be a hundred.

"The Hanovers, the Starlings. The usuals. The people you grew up with." Her mother tapped Eve's nose, and Eve recoiled.

"You can celebrate without me."

Her mother tsked. "Your father would be so disappointed."

She had to pull out that card. Eve wouldn't disappoint her dad for anything. He was the only one in the family who always said how proud he was of her.

"I mean, since you no longer intern there, you two hardly see each other anymore." Her mother tsked again.

"Mom. Don't." She was not going there. The woman knew the stories, the gossip that took little bits of her soul every time it magically drifted to her ears. It was as if the other interns were trying to make her feel bad. Not to mention over the years she'd done everything there was to do at her father's business—except gain a full-time position. But soon…

Her mother sighed heavily and raised a hand. "I'll say no more." Her face said it all. She wasn't dropping this.

"Okay. But only for a bit." Eve dropped her arms to her sides. Her mother wouldn't leave until she got what she wanted anyway. Two hours is all she'd spend there. She'd also invite Scarlett, who'd only decline in solidarity.

Scarlett had been to her family's parties before, and all the ostentatious wealth drove her nonconformist soul into a tizzy. Plus, now Scarlett would have to cover for Eve at Peppermint Sweet. Then again, Scarlett might be conveniently busy in order to give Eve an excuse to bail on this birthday shindig.

"And bring a date. You must have men lined up and down the street. A college student like you." She brushed dust off Eve's shoulder. "Though, the way you girls dress these days. You'll never catch a man looking like you just stepped out of a camp in the middle of the woods. Dear, more *lipstick*." She whispered that last word.

Like her mother would know what someone stepping out of the woods would look like.

"Hey, Eve…" Brent had appeared in the archway, one hand wrapped around the molding, making his forearm flex. The move, so innocent, caused not-so-innocent thoughts. "When you get a sec?"

Her mother's eyes darted between them. "Mr. Shadwell."

"Brent." He dropped his hand off the door jamb.

"Brent." She flashed him a smile. "How long have you been renovating homes?"

"Oh, on and off in between semesters. I'm at A.U. with Eve." He inched his chin toward her.

"Oh, really? Business?"

"Architecture."

Her mother's brow shot up. "Ooooh." She leaned back and twisted to face Eve. "How interesting."

Eve stepped between them. "He's getting his master's in architectural engineering. And he doesn't have much time. Let's let him get back to work?"

She wouldn't let her mother slowly unpack all the details about him. She knew this game, and she wouldn't have it—not with Brent.

If left to her own devices, her mother would drill him with questions until the guy had to admit he's either destined for greatness—by her definition—or was headed to a big life of nothing. Then he could be "slotted" into one of two categories, per her code. Find out if he can move you up the social ladder (*he wishes to design homes that could appear in Architectural Digest*), and if so, ensure his attention. If not (*he wishes to design strip malls*), dismiss him—immediately.

"My." Her feigned gasp made Eve's toes curl. "Your wife must be proud of you."

"Oh, no wife."

Oh, God, Katherine Chatham was in rare form. "Mom, we're in the middle of stuff. I'll see you on Saturday. I'll call Dad later." Eve hooked her arm to lead her to the door.

"Oh, no need. I'll do that. And Brent…" she slipped away from Eve and sidled up to him, "you must come to our little gathering on Saturday. Twelve noon. It's Eve's birthday celebration."

He fixed his eyes on Eve. "Your birthday."

"Mom. Brent is quite busy."

"I'd love to, Mrs. Chatham. I'll even pick up Evangeline." That smug smile on his face would not do. Her mother, however, positively beamed.

As soon as she clicked the door shut behind her mother, she leaned against it. "You don't have to do this."

He ran a finger over his bottom lip. "Uninviting me?"

"No, it's just… they are so different from me. You'll be shocked." She ran a hand through her hair. "I'm nothing like my mom."

His smile was back. "Pick you up, say, eleven-thirty?"

She was going to have to go and play the nice daughter or be super rude to Brent. "Noon is fine." There was no need to rush to her "party." In fact, she might fall ill that morning and not make it at all. Yeah, right. She knew she would go.

Now, how was she going to prepare Brent? "I promise you. There will be an open bar."

He shrugged.

"No. Trust me. You'll be glad."

# 13

The familiar gates of her parents' home slowly rolled open. Brent peered up the curving drive. "I always wondered who lived behind this gate."

Memories stiffened her spine. Even if they were going to a "party for her"—even her mind drew air quotes around those words—none of what was going on inside this house ever had to do with celebrating her birthday.

Her "birthday parties" were mini-carnivals that the adults took to with gusto once enough scotch and wine were consumed, like the time her Uncle Jerry had punched a hole with his foot in the bouncy castle from his alcohol-induced manic jumping.

"A lot of white furniture Thor's not allowed to sit on."

"Harsh." He nodded. "Still, lots of walls for him to hide in here."

"He hates it here." She didn't mean to sound like a crank, but there it was.

He peered over at her with brows furrowed. Close proximity to this house made her snippy. More than. It pitched her into stone-cold Bitchville. He was about to find out why.

All week, she'd debated about how much she should warn him. Then again, they'd been two ships passing each other in the night, which wasn't a bad thing because no more offers of kissing were made.

She had so many classes and work shifts, she'd given him a key. He could let himself in and get started on the list he'd amassed the day Thor took himself on a walkabout. He'd leave it on the kitchen table and cross out an item every time he completed it.

He'd cleared her sink and bathtub drains, leaving a note that Thor's fur was the culprit and it "rivaled my lab's fur." He'd assessed the floors of her kitchen and gave her a ridiculously low estimate of $1200 to take up the linoleum and sand out the "eau du poisson" plus tile the floor. Next, he patched up two tiles in her bathroom near the floor that kept falling off—always clinking to the floor in the middle of the night, making her jolt awake, sure she was under home invasion. That was "on the house," he'd written under the item. Plus, he'd fixed her garage door and offered to haul everything away in Hans, which she learned was his truck's name.

When she'd asked him about the whole "Hansel and Gretel" thing, he'd said they worked well together. One cut up trees and limbs and the other hauled it away. The fact that he used children's fairytale names for his things only made him more appealing—like he was secure in his masculinity, unafraid of losing man points.

All in all, the man deserved better than what he was about to encounter.

But what would she say? Gird your loins? Keep Hans running? Remember what I said about the bar?

It made her sound pathetic—or worse, churlish.

Brent pulled his truck up behind the Salingers' Mercedes and the Woodland's Jaguar. *Small gathering, huh?* She should have known better.

A valet ran to the side of the truck and another cracked open her door as soon as Brent had stopped. Other valets scurried back and forth, which meant cars were lined up around the back lot, designed for this purpose.

"Um, my family loves their parties. The bigger the better, says my brother-in-law. But you know what they say about over-compensation and size." Oh, my God. Another snort came out of her.

"No. I've not had that problem." He smirked and patted his truck's dashboard—his *enormous* dashboard. "What you see is what you get."

She scoffed and waved her hand, which he grabbed.

He arched a perfect brow, a smirk camped on his face. "You think I'd kid about something like that?"

"Ma'am?" The valet was holding out his hand to help her out.

"Remember, honesty is a virtue," she whispered to him.

"I know," he whispered back.

Oh, man. The size of his, ahem, *Hans* was now on her brain.

She let the valet help her out of the car. Her mother and father smiled at them from the top of the wide, front steps.

"There she is. My birthday girl." Her dad's face beamed as they took the stairs up to meet them.

Her insides calmed. "Hi, Dad." Her father somehow remained normal despite all the trappings of wealth. For one, he asked questions and listened to the answers.

He engulfed her in a bear hug. "You look wonderful. As always." Tension loosened in her shoulders.

"She looks tired." Her mother leaned down for a cheek kiss and dropped her voice to a whisper. "I see you chose to wear flats."

Eve rolled her eyes toward her father, who smiled back conspiratorially. Her mother should be glad she'd donned a dress, found still hanging in its dry cleaner bags from months ago when she'd worn the blue number to her cousin Margaret's wedding. She rather liked the daisies dotting the hem. Nice, simple flowers.

"And who is this fine young man? Nice truck. That an F-450 Super Duty?" Her father gave Brent a hearty handshake.

Eve had to stifle a laugh. "This is Brent."

Brent nodded once. "Yes, sir. One of their limited editions." He glanced her way and a tamped-down giggle erupted. Her dad and trucks didn't mix.

Her father still blinked at her. "Well, now I'm going to have to look into buying a truck." Her dad circled her mother's shoulders and squeezed her closer to him.

"Oh, really?" Her mother reddened a little—probably wondering how on earth she'd hoist herself up to the front seat in her Chanel heels.

"Watch me." Her father winked, and a pang went off in Eve's chest. Her dad had none of the airs of her mother but sure could pile on the charm when needed. That's why he managed to be such an ace negotiator, buying up companies left and right.

Eve pulled Brent toward the entrance. "We're going in." The faster in, the faster out. That was her strategy—expose him to the fewest people possible, make one round, and then she'd fake a headache—or a broken leg, if necessary. Or get drunk. They could do that, too.

Her mother's eyes squinched. "Yes, you two go inside. Everyone's been waiting for the birthday girl."

Her father's hand cupped her bicep, and he leaned down to her. "Everything going well with school? Work? Still got your eye on the ball?" He glanced up at Brent.

A childish zing of fear ran through her. "Of course, Dad. Everything's great." She glanced over at Brent, who was chatting up her mother. "Brent's helping me with house renovations. I won't let you down." He knew that, right?

Her father straightened and nodded once, a smile firmly in place. "That's my Eve-bee. Remember," He winked. "You'll be the first." As in the first female of the Chatham clan to graduate college—that was their shared dream.

"But I'm glad you're getting a little recreation in, too." Her father glanced over at Brent.

Her heart moved to her throat. It beat loud and fast, full of questions. Her father didn't golf, barbeque, or even go on vacations unless her mother dragged him.

"Ready?" Brent held out his arm.

"Bryson," her dad called to a rotund man attempting to lift himself out of a Mercedes. "Glad you could make it."

Brent pulled her inside. She would have to find her dad later and talk to him about what he meant by "recreation" because he had never been a proponent of it before.

As soon as their feet were through the entranceway, a woman in a maid's uniform held out a tray to them that carried champagne flutes. "Happy birthday, Evangeline."

"Thank you." Her mother likely handed out her picture to every person here—from the hired help to the guests—to make sure they knew what she looked like.

She turned to Brent. "Brent, listen…"

Brent took two flutes and handed her one. "Remind me to up my present game. I didn't realize you were a Tiffany girl." His chin dipped toward a large foyer table laden with colorful packages, some in bright pink with white ribbons, others in purples and greens, and a few of the telltale Tiffany blue boxes tied in white ribbons.

"I'm more of a stained-glass girl." She softened her eyes up at him. He'd also given her a birthday card—one with a beautiful watercolor scene picturing a large cat that looked like Thor. "Every year, I ask them to make donations in my name. They never do. I'm donating all of that," she inclined her head to the ridiculous number of presents, "to Catopia, a local rescue group, for their silent auction. I do it every year."

His green eyes fixed on her, warm and amused. "Good thing I drove my monster truck, then. Ya' know, to haul away the goods."

The stinging tightness in her shoulders eased a bit more. He was a lot like her dad—he knew what to say when. "You're not afraid your masculinity will be questioned hauling around pink and yellow boxes?"

"And Tiffany blue."

"I'm impressed you know that."

"I'll have you know my mother gets jewelry from me every year. Not Tiffany, but someday."

"I'm sure you will." She squared herself to him. "Hey, I probably should have told you some things about my family and their friends. They might cross some boundaries. They're a little…"

How did one say, *"Count your nuts on the way out because those manicures are sharp?"*

"Don't worry." He took a sip of champagne. "All families are crazy." He lifted his glass. "Promise me I'll find something that doesn't fizz to drink later?"

"Straight up," she promised.

Female voices sounded like they were growing closer. They had to move—*now*.

She hooked her arm in his. "Open bar out by the pool. Let's go."

"Evangeline!" A loud squeal bounced from the living room entrance. "Let me get a look at you."

Eve squeezed his arm and whispered quickly, "Know that once again, I'm sorry for what you're about to walk into."

Her mother's best friend, Carolina Salinger, teetered over. Within seconds, Eve's face was full of her stiff hair and Dior perfume. Mercifully, Carolina pulled back before Eve was about to launch into a wheezing fit.

Carolina bracketed her face with both hands, the cool metal of rings touching her skin. "Like I thought. Too much work. I took this face-reading class the other weekend. It was magical. Speaking of faces..."

At seeing Brent, Carolina's silicone lips curled upward like a duck. They failed to stretch wide anymore.

"My," she breathed. "Katherine did not do you justice." She ran her hand up Brent's arm. "No, she did not." Her hand squeezed his bicep. "So, you're Evangeline's renovation help. You look tired, Eve dear, can I make you a spa appointment? On me?"

"I'm good, I'm just—"

"She doesn't need a spa. She doesn't age—at all." Bethany Woodford's voice was laced with over-the-top excitement as she scooted up. "I'm Eve's fairy godmother." She offered a limp hand to Brent.

Eve tugged harder on Brent's arm. "We were on our way—"

"No, she does not. She's ravishing. Get in here, you two." Her Aunt Lillian stood in the doorway and cocked her head toward the living room behind her.

The entire Interrogation Brigade, the IB, was assembled: Carolina, Bethany, and Lisa in the hallway, and the rest of them, Aunt Lillian, Trina Palisi, and Cousin Helen Mallory, just inside the doorway.

Eve's heart slunk to the pit of her stomach. What did she do to earn this Karma? What did Brent do?

Then again, Eve should have guessed her mother would have made sure her friends, cousins, and aunts were positioned in the living room so there was no way they could have gotten farther into the party without being seen—as had been Eve's hope. Now, the IB could do the probing for her mother, reporting in later.

Carolina hooked her arm in Brent's and Bethany's wide hips booted Eve to the side so the woman could lay claim to the other arm. *Whoa there, fairy godmother.* Taking ownership of a new Gucci purse was one thing...

Brent's eyes colored with amusement as she and Brent were ushered into the main examination room, a.k.a. the white couches only despoiled with people's butts for super special events, like the unpacking of a new male in their midst. Swear to God, if any one of them made him uncomfortable, she'd be forced to say something.

Brent—the trusting man—smiled down at each of the women, introducing himself with an outstretched handshake. Each woman took their turn to clasp his hand with both of theirs. They sure loved to fondle people—especially men.

Carolina's upturned face beamed. "My, such proficient hands. Katherine tells us you're in renovations?"

And the interrogation had begun.

He scrubbed his hair because he'd finally gotten one hand free. "Something like that."

Carolina led him over to the white leather couch in the center of the room, perched herself on the edge, and patted the middle seat next to her. "Let's chat for a minute."

Brent, being the polite—and naive—guy he was, sat himself down, and instantly slid to the back on the angled seat. Eve quickly landed next to him—because a man needed protection in this den. She was smushed closer to him when Bethany wiggled down in the last few available inches of couch space.

Aunt Lillian, Trina, and Helen sat on the matching couch on the other side of the wide glass coffee table. Their trainer-toned asses perched on the edge, their legs crossed at the ankle. Crystal wine glasses and flutes dangled from manicured fingers.

For women who were married, thirty years Brent's senior, and not a single one needing renovation help, their fawning over him caused her internal organs to practically itch.

Aunt Lillian licked her lips. Fixing a leaky toilet or patching drywall was the last thing on her mind. She was on her third husband—fourth? Who could remember? One thing she did know, her aunt always went for younger guys, married or not.

In fact, all of them did little to hide the hunger in their eyes as they assessed him. Of course, Brent standing in all this feminine energy, his male side was highlighted even more—and he was a mighty fine specimen of manhood. Still, did they really have to salivate so obviously? Isn't this what women fought against for centuries? Where was their pride? Their feminism?

Then again, her own hormones had folded the second they met the man.

Why was she asking these questions to herself anyway? She knew the answer. They didn't have much else going on and didn't want much else. They might break a fingernail if they strayed too far from their spas and boutique shops and moved toward anything resembling work. Or, heaven forbid, needing their own bank accounts. Or, horrors, they'd have to pay attention to an ATM balance. They might have to do *math*.

Well, that math aversion she understood. But still…

A while back, Eve had overheard a conversation between her mother and Carolina about how Aunt Lillian's "*sloppy Big I*", which was code for infidelity, and "*getting caught like that*" being the reason for the last *Big D*—the label they used amongst themselves for divorce. The *Big R* was for rest, recovery, and rejuvenation—usually in the form of plastic surgery. That was followed by the *Big G*—or the *"big get"* of the next husband.

That was why she hated these gatherings. Her ambition, her wanting something more than the *Big G*, made her a foreigner in her parents' house.

Eve took a sip of champagne to give her mouth something to do. "How has everyone been?" Any "bigs" she needed to know about?

"We're all fine." Bethany fluttered her hand, her rings catching the light. "Except Hilton Head was such a true bore this year."

The other ladies nodded in agreement.

Carolina's cool hand reached across Brent's lap and touched hers. "How are you, birthday girl? When was graduation?" Carolina sent a hand to her breastbone. "We didn't miss an invitation, did we?"

"Oh, no," Eve shrugged. "Still in school."

Bethany's lips turned down. "How is living on your own? Are you lonely?" She tittered. "Oh, what am I saying? You have Brent here." She took possession of his wrist. "Brent, how many houses have you worked on?" Her knees pressed against his thigh.

Bethany made a flourishing motion with her hand. "Carolina, a man doesn't count his houses."

"Tell that to my first ex."

All the ladies laughed—a quiet, practiced cackle.

Brent set his untouched champagne flute down on the glass coffee table. The tall cut crystal looked silly in his large hand anyway. This man needed a tumbler of something super strong to continue. Eve glanced around. There had to be a bottle somewhere.

Brent cleared his throat. "Twenty-seven."

*Oohs* and *aahs* filled the room. Eve understood their reaction to his answer. Twenty-seven? And she thought she'd been busy.

Carolina's hand blew to her cheek. "My. You're practically a developer." Carolina's hand clutched Brent's bicep—again. "Tell us all about your work. I'll bet it's a terrific way to stay in shape."

"Oh, I'd say the man is already in shape." Aunt Lillian's eyes lazily drifted down his chest. She was so obvious in her check-out of Brent, Eve was embarrassed for her.

Brent scratched the side of his neck, clearly growing uncomfortable by this little exchange.

Eve cocked her head. "Aunt Lillian, where is Jerald?" As in, *"Why are you eye fucking my date?"* Yes, she was declaring him that today. A man like Brent needed a label—like a big circle with a slash through it. Or, better, police tape around him.

"Oh," her aunt scoffed. "It's not my turn to watch him. But check the maid's quarters."

More fake laughter.

"What? It's very hard work watching that man. Talk about lack of discipline. He can get himself to the bar—or zip up his pants on his own." She drained her glass.

"So few men are disciplined these days. It's wonderful to find someone willing to put in real work, you know?" Carolina would be frowning at that moment given her serious tone, but the Botox made it impossible for her to move her forehead.

"Yes, so few men work with their hands anymore," Bethany chimed in. As if either of them would know? One was married to a bank executive, the other owned a chain of convenience stores up and down the East Coast. Or was it the other way around?

Carolina ran her fingers back and forth on his forearm like she was petting him. He gripped his knees, and a flash of anger lit up Eve's insides. This man was not one of her Shih Tzus.

Before Eve could make a move to rescue the man, Brent tried to adjust himself on the couch. With so much female flesh penning him in, not much changed in his position. They needed to go and park themselves at the bar—outside.

Carolina lifted her chin and looked him at from under her lashes. "Yes. I think you're on your way like our Eve. Why, you two are perfect for each other. What's the next step?"

Step? What step? Eve moved to extract herself—and Brent—from the couch. "Brent, let's get you a real drink." They couldn't wait another second. Because whatever past life had either of them had that caused this? That penance could be paid another day.

Eve tried to stand, but Bethany's hand fell to Eve's leg immediately as if to say, *"Down, little puppy."*

Bethany twisted, lifted her arm, and waggled her fingers. "Malcolm, can you get this man a real drink? Let me guess, Brent. Scotch?"

Eve hadn't seen Malcolm standing by, probably given orders to hang where the Brigade were to count their drinks and then send a warning to her mother when they hit a certain limit—as if that stopped anything.

"Scotch is fine." Brent placed his hand over Eve's. "What about you?"

That noble move ignited a new level of interest among the women. They cast sideways glances at one another and nodded.

"Oh, you are a gentleman." Bethany's eyes widened. "Eve, dear, grab this one *now*."

Eve was being punished for something—something on the *universal* level, wasn't she?

"Evangeline is probably pacing herself," Bethany added.

"She is so… disciplined. No wonder she hasn't had a date in, what has it been, Eve dear? Two years?"

Oh, for Christ's sake. "I haven't exactly—"

"We understand." Carolina tucked a lock of Eve's hair behind her ear. She lifted her lashes to Brent and lowered her voice. "Brent, you are her *savior*."

Kill her now. Someone, please.

"I'd say Eve is pretty good at saving herself." Brent chuckled. "It's Thor who needs the help."

Six sets of false eyelashes blinked in confusion. "Who?" Bethany asked.

Never mind every single one of them had teetered on their heels to avoid him when Thor came down to rub himself on their designer outfits. God forbid a cat hair spoil their "look."

"My cat," Eve reminded them. "Listen, we—"

"Ooooh." Carolina tsked. "A cat." She nodded slowly, knowingly. The other women's lips pursed in understanding.

And just like that, Eve was a spinster with a stopped clock and a ruined wedding cake sitting in the middle of the table right out of *Great Expectations* or something.

She pushed herself to standing and held out her hand to Brent. "Actually, I do need a drink." Or a bottle. "What do you say we make a round and say hello to everyone? We don't want to ignore anyone."

"Yes, why don't you do that?" Carolina cooed. "It'll give us time to get to know Brent here."

"Ladies," Eve's father boomed from down the hallway. "I hear a man in here needs a drink. Brent, want to join me by the pool?"

God, she loved her father, and a raise to Malcolm, who must have alerted him to the fact a hostage situation was ensuing and Brent and Eve needed rescuing. If not, this crew would have the two of them engaged before they finished their champagne.

"Yes, well, I suppose the men must gather." Carolina smoothed down her bangs. "Eve, why don't you let the men go have a drink together? Stay. Catch up with us."

No. Way. "I need to go find Persephone."

"Always doing the right thing." Bethany touched her hand and winked. "Don't forget to have some fun, Eve. I know, I certainly would with…" she inclined her chin toward Brent, who strode over to her father, "that one working a hammer near me."

*Lady, keep your hands off his hammer.* Eve smiled down at her.

The party had officially begun.

# 14

Eve stepped out of the powder room and glanced up and down the hallway. She'd desperately had to pee and had trusted her father would spirit Brent away to the bar—and only the bar.

She ran smack into Persephone around the corner.

"Eve. Happy Birthday!" Her sister yanked Eve's arm and pulled her inside the powder room, barely large enough for the two of them.

"Whoa. Watch the nails." She rubbed her arm where Persy's manicure had scratched.

"I saw Carolina working you over in the living room. Hang out in here until she finds someone else to interrogate. Here. Put on some lipstick." She reached into her clutch and brought out a little gold cylinder.

She took the lipstick from Persy. A little color wouldn't be bad. "Thanks."

"I overheard mom filling in the IB earlier. She said Brent's an architect." Persephone leaned against the vanity top. "How long have you been seeing him?"

"We're friends."

Her sister snorted, which made Eve's heart sink. Maybe the nose laughter was hereditary. "God, Eve, do you know what architects make? When they're successful?"

Here they went—yet another conversation that screamed their differences.

"Don't know. Don't care. I have to go find him." She handed over the lipstick and tried to whirl away, but Persy's nails dug into her arm.

"Wait." Her sister then crossed her arms over her boobs. "Honestly, Eve. You will care when you're out of school and see how hard it is to get up every morning and go to an office and—"

"Persy." Her sister hated that nickname but Eve hated her tone. "Can I get through this day without having this conversation?"

"You know, Mom and Dad are worried about you. Living by yourself, never going out."

No, *their parents* weren't. "You mean Mom. I'm fine. I'm happy." Sort of. She wasn't *unhappy*. She was content with her choices.

Persy's lips drooped. She still looked like a model. She'd got the glossy dark hair and almond-shaped eyes. "You're not getting any younger. And it gets harder and harder, especially after you turn thirty." She turned to face the mirror to check her makeup under her eyes. It was perfect, of course.

She glanced at Eve in the mirror while she popped open her lipstick top. "One day, you'll look back on this and wonder why you didn't grab the first guy that I could see even across the hallway you like. I hear he's *handy*."

Her mother certainly had spread the word about Brent, hadn't she? And what was up with all this old maid talk? "I'm not exactly needing to apply for the *Bachelorette* yet." An exasperated puff of air left Eve's mouth.

Persy stilled, lipstick in mid-air. "That's not a bad idea. They get good-looking rich guys. I'll bet you could apply."

She was going to have to get drunk today, wasn't she?

"I mean," Persy returned to applying lipstick. She pressed her lips together and let them go with a smack. "Getting your degree is great, but you're my sister and I don't want you dying with just that cat."

*That* cat? Eve put her hands on her hips. He wasn't just "a" cat, and no one talked down on Thor. Not on her watch. "Thor is better company than someone who wants to talk accounting all night long."

"Kevin is a corporate tax attorney who made partner at age twenty-six." She fluffed her hair and yanked on the sides of her dress to reposition her perfect breasts—the mounds of silicone that she'd begged for as her eighteenth birthday present. If Eve recalled correctly, she'd whined to her mother that she couldn't go off to The University of North Carolina "looking like she balanced two strawberries on her chest." Mom was such a pushover.

Her sister dropped her chin. "Don't roll your eyes at me. Listen, I'm trying to spare you my mistake. I should have been with Kevin all along. We fit together. But I rebuffed him at first. Ended up with that *Peter* instead."

Eve crossed her arms. "I'd prefer it if we used his real name."

Persy's lips inched up, and together, they said, "Pecker head." They burst into giggles which quickly died off. Probably because it wasn't funny what he'd done to her sister. Not even a little bit.

"Eve, I need to tell you what I've learned. If you don't show interest in the great guys when you meet them, they *will* find someone else."

Eve couldn't believe her sister was telling her to play the

opposite of hard to get. Didn't she invent that little ploy? "He's welcome to."

"Are you sure?" Persy asked slowly.

She rolled her lips between her teeth. "Mmmm-hmmm." She wasn't—not really. Truth was, the thought of Brent with someone else made her feel a little sick. But the idea of getting romantically involved with him? Terrifying. The slide away from her goals could start so easily. Even Olympians say if you move your hand a millimeter or slow down for a second, you could lose the Gold—or not end up on the podium at all.

"Here's a little more advice for you. After my divorce mess, when Kevin finally got the nerve to ask me out again, he asked where I'd like to go to dinner. So I chose the most expensive place in town—"

"Persy, come on—"

"No, listen to me. He needed to know who I was upfront. When Brent asks you what you want, you tell him who he's dealing with. That's the key. So he knows what's important to you. Otherwise, no matter how great he is, it's not worth lying to him or yourself." She tsked. "Boy, did I learn that one the hard way."

Persy then yanked open the door. "Now, go find Brent. Show him the real you." She spun Eve by the shoulders and pointed her to the exit. "And rescue him from whatever interrogation is ensuing. If you don't, know that there are at least six single women here who'd love to check out a new man's skills." Of course, Persy counted the unmarrieds within a mile. She still had trust issues to deal with.

"He's fully booked," she said quickly. "I mean, his skills. With my house… and…"

"Oh, I know what you mean." Persy graced her with a knowing half-smile. "I saw you in there with the IB. Thought you were going to scratch out Carolina's eyes at one point."

"I was not." Yet Eve's stomach roiled with something she couldn't fully grasp. The bathroom door clicked shut behind her.

*Tell him who he's dealing with.* As she strode to the pool, those words rolled through her brain on a loop. When had Persy turned so thoughtful? Truth was, she thought she knew herself. Since she'd met Brent, however, she was becoming so… enthralled by him. Normally, she was much more clear-headed.

She knew one thing, though, that Persy had identified. She didn't want Carolina—or anyone—petting Brent again.

# 15

Her father and Brent weren't in his study, so they had to be near the pool.

As soon as she stepped onto the terrace, she caught both of her parents standing with Brent by the diving board. Her father's smile reached right into her heart. Thank God, he'd stuck close by Brent.

That didn't stop quite a few of the Interrogation Brigade from hovering nearby—or two teenage girls Eve didn't recognize who splashed in the pool, whispering to one another while eying him.

Brent truly was a chick magnet. He also was cool under pressure because the most seasoned FBI hostage negotiator couldn't out-interrogate the Brigade.

As soon as she made her way to them, her father engulfed her in a big hug. "There she is. My little college student."

She smiled up at him. "Almost graduate."

Her mother reached over to correct the neckline of her dress that—horrors—had gone askew from Dad's hug. "So long as she doesn't overdo it."

"Our little Eve-bee is going far, Katherine."

Her mother's eyes drank in Brent. "I'm delighted to hear you're helping Eve with some things around the house. I worry, you know. Her sister, Persephone, is finally in a good place, and I want my girl here to find hers, too."

The Eve-is-a-spinster vibe was alive and well. She needed wine—pronto. She looked around for someone holding a tray of glasses or where the bar had been set up. Ah, in the corner. Only twenty feet away—and yet so far.

Brent twirled the tumbler in his palm. Thank God, he'd got straight-up liquor. "She's got quite a nice place. A find on her hands. Those houses are in demand."

Brent didn't realize exactly what her mother meant. Until Eve was tagged and bagged into some marital bliss, Eve was considered unfinished by her mother. Unslotted. Adrift.

Her father shifted on his feet. "I was skeptical at first, but Eve here seems to have things under control."

"I do, Dad. My renovation class is—"

"Oh, Eve." Her mother scoffed. "That's what men are for." She smiled at Brent, who flushed. "In fact, Brent and I were discussing some changes to the pool house."

She groaned. "Mom, that pool house is fine." Where was a drink server when you needed one?

Katherine clucked. "Spoken by a woman who never uses it. Oh, there are the Moores. I wondered what had happened to them." She lifted her chin toward a man in golf pants and a woman in a long, flowy white dress. "Excuse us, will you?" She squeezed her father's arm. "We should go say hello."

Her father offered his hand to Brent. "Good to meet you, Brent. Eve." He placed a quick kiss on her forehead and lowered his voice. "She means well. I'm proud of you, Eve-bee."

Six words—that's all it took for warmth to swirl in her chest, replacing all the irritation her mother and sister had called up. Her dad could make things right so easily.

He then reached into his jacket pocket and drew out a pink envelope. "For later. And let's have lunch soon."

"Thanks, Dad." She rose on her tiptoes and kissed him on the cheek. She'd open his birthday card later when she had some privacy. Her father never failed to give her a special one with a little hand-written note inside at every major event—birthdays, Christmas, and even President's Day. It was their little secret.

Eve grasped Brent's arm and urged him closer to the diving board. She needed to get him away from any others who might have pool houses that needed renovating. "Sorry for whatever my mother said or asked you. And for all the others." She waved her hand toward the house.

"Nah, it's fine. And your mom's cool."

She grimaced. "That is not a word I'd use to describe my mother. And seriously, double sorry about the Interrogation Brigade—and how they instantly started feeling you up."

"Hey, what can I say? I'm cougar bait."

A giggle rose in her throat followed by a god-awful snort.

He slapped his hand against his chest. "Wound me with your laughter, why don't you?"

She bumped her hip against his thigh. "So sensitive."

"Me?" He pointed one finger, the others holding his glass. "You were jealous."

"Was not." Maybe a little, which was odd for her.

He leaned down and whispered. "I liked it." When he rose back to his full height, his eyes sparkled. "You're competitive."

Her chin rose. "Am not."

"Are too." He bumped his shoulder against hers.

"I'm independent. I now have my own house, and in six months I'll have my degree. 4.0 average, and I'm going to have marketable skills that will be with me forever." She clasped her bottom lips with her teeth as if that might stop any more gushing of words. She hadn't meant to sound defensive.

"And you're not competitive?"

So amused. He didn't understand. She needed to prove to herself she could do this. And to her father. If she didn't, she wouldn't have anyone in the family who was proud of her accomplishments, who measured her worth by actual goals achieved and not how good she looked and what man she snagged. "I need to know I can take care of myself. I am not going to end up like them."

"Them?"

She hitched her thumb toward the Brigade. Over by the bar, Aunt Lillian fake-laughed at something a man said, and her long red fingernails trailed down from his bicep to forearm. Eve had seen that move a hundred times—and dozens of others meant to do one thing: keep a man close. Or, should she say, keep his bank account open?

He nodded slowly. "Success, then. You're not like those women at all."

"You say all the right things. Ah, finally." A woman in all black had appeared and presented a tray of full wine glasses. Eve grabbed a white wine. "Let's sit." She plunked down on the diving board and set the card from her father in her lap. "First, I should have filled you in about my family for your own protection." She took a big swallow and instantly felt the tension float right out of her.

Brent settled next to her and placed his elbows on his knees. "They're not that bad."

"My dad's pretty cool. He likes you." Across the wide patio, her father bent down and kissed her mother's cheek as she continued to chatter with the Moores.

"It's the truck, isn't it?"

"Totally. And the fact you own a chainsaw and know how to use it."

"He did seem awfully interested in Gretel."

"Can I ask you a question?" She had more than one, but a particular question was burning in her gut. "How are you single?" The wine had taken hold—clearly. She took another big gulp. "I mean, really?" She motioned toward the women who were *still* staring in their direction. They didn't even avert their eyes at her wild gesture.

He set his tumbler down next to him. "Been busy. The question is how are you?"

A rumbly snort rose up in her, naturally. "Been *really* busy. I don't have a lot of time for…" She waggled her fingers back and forth between them. Words were beginning to fail her. She hadn't eaten much that day, and wine made her stupid under the best of circumstances.

Brent interlaced his fingers through hers, warmth spreading across her skin. "Then you'll just have to use me for my skills—and sex."

A huge laugh followed by a honk—dammit—flew out of her. She slapped her hand over her mouth and nose to stop any more embarrassing noises coming out of her.

"You think I jest. It's okay if you want me for my body." He pointed up and down his torso. "Really. I mean, apparently, I'm in great shape, according to the judges." He tipped his head toward Aunt Lillian. "I can tell she's a harsh judge, too."

Hardly. But this man couldn't be for real. "You just want my house… or maybe you want to hang out with Thor."

"It's Thor." He hung his head but then turned his face toward her. "So, what do you say? Think you might go out with me again? I like you, even if you are competitive. You're smart and capable as well as beautiful. Yes, you are. Don't protest. And it's a rare combination. We'd have fun together. All three of us, actually."

"Date you?" She crossed her arms. This was not how

things were supposed to go, but honestly, he seemed to understand her more than most. "Hmmm. You may be good with a screwdriver, but how are you at scooping out kitty litter? Cause if you won't do that, Thor will *not* want to hang with you. He's particular."

His eyes peered up into the sky in thought. "Hmm. Anything else I can contribute?"

Persy's advice rose to the surface. *Tell him what you want.* "Show me how your power tools work."

"Consider it done."

Oh, points for Persy. "You really do know what to say to win a girl. One thing, though. We go slow. Take our time."

He nodded slowly. She should have never doubted her sister. If anyone knew men, it was her.

"Oh, and despite us being casual, my family will continuously question your ability to keep me in the lifestyle I've grown accustomed to." She raised a finger. "But know I will never *need* you to finance, support, or give me said lifestyle."

"Your lifestyle? De-skunking agents, power tools, and cat litter? Those, I can do. So, deal." He offered a handshake, which she took.

For a long minute, his hand heated hers and they stared at one another. What had she agreed to? A little innocent fun, that was all.

More tension loosened inside her like a coil she hadn't realized was wound up. He was fun, but even greater, he was trying to understand her—like really get to know her. This is what she wanted eventually—someone who didn't judge her choices yet still wanted to be with her. She'd never met a guy like Brent before. Getting to know him better didn't *have* to mean she'd suddenly grow helpless or lose her momentum. She could keep it under control. It didn't have to take over her life.

When she went to free her fingers, though, he yanked her closer to him.

He tsked. "Uh-uh-uh."

She should draw a boundary right now: no surprises, no assuming anything. "What are you doing?"

"Letting you win… my body. Steel yourself. I'm moving in for a public kiss, the one that I wanted to give you in your garage. Which, by the way, I'm adding its roof to the renovation list."

He couldn't be serious. She playfully slapped him. "We shouldn't."

"Are you sure?" He moved his gaze around the pool area "That woman over there is eyeing me like she wants to climb into my truck bed."

"That's Trina. Only if you have 1000-count Egyptian cotton sheets in the back would she consider it. Plus, I don't think she'd appreciate Gretel like I would."

"Ah, another reason to like you." He leaned closer. He was going to kiss her.

The thrum of her blood pulsed in her ears as she met him halfway and let their lips collide. It was supposed to be a peck—something simple, chaste.

Chaste, her ass.

His arms wrapped around her and pulled her even closer and sparks flew up her spine. His lips slid across her mouth, fitting so beautifully. His hands slid further up her back, and sweet Jesus on high, the urge to be manhandled grew like fire over prairie brush.

When she pulled back, a satisfying flush colored his face. "So," she said.

"So."

"We'll go out on a date sometime." She could barely get the words out, but that's probably because his thigh pressed warmth into her leg—and other places.

"If you don't mind being driven around in a truck."

He had to bring up the truck because now her mind filled with visions of its considerable size. "I insist. I might be using you for it, too."

*Don't glance down at his crotch. Don't do it. Just. Don't. Look. Down.*

*Oops.*

The bulge in his jeans spoke volumes. He'd enjoyed their kiss as much as she had.

He tucked hair behind her ear. "Good. You're real, Evangeline. Authentic."

Her last wall of resistance fell with a loud crash. "Call me Eve. I hate my full name."

He fingered a lock of her hair. "Evangeline is elegant."

"It's pretentious." His scent and the heat from his muscled leg pressed in on her. *Please take me to your truck.*

His gaze flicked to her lips. "It's beautiful."

"It's ridiculous." Her words were a mere whisper. "I don't want to be ridiculous." That's what it was, wasn't it? She would never be made a fool like too many women she'd been around had.

His arm snaked around her waist. "You could never. But you *are* beautiful. And you can get jealous over me anytime. I don't even mind if you just want me for my bod." He winked.

"Don't forget your power tools." And maybe his truck. "And I wasn't jealous." Yeah, she was. "But I know I can sometimes be…" She couldn't even say the word. *Competitive.* But it was a good energy to tap into when trying to get things done.

"Can't say it, huh?" He arched an eyebrow.

Damn mind reader. "I'd rather not talk."

She silenced him with her lips, this time lingering long and dipping her tongue into his mouth as they sat on the diving board, surrounded by the crème de la crème of Bishop's Gate society.

Brent's lips inched up into a cat-like grin. "I knew you couldn't wait to do that."

Their lips were still touching. His breath was full of scotch and peppermint. "Maybe."

"Hey, ready to grab the loot pile and run?" He didn't wait for her answer. He stood and held out his hand. "Let's not be like them and rudely leave early. I have another present for you."

A drive would be good. She'd regain her composure on the way home.

She would.

# 16

As soon as they stepped inside her house, Thor began his usual ritual—rubbing up against her in a demand for dinner in a symphony of chirps and purrs.

Brent's lips returned to hers as he backed them both down the hall. "Looks like there are two of us into you."

At every stoplight, he'd either kissed her or kissed the back of her hand which he'd captured in his for the entire ride to Catopia— who were beyond thrilled at the piles of jewelry, scarves, and other trinkets they could auction off at their annual Critter Ball. The closer they got to her house, the more urgent his hands grew, squeezing her fingers, trailing his down to her thigh. The man had great hands and a smile that turned her insides into goo.

So much for regaining her poise. People kissed when they dated. It was okay. Only his kisses were more than okay—they were mind-numbing, body-igniting *sledgehammers* to good sense.

On the way home, she made a deal—no full-sex business. Not yet. They'd only started getting to know one another.

Her hand landed on his pec, an attempt to put some

distance between his hypnotizing lips and her growing neediness. "I liked our kiss, but we shouldn't get into any… funny stuff." Oh, jeez, she waggled her finger at him.

He laughed. "But do you find this funny?" He placed his hand against her cheek. *Feelings* crowded in around her. All kinds of mushy, messed-up, please-kiss-me-again thoughts stirred and whirled under her skin. But they would. Today, he'd dangled the greatest aphrodisiac in the world—being desired for who you really are. That's what he'd really done. She'd shown her hand, and he wanted to keep playing.

Thor meowed a protest at being ignored.

"I have to feed him or he won't stop."

Brent nodded slowly, his smile still camped out on his gorgeous face. Yep. This man did *not* play fair. Driving a monster truck, waltzing into her home with those gifted hands, good looks, *understanding*, and a drywall saw.

He was going to be amazing at the funny business, wasn't he?

He chortled. "What's going on in that head of yours?"

Uh-uh. She wasn't telling or he'd get funny stuff *ideas*. "Nothing."

"Do you want to know what I'm thinking?" He looked down at Thor. "He's definitely jealous of me."

A snorty laugh burst from her throat. "You're standing between him and food. That's what's going on."

"Mmm-hmm." Brent closed the final bit of distance between them, her breasts now mashed against his chest. "You want to kiss me again, and he doesn't like sharing you. I know the feeling. How about you feed him and then you can again."

"Can what?"

His hands wrapped around her waist and squeezed. "Kiss me."

"I already did on the diving board," she said, all breathy

and bothered. And in his truck. And standing here in her hallway.

His clean scent, like sawdust and fresh air, was making her dizzy. Or she was hyperventilating. Her chest was rising and falling like she'd run home and not been driven here.

Gah, she loved Hans. A big, manly, masculine-smelling, tool-carting hunk of steel.

Slapping his pecs again to keep him from drawing her closer only made it worse. All. That. Rugged man muscle. Her fingers curled into his shirt. He had good taste, too. Finely woven cotton rustled under her grab.

His lips twitched up into another half-smile. "Your call if you want to again, of course."

"Yes."

"Yes, it's your call, or yes, you'll kiss me again?"

"Yes, yes." She did *not* say that, or, in reality, breathe it out like a wanton puddle of consent. But yes, she had, and now, he was slowly and deliberately backing her up the hallway toward the kitchen—with more lip-locking on his mind. She'd forgotten how wonderful kissing felt. Such a strange thing, to put your mouth on someone else's and have sparks fly through your whole body.

As soon as her feet hit her crappy kitchen linoleum, she pushed him off her. She held up a finger and attempted to catch her breath. "Wait. One second." She had to remember how to breathe. Air in and air out.

She backed up toward the kitchen cupboard where Thor's food was stored. She hadn't wanted to break his gaze so she kept her eyes locked on him. All that green flecked in gold was drinking her in, and it was as if her insides were being pulled toward him even as she stepped backward.

She fumbled behind her to open the cupboard, but then his hands were on her waist again and he pressed her against the counter. His lips found hers again. Jesus, the man's skills list was growing.

Finally, she broke free, spun, and grabbed Thor's bowl and the Meow Chow. She couldn't look at Brent anymore or she'd dissolve like a marshmallow in hot chocolate. Kibble pinged like tiny chimes into the bowl.

She startled when his fingers circled her front and his hands palmed her breasts. Thor's chow bits skittered across the counter and onto the floor as her hand shook and she missed the bowl. Whatever, he'd eat the rogue kibble off the floor.

Brent murmured. Was he appreciating? Disappointed? She wasn't Dolly Parton in the breast department, but she wasn't sporting two strawberries, either. Her worries vaporized when warm lips met the back of her neck.

"Mmm, sweet," he said into her hair.

She lowered herself slowly to set down the bowl, and Thor attacked his food.

As soon as she twisted to face Brent, his mouth crashed down onto hers. And God help her, she loved the way he practically devoured her and pressed her against her counter.

For long minutes, they stood in her kitchen, his mouth on her lips, her neck, even a few pressed to her eyelids, which was so tender and so erotic she nearly slithered to the floor in full surrender.

He scooped her up and took her into the living room where they landed on her couch.

His body lay on top of hers, one leg hitched over his hip as his cock, trapped behind his jeans, ground against her. Now she understood the truck reference because holy mother of God. His hips arched into her... then again...

She must have left her brain in the kitchen because they were dry humping like teenagers in the basement of their parents' house. He didn't try to take her clothes off—instead, he drove her mad until she came, completely clothed.

They stared at one another for long seconds, panting. He put both his hands on either side of her head. "I want to give you more."

She nodded because *more* sounded great despite her earlier promises to herself. A restless, sharp ache grew inside her like a storm was building.

His lips curved into a smirk worthy of Rhett Butler. The man really did good things with his mouth. His hands trailed down the sides of her body and then slipped between her legs.

She swallowed. They were going to have sex. The horizontal cha-cha. The live power drilling. Had she shaved?

He unbuttoned her jeans and slipped his hand inside so fast, she gasped. She hadn't been touched there in millennia. His finger slipped inside her easily since she was soaking wet from coming.

"I'm upping my present game," he growled.

And then she was releasing again, her hot breath moving across his cheek. Mind blank, body shaking, she'd let this man do anything he wanted to her. *Anything.*

"Happy Birthday, Eve," he whispered into her ear.

*Definitely better than Tiffany.*

He laughed. Oh, she'd said that aloud.

"Better than that pink thing," he said.

He had to bring up the Vibrator Incident. "Glad to hear you're confident."

Green eyes cast mischief down on her. "Want me to prove it again?"

She nodded vigorously.

# 17

Eve's heart nearly shot out of her chest. Her eyelids flicked open. Thor was kneading her chest and purring loudly—code for "me, me, me."

She'd fallen asleep. What time was it? Through the windows, the sun hung low in the sky giving off that flat, warm glow of a summer exiting and a fall entering.

She righted herself, and her snuggly ivory blanket slipped down to her waist. Her hands shot to her chest. She'd fallen asleep after the smutty shenanigans, but she had her clothes on now. That was good.

Thor plunked to the floor and swung his tail at her as he strode to the kitchen where she could hear Brent whistling—and the scrape of a pan on her stove.

Her thighs ached a little as she swung herself off the couch. She should go see what he was doing. Lord knows because Brent knew how to do a lot of *things*, like cause her to engage in an orgasm-a-thon. She'd fallen down the erotic rabbit hole fast.

Not her fault.

Maybe it was half her fault. Two to tango and all that.

She could be sorry she caved so quickly to him or enjoy the fact she'd met a guy who seemed to get her. It wasn't like he was a one-night stand or she'd blown off work or a test or anything for the guy.

You know what? She shouldn't be so hard on herself. She deserved to have fun. Scarlett and Persy were right. Eve had been living like a monk on a deserted island in the middle of the Pacific Ocean. It was her birthday week, too.

Right. Big breath in. She wasn't sorry. The only thing she wished was that he'd gotten his fair share of the sexy times. He'd used his hands and mouth—both of which should be bronzed—but left his cock out of the action.

She found Brent in her kitchen, lording over the stove, barefoot and wearing nothing but jeans. The smooth skin of his back glowed. Only someone who worked outside shirtless ever got a gorgeous tan like his.

Thor circled her legs. She reached down to pick him up and sidled up to Brent. "Please tell me those are pancakes." Her stomach rumbled.

He practically jumped a foot, the skillet in his hand banging back down to the stove. He'd had earphones plugged into his ears.

"Hey." He pulled out the little buds and grinned at her. "I noticed you didn't eat at your own birthday party. So," he spooned pancakes onto a plate, "get ready for the most magical carbs on the planet."

She dropped Thor to the ground, seeing he had plenty of kibble in his bowl, and settled her butt on her kitchen chair. "Okay, seduce me with your carbs." He'd seduced every other part of her already. Again, not sorry.

Brent spooned silver dollar-sized pancakes onto her plate. "The trick," he said, "is not to make them too large. Syrup?"

He picked up a bottle. He most certainly had made

himself at home, rummaging through her pantry. She didn't know what was in there.

Her mother had stocked it up when she'd first moved in, though she doubted her mother would have ever bought maple syrup. *"Too much sugar,'* she'd have declared and nibbled on a piece of melon for breakfast.

She took the bottle and spilled a small amount onto her pancakes.

Brent slung his long leg over the chair back and straddled the seat. He then doused his own plate with the syrup and sucked on one finger while screwing the top on with the other hand. That finger had been inside her, what? Two hours ago?

Thor meowed loudly. "No, you can't have any," she said to him. "Go eat your yummy kibbles."

He mewled again in protest and sulked off.

Brent chuckled. "Can't say I blame the guy. I'm a pancake master, and no one should be without a little sugar." He winked her way and lifted his fork.

"Oh, I'll be the judge of that." She forked four pancake rounds and stuffed her mouth—too much because her cheeks bulged out. She covered her mouth with her hand as if that would hide the chipmunk resemblance.

His eyebrow shot up. "Well?"

They'd melted on her tongue, all buttery and sugary. Once she had swallowed enough of the wonderfulness, she took a big gulp of milk. "Mmm. Master-level carbs right here." She pointed down at her plate with her fork.

"Glad you enjoy my skills." He slid his fork through his lips, and her lady bits jumped to attention.

Oh, he had skills, all right, and not just with pancakes. She squirmed.

What did he think of their, ahem, time together? She

could ask, but how did one ask *that? So, great pancakes, and by the way did you see stars? Hear music? Go take care of yourself in the bathroom because clearly, I got the better end of the deal?*

Instead, she concentrated on her plate until there was nothing but a smear of syrup left.

It was strange to be sitting in her kitchen like this—with a man, eating pancakes he'd cooked, shirtless and comfortable. Like they were a couple who did couple things.

"Um, thanks for coming with me to my parents'. Sorry about being such a crank, too. My family puts me on edge." *Thanks for taking me off the edge with your magic fingers.*

"That's family for you." He suddenly rose. "I've got to get going. Mind if I take a quick shower?" He picked up a duffel bag she hadn't noticed near the back door. A shirt and pair of jeans peeked out the top. "I have to go cover for my dad tonight."

"Oh, of course. Go ahead."

She busied herself with dishes and tried hard not to think about what was going on in her bathroom. Because as soon as the water whooshed, a picture of what he might look like nude broke into her mind. He was in her shower. Alone.

Maybe she should strip everything off and jump in there with him. Ya know, slither in like those girls did in the movies. Make sure he got more out of today's sexual festivities. It was only fair.

The water shut off suddenly. *Ooo, fast.* Maybe he did just want to get clean and head out.

He had his clothes on within minutes, drips of water on the ends of his hair that he slicked back with his hand. He hadn't shaved, which meant he was rocking that Thor god thing—again—which was so wasted because now she really wanted to be in the shower with him. To make stars and music happen.

At the door, she leaned against the jamb between the hallway and kitchen. He pulled on his T-shirt. "I'd like to see you soon, but my dad..."

"Of course. I really hope he'll be okay. Anything I can do to help?"

"Nah, between me and my mother, we've got it covered. She's a retired nurse."

"Retired?"

He shrugged. "I was a late-in-life baby."

Oh. They really knew so little about each other, except he was into old houses and knew how to use his hands—well. That hadn't stopped her from dropping trou, though, had it?

"I'll try to get back Monday." His serious tone was casual. "I see your stove is a bit lopsided. I'm worried about the floor."

"Oh, guess I should add it to the list."

"I'll handle it."

Something twisted inside her chest at the possession in his voice. "Hey, I need to pay you. For this week."

"We can wait on that."

"I'd rather handle it now." She reached for her purse and pulled out an envelope of cash she'd been stuffing bills into every day after calculating his hours. She wanted to be ready to hand it to him at a moment's notice.

He took it and peeked inside the envelope. "This is too much."

"You deserve it, and I figured—"

"I mean, I get it." His hand moved through his hair. "You're rich. But I want an honest wage, not because you think I might need it." He stared directly into her eyes, unsmiling.

Excuse her? His pride practically stifled all the air in the room. "I'm not rich. My parents are."

His mouth twisted into a frown like maybe he didn't believe her.

"It's too much." He pulled out $200 of the $500 she'd put in there and put it on the console table by the door.

Heat crawled up her spine. "I was trying to be fair. Pay you what you're worth."

"I know my worth." He pocketed the remaining $300 then focused down at her again.

"So do I."

She crossed her arms. He mirrored her gesture and showed no move to leave. They stood there in a stand-off, like who could blink first.

He broke first. He turned to the door and placed his hand on the knob. "See you Monday, Eve."

"Yeah, Monday, for my floor. And thanks… for coming today." Though she'd done most of the *coming*. "I mean, I had a good time, and I'm glad we talked and…" She should stop talking.

"Me, too." He lurched open the door and strode out.

She moved to her couch to watch him from the front window. He sauntered to his manly, chick-magnet truck, arm muscles flexing under the weight of his duffel bag. He didn't look back.

Maybe they shouldn't have fooled around so soon. Time with family made her do crazy things—like have someone she'd known for two weeks prove he was better than her vibrator. (He was.) That even sounded weird in her head, but it was the truth.

A cooling-off period was needed. They'd agreed to go slow, after all, and a deal was a deal.

Thor jumped up onto the back of the couch and flicked his tail in her face as he pranced by.

She waved it away. "Thor, you heard and saw nothing today."

He meowed.

"Well, don't tell anyone."

She maybe, sort of, had a boyfriend. Except he seemed miffed at her giving him money.

She grabbed her abandoned purse and plopped herself in her—or Thor's—chair. She pulled out her father's birthday card. Seeing his handwriting would ground her a little. He always included a special note for her and didn't rely on the pre-printed message to convey his thoughts.

She ripped it open. A giant bee smiled at her from the front with "Hap-bee Birthday" scrolled in script under its fat belly. Inside, her father's sprawling writing filled the left side.

*To Eve-bee, my beautiful and talented daughter,*

*This is your year, the culmination of everything you've worked for. I couldn't be happier for you.*

*I am so proud to be your father.*

*Love, Dad*

Her eyes stung, and her fingers drifted to her kiss-bruised lips. Would he still be proud if he knew how quickly she'd given in to Brent today? She'd done no more than any other almost-thirty-year-old girl did when they dated. Only her dad didn't want her to be ordinary, did he? He wanted her to stay focused and set herself up for a career and independence.

Maybe the nerves in her belly danced because she'd acted a little bit more like her sister today than Eve cared to admit. Persy would most definitely have flirted at a party, caught a man off-guard, then sort of give in to sexual stuff but not completely so he'd want to come back for more. She was great with men—except for the peckerhead, but his lack of ethics wasn't her fault.

These mental gymnastics weren't good.

She was fine. Everything was fine. Brent would be back—or not. And she'd be *fine*.

Thor jumped up to claim his spot on her lap.

"We can do this, Thor." She ran her hand down his back, his spine arching in pleasure. He turned around, his big yellow eyes blinking up at her a few times.

"Don't lecture me, please. I know what I'm doing."

# 18

Maybe she didn't know what she was doing. The next morning her situation should have been clearer, felt calmer. *Not.*

Eve returned her attention to the book in her lap and attempted—for the fourth time—to read the paragraph on statistical anomalies in market research. She had a quiz the next day that was twenty-five percent of her grade. Bomb this, and she'd never make up the loss on her average. Talk about being screwed.

She also could not stop thinking about screwing. It was like one orgasm—okay, *three*—with a real live man and her body was now addicted. Effing Chatham DNA.

Her hand drifted to the curtain over her shoulder. She stared out at the street. Sheets of rain poured over the gutters of her house so thickly, Eve could barely make out the lights of the other houses. Despite it being Sunday, it was too quiet. Not a soul had driven down her street in over an hour.

She shifted to Thor's favorite chair. He lay sprawled over the back, his legs dangling down on all sides. He shifted his head next to her ear and purred loudly. That would fix it. His purring was better than a white noise machine.

Her gaze returned to her textbook. The words still made as much sense as reading Japanese would have.

She slammed the book shut and let it slide close between her thighs then picked up her phone and glanced at her messages. Still no call or text from Brent. But why would he? Because he'd shared his mad finger skills with her?

Why, yes.

How quickly things had turned. Forty-eight hours ago, she and Brent were new friends and he was someone who'd agreed to help her fix the place up and be paid for it. Now, the man had been gone for less than twenty-four hours, and she couldn't stop thinking about him, about how they'd left things. It niggled at her.

He'd said he'd return to her house on Monday. It was ridiculous she kept thinking he might reach out to her beforehand. But then again, the man moved so fast, deciding he

wanted to do something and—bam!—it happened. Now, nothing.

She tossed her phone a few feet so it landed on the couch. She needed to get away from that thing—and its siren call for desperate women everywhere. She wasn't desperate. She'd been lonely, that's all.

A splash from tires sounded outside, a squeal of brakes, and then a big *ka-thunk* as someone turned into her driveway at an alarming speed. She made a mad dash to the front door's side window to see who'd arrived.

Scarlett and a familiar-looking guy jumped out from a blue sedan. They had rain slickers pulled over their heads and were laughing and running up to her front door.

She opened the door before they could ring the bell.

Their hoodies were pushed back and Scarlett grinned at

her. She dangled a frosted cookie in front of her face. "Red velvet," she sang. "Your favorite. It's a reward for surviving yesterday."

Eve snatched it and gestured for them to come inside. The guy pushed back his hood. "Uh, hi, Mark." It was her de-skunking rescuer—in the flesh.

"You remember him, right? We're dating," Scarlett announced.

Mark colored. If he was seeing Scarlett, he'd better get used to her communication style—as in, the woman's mouth had no governor.

She bit into the cookie. "Nice to see you guys."

"I needed to see your face—proof of life after family time. We're also kidnapping you. We're going bowling."

Eve did that stupid nose-honk thing. "Bowling?"

"Don't be a snob. What's not to love in a place where adults can play games, eat and drink cheap beer, and having a manicure is an obstacle? Or we could do that escape room thing outside in Marion Park—"

Mark's eyes glowed. "Yeah, at that new place with the tree houses."

They might be perfect for one another.

Mark smiled down at Scarlett. "After I kick Brent's ass at the lanes, of course." He looked at Eve.

Eve lowered the cookie and stepped closer. "What do you mean about Brent?"

"Mark texted him, told him to meet us for a late after-noon bowl-a-thon. He said he needed to run some errands first, but he probably would." Mark winked, so similar to Brent. Maybe it was a modern man gesture.

So Brent didn't need to work today after all? "I'm a terrible bowler." She wouldn't be caught dead in those god-awful bowling shoes with her size ten foot proudly displayed on the back. Brent would see it.

Scarlett gave her a scolding look. "Have you even ever been bowling, Eve Chatham?"

Busted. Scarlett knew she hadn't.

Eve grasped her arm. "Hey, Mark, can I steal Scarlett for a minute? It's a work thing." Liar.

"Oh, I seeee," Scarlett sang. She turned to Mark. "Babe, I'll be right back. Remember Thor? He's probably in the living room. Don't sit in his favorite chair and you'll be fine." She patted the guy's chest.

Scarlett followed Eve to the kitchen.

"What happened?" Scarlett glared down on her like a scolding mother. "Did Brent try to kiss you or something equally heinous?"

"No."

Scarlett made come-here gestures with both hands. "Spill."

If she thought about it, Eve could easily call up how his fingers had deftly moved from her neck, down her torso, and dipped inside her panties. "We did more than kiss."

Her eyes widened. "You slept with him. That perfect butt is real, isn't it?"

"Not exactly."

Scarlett tapped her finger on her lips. "Hmm, I usually can call a thing like that."

"No, I mean we didn't sleep together." Or rather, she slept and he made pancakes. "We did… some things."

Scarlett waggled her eyebrows. "About time."

"It's just, we might have had a teeny, tiny argument—"

"What did you say?" Scarlett's mouth screwed into a frown.

Eve scoffed. "Me?"

"Never mind. What else?"

"As you know, he met my family yesterday… and the Interrogation Brigade…"

Scarlett gasped and waved both hands in the air. "Say no more. They were all there?"

Eve nodded. "Carolina was in fine form. Aunt Lillian was, well, Aunt Lillian."

"Did she get a feel in?"

"Maybe a little. Anyway, we came back here and did things. But that's not the issue. You know I'm terrible at this dating thing. So, I went to pay him—"

Scarlett gasped. "He's a hooker?"

"Nooo." She slapped her friend's arm, probably a little too hard because she winced.

"You're the one who brought up money." Scarlett rubbed her arm.

"It was for the work he did. But it irritated him for some reason."

"I'll bet."

Eve dropped her chin. "What do you mean?"

"With those arms? He can probably start a Husky 3120 XP chainsaw in his sleep. He's got pride, and after getting personal, then to bring up money? It mixed things up."

Rather than question Scarlett about her chainsaw knowledge, Eve pressed forward. "I'm not going to use him for labor. I have pride, too."

"No joke." Scarlett smirked.

"Hey, babe?" Mark's voice boomed from down the hallway. "This cat is hissing. Is that a bad thing?"

"Don't. Touch. The chair," Scarlett called into the hallway. "He'd be lost without me already."

Eve heaved a sigh. "He should be paid for his work. And my real problem is we've been out once and I'm already checking my phone a thousand times for him, and that Chatham female thing might be hereditary. I can't give in to it." Talk about letting pride slide.

"Why not? You like this guy."

"I do." Gah, she'd whined. "I don't want to seem too eager. Do I go bowling and look like the besotted puppy? Or do I not show up and make him see I'm no pushover? Persy told me to tell him who I really am—"

Another gasp sounded. "We're most definitely in an emergency situation. You took advice from your *sister*."

She had. "I should run my brain through the car wash, shouldn't I?"

"That, I can't help you with. But I can help you assess this situation clearly." She took the last bite of cookie Eve was holding and popped it into her mouth. "Fortification. Now," She tapped her finger against her cheek and her eyes grew a little distant in thought. "He didn't come here to pick you up for bowling after you did sexual things with him yesterday. Dispute or not, he should have." Her tone was so prim—like Dr. Ruth.

"And I have a big test tomorrow. I should stay and study. If I don't go, it doesn't mean anything, right? The fact that he didn't call me today and ask me himself doesn't mean—" She stopped herself. "What am I doing? Did you hear that? I sounded so *desperate*."

Scarlett grasped her shoulders. "You, Evangeline Marie Chatham, are the least desperate female I know."

Eve shook herself a little to recenter.

"Now, Brent is too cool to lose. Your babies are going to be gorgeous. And my future goddaughter, Little Scarlett, is counting on you."

A long *gah* left her throat. Scarlett and her imagination. As if she was any better?

"Text him that you're studying and he should call you after bowling. Then, when he does," she nodded like a schoolmarm, "you have phone sex."

Strike that. Like a *naughty* schoolmarm. A half-laugh burst from her chest. "I don't know how to have phone sex."

"As soon as Brent says hello, you say, I'm nude."

"Oh, my God. I am not doing that."

"You worried about acting like a typical Chatham female?" Scarlett raised an eyebrow. "Persy would *never*."

Okay then, maybe Eve would.

# 19

“No, no, no.” A stuttered cry shook in Eve’s throat. As if wailing at the hot water handle that now lay in the bottom of the tub would magically make it reattach itself? The old-fashioned handles that read “hot” and “cold” on their respective tops were charming—or so the realtor had said. Eve was learning nothing was charming if it kept breaking down.

She was all set for a long, hot soak in the tub to ready herself for phone sex with a comic book god doing things to her body through phone lines. Instead, she rested both elbows on the edge of the porcelain lip and put her head in her hands. “Why? Why? Why?”

It was official. This house was cursed—and it agreed with her that she should not be readying herself for phone shenanigans.

Something loud creaked in the house from a wind gust as if in answer to her thought. Rain peppered her window, and a louder howl sounded as if an air current was caught in the eaves.

She pushed hair off her face and peered at herself in the

mirror. "It's the wind." She mentally added *"check insulation to the attic space"* to her dreaded renovation list.

Her phone buzzed.

**<Hey got called into work. Sorry I couldn't join you for bowling.>**

Hold the Sam Hill up. He hadn't even gone? He also didn't seem mad anymore. So, all these mind machinations had been for naught.

She didn't text him earlier. Instead, she decided she wouldn't show up, which was immature and such a bad thing to do, but she had to have some semblance of control here. She would text him later with a scintillating message. Something provocative. Something… she hadn't figured out.

Thor mewled at her feet. She looked down into his huge yellow eyes. "No way, Thor. We're not ready." She saw how he was looking at her. *Call him,* his eyes said. Except she'd wanted to develop a script while she was soaking in her tub.

Maybe Scarlett could come up with one for her, though Lord knew what she'd write.

She sat and put the phone face down on her bathroom rug. She couldn't even think about saying dirty things aloud without blushing like a Victorian lady who'd been asked to get naked.

The wind howled outside. Oh, for crikey's sake. Forget the house breaking down for a second. Returning his text might be the best course of action right now.

She typed. *I stayed home and studied. Hard to concentrate thinking of you fingering a bowling ball.*

That was pretty terrible. She backspaced like mad.

**<I stayed home and studied. Hard to concentrate when I was imagining you…>**

What to say? She dropped her phone to her knee and a *bloop* sound went off. She held up the screen to her face. She *was* cursed. She'd hit send by mistake.

The phone buzzed an incoming message. <**Yes?**>

Details would be the next thing to give him. A burn rose in her chest when the words arose in her mind. *Your fingers. Your lips. Your... tool belt...* that she had yet to fully check out except she could already tell Thor's hammer had nothing on this guy.

"Rock You Like a Hurricane" rang from her phone. Brent's ringtone.

Her grip slipped, and the phone bounced on her bath rug —new, thanks to the skunk incident. She scrambled for it as her fingers shook like a chihuahua.

*Oh, man. Oh, man. Oh, man. Not* answering wasn't an option, yet what could she say?

After taking a big swallow, she accepted the call. He didn't even wait for her to say anything.

"So, T-shirt or nightie?"

She switched the phone to her other ear. "What?"

"What you're wearing. Isn't this the part where I ask?" A slight suppressed laughter shook in his voice.

Scarlett wouldn't have given him a heads up, would she? Eve sat up straighter, her robe slipping open to let one of her boobs slip out. "Who says I'm wearing anything?"

An audible swallowing sound came over the phone. She was woman enough to admit and own the self-congratulations that filled her veins over his reaction. Maybe Persy was on to something.

"If you aren't, it's going to be really embarrassing when I hobble to my truck later. When I get off, want me to come by?"

"Oh, no. It's a Sunday—a school night." Plus, she hadn't spent at least two days doing all the shaving-washing sheets preparation things that one did. They did those things, right? Her legs vehemently disagreed with her delaying by the way they began to scissor like crazy over her nubbly blue bathroom rug.

She clutched the lapels of her robe together. "But what would you do when you got here?" Mouth. Traitor. But the idea of him pulling up in that monster truck, rushing in to…

Maybe that'd be his Avengers name. Yeah, Monster Truck God.

Thor began rubbing himself all over her legs, which also was distracting as hell.

"How much do you want to know?" His voice had dropped an octave, which was something given he already rocked the omnipotent god tone most of the time. "I mean… the details."

"All of them." More smug satisfaction at even voicing that set in. Let the Scarlett channeling begin!

He cleared his throat. "I'm a man of few words. I rather like showing more than telling."

"I don't get a heads up?"

He laughed. "Oh, a *head's up* for sure."

Gah, her legs began to dance on the carpet now, and Thor meowed loudly at being jostled.

"Thor's not invited," he rasped.

She pushed at her cat to go find a cat toy or something. It was a little weird Thor was getting clingy suddenly. "He'll have to learn to share."

"Oh? I'd hope he wouldn't watch."

*Ewwww.* A scoff followed by a snort echoed in the bathroom. She slapped her hand over her lips. Embarrassment whacked her libido right down on the image of Thor fixated on her and Brent.

But then Thor headbutted her boob and howled.

"Wow," Brent laughed. "He *does* want to watch."

Oh, my God. This was terrible because now all she could think of was how she and Brent would *fit* on her mattress—

and with each other—and two big yellow eyes staring at them. "Um, how about we talk tomorrow? It's late, and..."

A phone rang in the background. "Sounds like a plan. Listen, I gotta pick up this call."

"Of course." Thor climbed into her lap.

"But Eve? I'm way better in person than on the phone."

"I'm sure. I'm sure you're... great." She was an idiot. She tossed Thor onto the carpet and stood. "I mean..."

"I know what you meant. And about yesterday..."

"I'm sorry," she said quickly.

"I am, too."

Silence filled the phone. Now what?

"See you tomorrow. I'd like to get started on that floor."

"Right, the floor. Yes. Good plan." She smacked her forehead at her wooden words.

"Have a good night, Eve." Then the phone was dead.

Phone sex, pfft. What was she thinking?

And she hadn't brought up her new bathroom leak because they'd gotten over the little blip from this morning and launched into almost-sexy times. Except that last part, they didn't really, and why was it complicated all of a sudden?

She looked down at her cat, who blinked up at her as if to say, "*What?*"

She should go to sleep. She had to be at Horace's Dry Cleaners at nine a.m. Then Peppermint Sweet by one p.m., and then class from six p.m. to nine p.m. She'd squeeze in a trip to Martin's Hardware between *one* of those.

The problem was she was wide awake. What the hell. She moved to her computer and pulled up YouTube.

After spending thirty minutes scrolling through a number of "how-to" videos, she figured out that screwing the handle back on worked. Except the second she gave it that final crank, water ran down the side.

She headed to the basement to turn off the water so the leak didn't continue all night. That jug of distilled water meant for ironing could stand in for a quick shower in the morning. She was getting pretty good at improvising.

Except for the phone sex part.

# 20

Eve tore the ticket off the pad and handed it to Mrs. Bateman. "Glad we could get your suit back in time for you."

"Eve, I don't know what I'd do without this place."

Eve had heard that a million times about Horace's dry cleaning magic. "*We kill grime so you shine*," was his motto.

She lifted the hangers off the silver rod of the rack and, in a rustle of thin plastic, handed the woman's outfit to her, apparently needed for her daughter's wedding tomorrow.

Mrs. Bateman turned and nearly ran over a stooped, overly frail-looking man. "Pardon me." She scooted by.

The man shuffled his way up to the counter.

"Can I help you, Mister..." Eve didn't recognize him, and she prided herself on knowing everyone who came into Horace's.

"Name's Shadwell. James. Got a black suit here." He slapped a worn leather wallet down. His fingers shook horribly.

When he lifted his gaze to her, Brent's eyes shone back at her. He was Brent's father.

When she saw the name in writing on the computer

tablet she took in a long breath. Sure enough, Brent's name was alongside James though he hadn't dropped any clothes off in almost two years—before Eve started working here.

"Um, coming right up, Mr. Shadwell." She turned and flipped the switch to make the carousel begin its creaky snake movement, plastic bags holding dresses, blouses, and pants swinging by in a loud rustle.

When she finally stopped at the "S" section, she found his suit. She turned to find Brent standing by his father. "Well, well. If it isn't my favorite dry cleaning doll. Dad, this is Eve Chatham, the girl I told you about." He took the suit from her. His eyelids hung heavy and his shoulders were hunched as if he hadn't slept in days.

"Hi," she held out her hand to the frail older man. Cold, shaky skin met hers.

"Good to meet you. We were beginning to think Brent had made you up."

"Oh, no. Here I am." She lifted her hands in a pose. "Live girl. Real." Crap, his dad might be dying and she was blubbering about being alive.

For a long minute, Mr. Shadwell fumbled with his wallet. Brent reached over and helped him pull out a twenty-dollar bill. She took it, made the requisite change, and handed it over to the older man.

When Brent reached out for the money, he angrily jerked his wallet back. "I got it. I got it."

He gave her a wry smile. "Thought I'd start sanding your floors later today."

She glanced at his father who was still trying to get the bills into his wallet. "I'll be at Peppermint Sweet later and then class tonight. We can postpone."

"Nah. I can let myself in. You gave me a key, remember?"

Oh, yes, she had done that when she'd first contracted

him. Why? It was those green eyes, wasn't it? They said *trust me,* and she had.

"I should be there, though. I wanted you to show me how to work the sander, remember?" No way would she be left out of that demonstration.

Mr. Shadwell, who'd finally gotten his money into his wallet, looked up at her. "Heard you hired my boy here for some renovations." He glanced at Brent. "Finally. A girl who wants to learn to do something useful for a change." He chuckled. "Brent here can show you anything, Eve. Brent's got good hands."

Brent's eyes sparkled. "Eve knows, Dad. We've already done things together."

His hands were skilled, indeed.

Mr. Shadwell stuffed his wallet into his jeans back pocket. "He's especially talented with a drill. Not everyone can drill straight."

"We haven't gotten to that part yet." Brent shifted the dry cleaning he'd slung over his shoulder and grinned at her like he was reading her thoughts. Or maybe he was reading her body that had grown clammy, her thighs tensed as if waiting for action because of all the hands and drilling talk. "But Eve here is taking a home remodeling class. She's very interested in outdoor power equipment in particular." He winked at her.

It was too hot in here—like way, way too hot.

"That right?" Mr. Shadwell asked.

She nodded. "I, um, want to know how to do stuff." Stuff—could she sound any more simple? "Like basic home repairs. Like my tub's hot water handle that's now leaking."

Brent's brows furrowed. "I can swing by after I drop off Dad and handle it for you."

"No, that's okay." His dad didn't look good, a little gray

around the edges. "You do what you've got to do. I found a YouTube video. It's probably the washer."

Mr. Shadwell chuckled a little. "You're the giant-cat-in-the-wall client. You consulted that tube video place."

It was uncharitable for her to grow irritated at a man who was clearly ill, but annoyance arose inside her anyway. "YouTube can be useful." She prayed her words came out gently. A little fake laugh followed. "But yeah, that one time it didn't work out too well."

Brent grinned down at her. "But it's how we met, so I'd say it worked out okay. Now I can show her all kinds of my skills, Dad."

Irritation gone. "Your son has amazing skills, Mr. Shadwell. He tells me you taught him a lot of it."

"Boy likes to work with his hands. Lost art there."

She nodded and smiled up at Brent.

"So, later," he said. "I can fix that washer in two seconds flat. I'll remember to keep the back door closed so Thor doesn't go on another walkabout."

"I'd really like to do it myself. To see if it works, though." She couldn't help herself.

Brent nodded. "Talk later? Come on, Dad, I'll get you to the car."

"Nice to meet you, Eve."

"You too, Mr. Shadwell."

He angrily swiped at Brent reaching out to steady him. "I got this." But Brent prevailed, and good thing, too, as the man didn't look too steady on his feet.

She needed to call her own father. Today.

# 21

Greta was a saint. She'd let Eve leave early thirty minutes so she could run to the hardware store to get a washer for the tub's hot water handle—and to quickly try it before class.

Her boss still asked her why she didn't get her "handyman to take care of it to spare her manicure." It was an offhand comment which should have meant nothing. Except the suggestion of sparing Eve's quite frankly non-existent manicure made Eve wonder if Greta was channeling her mother or sister.

That was the beginning of the downward slide of what should have been a decent, ordinary day. First, she'd prayed she'd make it to the gas station since the needle on her fuel gauge was below the empty line. She did but had to fish all the change she could find in the car console to pay for a few gallons since the credit card machine wasn't working.

Eve was pretty good at shaking all that off—at least, until she turned the corner of Magnolia and Vine streets and her house rose into view.

Brent's truck was parked in her driveaway. Heart

hammering, she slammed on the brakes, and her cell phone tumbled to the floorboard. “Dammit.”

A loud honking sounded behind her.

“Sorry, sorry!” she said to her rearview mirror at the car behind her, though they were far too close for her taste.

Seeing no room was left for her to pull into her own driveaway thanks to one ginormous truck—Hans—she parked at the curb, unclicked her seatbelt, and sat there. A knot squeezed in her gut. Brent shouldn’t be here. Had she not made that clear this morning? She cracked open the door.

The whirring of a sander sounded when she stepped inside. Thor was nowhere in sight—likely upstairs, spazzed out, under her covers. Cats were good self-preservationists.

She moved to the kitchen, stood in the doorway, and waved to get his attention.

He reached over and turned off the machine. “Hey. Didn’t hear you come in.”

“What are you doing?”

“Thought I’d get started on this.” He lifted his safety goggles to the top of his head, which pushed his blond hair up and out in adorable tufts.

“But we discussed waiting until I could be here.”

A huge mass of fur in her periphery stood up. She jolted backward. A giant yellow lab panted in the corner, stretched himself in a downward-facing dog move, and then moseyed over to her.

“Hope you don’t mind. Homer’s been home alone a lot lately and I thought it’d be okay.”

*Oh, really?* Homer appeared more apt to take a nap than chase after a cat. Brent still should have asked first.

“Where’s Thor?” Thor had met few dogs in his lifetime. There was no telling his reaction to their surprise visitor.

“He’s upstairs. I shut the bedroom door so he’d be undisturbed by him. Homer would never bother him, though, if you're worried. He grew up with some barn cats next door."

Small favor, she supposed. "Um, thanks, but Brent, I really want to be here when you're doing stuff. Don't show up without telling me. Like, call first or something?"

He rose up and took off his gloves. He didn't address her direction, rather pointed at the bag dangling from her hand. She pulled it behind her before he could read Martin's Hardware on it.

"Something else break?" He inched his chin up.

"I need to replace that washer I told you about."

"Yeah, I saw that the water was shut off. I can take care of it. Leave it with me." He reached for the bag.

She pulled it back out of his reach. They'd had this conversation already. "I'll do it. I'll consider it a lab exercise for my class." They hadn't ventured into plumbing work yet, but how hard could this be?

He huffed and his hand reached out for the bag again. "Don't be silly."

"Did you call me silly?"

"I didn't mean it like that. You did hire me to help you."

She had. "Yeah, but you surprised me—"

"Next time I'll send a messenger beforehand. You did give me a key, remember?"

She had but not so he'd let himself in whenever he felt like it. "Come on. A text at least—"

"I've been a little distracted. With… things."

The tension in her face softened. She looked at him—like really looked. Lines were etched deep in his forehead, and he was pale.

Her shoulders dropped an inch. "Everything's not okay with your dad, is it?"

"No." He rubbed his hands over his face. "He's getting worse."

"I'm sorry." Homer nudged his wet nose under her hand. She stroked his head, and as only a fur baby can do, her worry about him being here dissolved. He was a handsome boy like his owner, and it made sense Brent would want his dog around. Thor had comforted her a million times. Homer might do the same for Brent.

She bypassed Homer and grasped Brent's arm. "You all right?"

"That suit he picked up today? He said it was for his funeral. Just in case." Brent's voice cracked. He cleared his throat. "He laughed when he said it." He slapped his gloves on the counter.

A trill of nerves climbed up her legs, through her torso, and up to her heart which began to beat wildly. His father deteriorating had to be super-hard. She couldn't imagine her father not being who he was. But have him say *"his funeral?"*

Brent yanked his goggles off his head. "It's hard. Watching this completely capable man start to wither. He used to be able to do anything, and now? I'm not sure if it's the effects of the chemo or if he's really declining." Homer inched his head under Brent's hand like he understood the conversation.

She engulfed Brent in a hug—or at least as much of his body she could hold on to. He was stiff under her arms. "What can I do to help?" she asked, trying like hell not to focus on how hard and muscular his chest was under her cheek. Hormones had no sense of propriety—or boundaries.

"Nothing." His big hands gripped her shoulders and pushed her back so he could peer into her eyes. "No, actually, let me fix your tub. Working helps. Gets my mind off things."

She nodded slowly. "I know the feeling." They had the need to stay busy in common.

"Yeah. I can tell." His hands dropped to his sides. "We're the same like that. No laying around a pool for us, huh?" His lips started to turn up but then collapsed. His eyes drifted down to her clutch on the bag.

"You can fix my tub handle." A grin returned to his face at her offer which sent a satisfying bloom of heat across her chest. It made him happy. She reached in and took out the little handle and placed it in his open palm. "But I could have done it myself." She still had to set those boundaries, didn't she?

Homer's tail brushed past her, and Brent craned his neck to watch him disappear behind her.

"Homer, stay," he called over her shoulder. Brent sighed when he didn't respond, his tail disappearing around the corner, nails clicking on the floor. "I know you can do anything, Eve. You *YouTube*."

"It's more than that. I'm not a damsel in distress."

"That's good because I'm not attracted to those kinds of girls. You're the super independent woman who refuses to become her mother."

She could let that comment slide. Her mom was annoying but she did mean well. Her pride, however, rose up, stretched its wings inside her, and pressed against her insides. She did a reasonable job of holding the beast inside though a little scoff left her throat. They'd both had long, tiring days—no need to pile on more.

A loud whimper sounded from the living room, followed by an angry hiss. Brent stiffened and then bolted past her. She followed.

Homer was in the corner of the living room that Thor loved, his paw over his nose. Thor streaked past them and up the stairs, ostensibly to hide in her bed again.

"My bedroom door doesn't stay shut. It pops open. He must have heard me come home and he came down to see me."

Brent kneeled down toward Homer. "Lemme see, bud. You get close to the cat?"

She peered over his shoulder. Yep, a big, angry scratch laced his nose. He looked up at Brent with big doe-eyes. *Kill me now.*

"I don't know what happened. Homer isn't one to go after a butterfly let alone someone like Thor."

At least Brent called Thor some*one*. In fact, he was being completely cool about things. She wouldn't have if the scratch was on the other animal, her *baby*.

"I can see how." She pointed at the scene of the altercation. Homer's fur was all over the chair Thor liked to nap on. "Thor claimed that chair, and Homer must have gotten close. Sorry."

"Don't be." Brent stood up and motioned for Homer to follow. "He's fine. It wouldn't be the first time he's gotten a paw swipe. But let me handle your tub, and then we'll go. I can finish the rest tomorrow."

That's what she wanted, right? For him to go? While Eve checked on Thor—found under her bed, appearing fine but ticked off—Brent took his toolbox to her bathroom and fixed her tub handle in under fifteen minutes.

Eve leaned against the door jamb and watched him do it. It was for *learning*. Watching his arms flex was merely an added bonus.

He rose and moved immediately to her sink to wash his hands. "That should hold. You were right. It was the washer. A plus on the diagnosis."

"You do know how to sweet talk me." She handed him a small towel to dry his hands. "Thanks, Brent. Again."

When he didn't answer, an odd guilt arose. He was dealing with a lot, too.

"It's no big deal." He folded the towel and laid it on the sink.

"It is. I don't accept help very readily."

He chuckled under his breath. "Hadn't noticed."

She should be honest with him like Persy said. Let him run if he needed to. "I don't want to lose myself, and when I think I might, I push back. Sometimes hard. Even if that person…" she closed the final distance between them, "is being really kind to me."

"I know." He shrugged. "Still here." He peered down at her, his eyes still drooping a little.

His sadness tugged at the softest part of her heart. "You know what, Brent? I don't have to go to class tonight." She'd hardly ever skipped a class in her life, not even when she'd had the flu last winter. What was the harm? It'd only be the second time this semester. Besides, she would already miss at least half of it at this point.

"No?"

"No." She wrapped her arms around him. This time, he relented to her hug and relaxed against her.

She bent her neck to look up at him. "How about I make you dinner? Not pancakes."

So, she did—a frozen pizza found in her freezer, which he seemed perfectly happy about.

Homer got a leftover piece of chicken, and by the way he looked at her with his big, chocolatey eyes, she was his new best friend. Thor would be thrilled—not. Then again, he may never come out from under her bed. A can of tuna fish didn't lure him out. He simply put his paw in it and pulled it further under the bed as if he was owed.

Still, the longer Brent sat at her kitchen table, the better she felt about her decision to take a night off. They fell into an easy conversation about little things, like how Brent had once stuck a fork in a socket as a kid which is why his one fingernail was messed up. She hadn't noticed before. That his favorite color was green, and he'd found Homer as a puppy, abandoned on the side of the road years ago.

It felt good to learn a few things about him. Brent's casual lean in her chair that was a size too small for him and the way he cast his warm eyes her way quieted everything inside her.

Almost everything.

One part of her wanted to crawl across the table and straddle his lap. Who knew kindness also was such a libido stimulant? Good looks notwithstanding, Brent wasn't like any man she'd met before, other than her father.

An hour later, he granted her a good night kiss. Or rather, she kissed him.

Unlike their conversation, his lips were not laid back. They were kind of rude. Manners had no place in the kissing business anyway.

As she peered through her front window at his disappearing taillights down Magnolia Street, she told herself his kiss would be enough for now. After all, she was the one who wanted to go slow.

# 22

Eve pushed open her door and nearly tripped right over Thor. Her box of lasagna noodles went sailing off the top of her grocery bag and landed with a crackle and thud on her hallway floor.

"Thor! If I broke any of those..." She scrambled to get inside before the wind and rain destroyed what was left of her hair, done that morning for the first time in ages. Dang it. She'd wanted Brent to at least see the loose and flowy style like her hairstylist Trenton envisioned. Trenton had dubbed her new hairdo "Goddess hair."

"Finally getting rid of the Ponytail Express," he'd said to her as he spritzed hairspray over her head. She'd whined that tying back her hair every day had been practical and then watched him snip her hair elastic in two with his scissors. The man was such a drama queen.

She set the bag down on the floor and shuddered at the rain outside, glad she'd be in for the evening. So what if she was skipping her renovation class again tonight? It was on hanging and removing wallpaper, and she didn't *really* need to know how to do that.

What she really needed was Brent to share some of his magic finger skills with her. It was like a seal had been broken inside her. It was all she could think about.

A girl can't watch a guy like him—all capable and charming and smart— pull up in his huge truck and flex his arms working power equipment like he'd done the last three nights and be expected to behave. Come on.

Only it wasn't just the handyman porn he presented.

She'd learned more about him over the last few days. He told her he'd once stopped on a Chicago freeway to help a woman with a flat tire, and everyone in his office told him he was crazy because it could have been a setup to rob him. He didn't care. He'd have done it anyway.

He also did work for Habitat for Humanity, building houses for people without means, for fun. And he regularly picked up stray animals left on the road where he lives—a known place for animal dumping—for a no-kill shelter two counties over.

He was amazing. In fact, she was… *staggered* by him. That was the word.

All week, a low glow grew under her skin at the thought of him. To think she once knew a world where Brent Shadwell didn't exist. Now that she did, she wanted to shed all her clothes and press herself against him. Get at close as humanly possible to breathe him in.

Eve picked up the lasagna box. Yep, they'd cracked in half, the pieces floating free behind the little plastic window. They'd still taste good and, with any luck, do the trick.

Cooking had turned out to be fun—something she'd completely forgotten about in the last few years of swiping food from Peppermint Sweet or going through a fast-food drive-thru.

Tuesday, she'd picked up Chinese take-out for a late-night dinner because the tile in her kitchen was setting.

They'd sat on the floor on pillows and blankets in her living room to eat it straight from the containers—and then he went home. Wednesday, she'd grilled salmon and asparagus on her backyard grill; she'd been banished again from her stove because the floor tile grout needed to set. He left right after. But tonight? She was making Italian, Brent's favorite, in her finished kitchen, *finally*. And she really, really hoped he'd spend the night.

In fact, bring on the full-on passion—even if it involved a ton of garlic, which her recipe called for. Adding a little romance to her schedule was merely taking care of herself. Spirit, mind, *and* body, right?

She set the food down on the side table, and Thor threaded himself between her ankles. She sat on the stairs and he climbed into her lap. "Baby, you're being awfully affectionate tonight. You glad Homer's not here?"

Homer hadn't visited since the chair incident, but Thor had taken to hiding his favorite toys in her bed and spending more time under her comforter than anywhere else.

This evening, however, Thor was getting displaced—and so were the cat toys. She needed to snuggle up to a particular man, feel all his warmth.

A slice of light ran up the hallway from her kitchen light. The crackle of a tarp sounded and she startled, but in a good way, like a little trill of excitement. Brent was here. This coming-home-to-someone thing wasn't so bad. Nice, actually.

Brent's huge frame filled her kitchen archway. "Just in time. Grout's finally set and sealed, and I moved your table and chairs back in." He wiped his hands on a hand towel.

She rushed to his open arms. She inhaled his scent—all that clean cotton, tonight mixed with something caulk-like. Who knew construction material scents were sexy? Either that or her hormones had decided *any* part of him would do.

"Thor will be thrilled. He'd like his house back." She peered up at him. "Wait 'til you see what I got us for dinner. This girl is making you lasagna."

His eyebrows arched dramatically. "With ground beef? And four kinds of cheese?"

"And not the low-fat kind."

"You are a goddess." He swooped down for a wet and noisy kiss. She could lip-lock this man for hours. His mouth fit against hers so perfectly.

"You said you finished. Show me?"

He pulled her into the kitchen and she gasped. For days, he'd been laying some of the tiny, white, hexagon-shaped tiles, but he'd banished her from the kitchen when he was working on the grout. It looked so much better than she could have imagined. Neat rows of tile were broken up every foot with a snowflake pattern of smaller, dark azure ones.

"It's gorgeous." The flooring instantly lightened the kitchen. "It looks like it…" She didn't quite have the words, plus her throat was tightening a little in pure joy.

"Like it belongs?" His grin was worth every second of the last week of listening to sanding and grinding and being exiled from her own kitchen—even more than having a gorgeous new floor. She'd been planning on going for wood, but he was right. Tile was much better—and more practical.

"Yeah." She drank in his shining green eyes. "Like it belongs."

Brent looked good in her kitchen, too.

He pulled her into him. "Sure you don't want to do the rest of the floors? Now that you know how to work the sander."

"I think I'll leave that job to the experts." After working the sander once, she'd turned it over to him. It wasn't that fun, and he was much faster at it. In fact, he was fast—period.

He pressed a kiss onto the top of her head. "Heads up. I

won't see you this weekend. I'm going to help my mother out. She's another one who doesn't like to get help much," he chuckled.

"Thank you, Brent. For everything. Do you need to go there tonight?" She could be a big girl about sleeping alone again. Really. But if there was a God…

He pursed his lips and shook his head slowly. "I'd say lasagna calls for me making good on my promise."

She sucked in air. "Does this mean I get to start using you for your body?"

He leaned back against the sink and placed both hands on the lip. A deep gravity set in his face. "I don't know. Did you get dessert, too?" One of his eyebrows arched upward and his lips threatened to twist into a smile. She really wanted those lips on her again.

"And red wine." Boy, was she ever glad she'd brought home some tiramisu from Peppermint Sweet and stopped for two bottles of Chianti. Her nerves hummed as if they'd been zapped, and maybe the wine would calm them. Ha! Seeing his smile? Be still, her throbbing ovaries.

He slapped his chest, his eyes twinkling with something she'd hoped—no, prayed—fell into the lascivious category. "You're too good for me."

Truthfully, he might be too good for *her*. The guy had manpower-tooled his way through her house, kissed her every night until she was putty in his hands but not pushed the sex issue (but really he needed to start pushing it), and he made her smile—a lot.

Their eyes locked on one another, a secret message perhaps being shared. *"They'd gone slow long enough,"* it said. Sure, she was doing a 180 on herself, but smart girls took advantage of good things when they came their way. Brent was a very good thing.

She broke eye contact first. "Then let's get you powered

up." She hurried back out to the hallway to retrieve her groceries. She bent down, and when she rose, Brent's whole body engulfed her from behind. His strong legs pressed against the back of her thighs, his chest against her back. His arm caught her around her waist, and his face buried in her hair. "I'm already powered up. I have the whole night off. Care to build up an appetite?"

He was big and hard and smelled good. Who was she to think about food at a time like this? She twisted to face him, and he wasted no time erasing the last bit of space between their bodies. Her hands tunneled into his hair and she attacked his mouth.

Ferocious didn't come close to how he met her attack-kiss. That ache between her legs every time she thought about being with him, that glow under her skin grew so sharp, so clear. If she didn't get naked with this man in the next five minutes, she would explode. She wanted more of him, wanted to be as close as possible to him.

He began to back her up toward the staircase landing when the doorbell gave off its shrill buzz. Loud fist-pounding on her front door followed.

"Eve!" Her sister's shout was a little muffled, but there was no mistaking it was Persey. "Are you in there? Let me in!"

Brent pulled back, his nostrils flared, his chest heaving a little. Eve shook her head rapidly as if that would change the fact that Persephone stood on her porch being… Persephone.

Her sister banged again. *"Eve."*

Eve opened the door. "What are you… Persy, what *happened*?"

Rivulets of mascara ran down her cheeks, her eyes red-rimmed and watery, and… no lipstick. She hadn't seen Persephone without perfect makeup in years. Her sister's hair hung in wet strands and she didn't have a coat on;

rather, she hugged her thin arms, her purse dangling off one shoulder.

Eve's thoughts instantly jetted to her family. "Is it Dad? Mom?"

"C-can I come in?"

She stepped back and dragged her sister in by the arm. "Wait here. I'll get a towel."

"Everything okay?" Brent asked.

She led Persy stepped deeper inside the vestibule, taking her purse from her and laying it on the small table by the door. "Be right back."

When Eve returned with a towel, she wrapped it around her sister who shivered. A puddle of water had formed at her feet. Brent hadn't moved from his spot

"Let's go to the kitchen." It was tiled now, and her sister could drip to her heart's content there. "Um, Brent, give us a sec?"

He nodded, brows pinched together.. "I'll load some stuff up in the truck."

Eve gathered the groceries and gestured for her sister to follow.

Once they were alone, her sister lowered herself to a kitchen chair. "You got any hard liquor?"

Calorie consumption. Something bad happened, all right.

Eve pulled a bottle of vodka from the freezer, poured a small amount into a glass, and set it before her sister. Persy tossed the entire thing back then wiped her mouth.

*Who is this stranger sitting in my kitchen?*

Persephone looked around. "Wow. Nice renovations, I see."

"Yeah. Brent is helping me. He's really good at it. Now, what is going on?"

Her sister uncorked the vodka bottle and poured herself more. "Kevin couldn't tell the difference between an electric saw and a drill. Then again, he couldn't tell the difference between his assistant and his wife, either." She drained her glass in one gulp.

So, Kevin had been sleeping around. "An affair?" Persy always went for men who were successful and handsome. They were targets for other women, though she'd hoped Kevin was a tad better about taking up other women's offers than husband number one. According to Persy, the man had pined for her for years.

With her glass in her hand, Persy pointed a finger at Eve. "You were smart. Never get married." She poured herself yet more liquor. Eve grabbed the bottle and pulled it closer to her in an attempt to slow her sister down.

Her attitude was bad. Worse, it was unrecognizable. "Hey, Persy, let me make you some dinner. I'm making lasagna."

Persephone jutted her chin back in one of the most unattractive faces Eve had ever seen on her sister's face. Like a cow. Or a baboon. Turns out vodka's influence was no match for the best beauty products money could buy.

"When do you cook? Wait, let me guess. Feed the man, get access to his..." she spread her fingers wide in the air, "tool."

"No, not exactly." But his tools certainly helped paint smutty pictures in her mind. She rose and started unpacking the groceries. "Want to tell me what happened while I cook?"

"No." Her lips screwed into a frown as if holding in her words. "The fucker. A year, Eve. A whole fucking year he's been nailing *Amanda* all over his Parnian cresent desk that *I* picked out. Beautiful mahogany and maple..." She lowered her voice and sniffed.

"Also, in his Jaguar. In our condo in Miami. And probably in the Aspen house, too." She slammed her hand down on Eve's poor table. "A place he refused to go to with me last Christmas, which meant he wanted to stay here to be close to *Amanda*. She showed up at my house and bragged about his prowess. Apparently, they're in looove." She sang that last word and waggled her chin.

So much for not talking about her situation.

"You know what?" She banged her glass on the poor table. "Screw him. Screw husbands. Screw putting myself on hold. I'm going to go back to school and get a big fancy office with my big fancy degree." She stared out the window, lost in her misery.

"I can support that plan." Eve placed her hand on Persy's arm.

Her gaze shot to Eve. She jabbed her finger in the air. "I could do it, too."

"Of course, you can."

A rap on the wall made her turn. Brent had his hands stuffed in his pockets. "I'll see you tomorrow, Eve."

Her heart fluttered. "No, don't go. I'm making enough for an army." She wrung the tea towel in her hands.

"No." Persy twirled her hand in the air. "Go now, while I can still save my sister from my fate."

"Persephone!" Eve glared at her. She strode up to Brent. "Don't listen to her. That's the vodka speaking." Though Persy rarely let liquor speak for her. She spewed insults fine on her own.

He huffed. "I'm fine. But I should get back and see about Homer at least."

Oh, yeah, unlike cats, dogs needed way more attention. "Hey, how about I bring you some by later?" She could get naked at his house instead. Let Persy sleep with her vodka bottle.

He pressed a kiss onto her forehead. "I'll get some tomorrow."

A bottle clanked behind them. "Tomorrow is more of the same," Persy growled. "Amanda and her little keyboard-tapping fingers." She made wiggling motions with her fingers.

Eve curled her hands around his bicep. "She never eats, so a wine spritzer makes her mad drunk."

"Sounds like you two have stuff to talk about. Rain check for us." He lifted his hand in a wave toward Persy.

Eve fought the urge to clutch at his shirt to keep him here, but she understood. Her sister's attitude could scare paint off walls.

Plus, Brent had his furry companion and his family to contend with, and she had hers. The clink of the vodka bottle against Persephone's glass rang in the air once more. She was having more. Brent needed to save himself—now.

"Tomorrow then." She walked him to the door.

When she went to kiss him, he pulled back. He'd never done that before. But then he smiled and leaned down to give her a halfway-decent kiss. Except he didn't usually give her halfway-anything. It niggled.

"Eeeeve."

Jesus, her sister could win an Olympic whining contest.

When Brent's truck had pulled away, she went back to Persephone, who then spent another hour railing against her husband. Eve made dinner that would hopefully soak up some of the alcohol in her sister, but Persy was two seconds from passing out at her table by the time the buzzer went off on the oven.

"Come on, Persy." Eve lifted her from her chair and half-walked, half-dragged her to her guest bedroom. After leaving a glass of water, two Advil, and Persephone's cell phone next to her on the nightstand, she left her sister to sleep it off.

*Dammit.* Here she was, all set to have a celebratory dinner with Brent and finally get some live tool action, and her sister had to douse relationship drama over it. She felt bad for Persy, really, but what could Eve do to help?

You know what? Her night would be put back on its train tracks with a one-way ticket to hot, steamy country if it was the last thing she did.

With her sister ensconced in her guest bedroom on the futon, she wrapped up the lasagna in tinfoil and then dialed Scarlett.

"Hey, by any chance, do you know where Brent lives? Or could you get it from Mark?"

How she'd neglected to get Brent's address, she'd never know. He knew so much about her, yet she knew so little about him. Time to end *that*.

# 23

"Hey, babe, what's Brent's address? Eve needs to get laid."

"*Scarlett.*" The woman seriously had no filter.

A scratching sound went off in the earpiece. Scarlett must have adjusted her phone against her hair. "What? That's why you need it, right? He didn't come over after all?"

A low male voice rumbled in the background.

Eve would not answer. It'd take too long, for one. How did she explain all the mushy feelings that were developing? She herself didn't quite get why she missed him the second he walked out the door, and explaining her sister parachuting in to ruin her night's plans wouldn't help. "Does he have it?"

A long sigh escaped from her friend. "Mark says 1418 Stonefence Road. Whoa. Nice neighborhood." Another rustle came through the phone. "Seriously? Brent lives there?"

A deep male, "*Yeah,*" reached her ears.

"There you go. Remember to practice safe sex, little one. And don't hurt him. We play nice with our power tools." Scarlett laughed soundly, amusing herself.

Mark's laughter in the background joined with hers.

Guess those two got close fast given that he was at her house at nine p.m. on a Thursday evening. That meant what Eve was doing now wasn't bad. Look how fast Scar and Mark moved. She and Brent, however? Despite her wanting to go slow at first, things between them had ground to a halt. The U.S. Congress moved faster. Or icebergs. Either would do as a metaphor.

After she ended the call, she gathered her things and headed to the door. At the very least, she'd leave the lasagna at Brent's doorstep in her cooler, which she retrieved from the icky basement (and washed off). Presentation counted when one was trying seduce—or so she thought. She'd never really done this kind of thing before.

Thor stood at the doorway. "Sorry bud, you're not going outside right now."

He left off a loud meow.

"Don't lecture me. I have to go do… human things."

His house turned out to be about thirty minutes away and down two very dark and narrow roads. She passed the entrance—twice—because it was hard to see with the rain coming down. She managed to finally find his drive and pulled up behind his truck.

Score, he was home.

Her headlights illuminated the stone front of the two-story house. She'd imagined something much, much smaller. Rather, this "carriage house" looked like it could house a whole family. White shutters lined a red door, and warm light spilled from the front windows of what she guessed was the living room.

She cracked open her door, snaked out her umbrella, and popped it open. She then stepped out, her foot landing in a puddle. "Gah." Her shoes would be ruined in the muddy gravel of his drive.

The umbrella kept tipping as she pulled out the cooler,

which sent a long stream of water down her back. She jogged up the two stone steps and set the cooler on his stoop. It was dark and she couldn't see a doorbell.

Someone moved inside behind the open curtains of the front window. A fire blazed in a stone fireplace behind a wingback chair. She craned her neck to take in more of the scene.

A woman with long, glossy brown hair came into view. She dropped herself into the chair with a wine glass in her hand. *Who the ever-loving hell is that?*

Eve's hand curled around the metal banister, and another stream of water doused her back as the umbrella tipped upward. She swiped at her now-soaked butt and wiped hair out of her face. Who was she seeing?

The woman tucked her feet up under her and laughed. Brent's back appeared, blocking Eve's view of the, quite frankly, gorgeous woman. His rumbling laugh came next.

His sister, perhaps? He'd never mentioned one, and honestly, that little detail would have come up by now.

He shifted and placed one hand on the arm of the chair. The brunette leaned closer and he kissed her on the forehead. Just like he had to Eve before he left.

Her heart thrashed inside her chest, and she struggled for breath. Rain pelted all around her, the slight whooshing sound of it being collected in gutters and spat out through a downspout a few feet away, the ping of droplets hitting the plastic cooler.

Yet she couldn't stop staring into the window. Brent turned a little so she could see his profile. Then he did something worse than put his lips on that woman. He winked down at her, that little scrunch of his beautiful green eye with all those damned, seductive, gorgeous eyelashes that... that...

Her throat wasn't letting enough air inside her lungs. She tapped on her chest as if that would open up some room.

*Goddammit.* She spun and nearly slipped on the wet concrete on her way to her car. Her umbrella lowered and she was pelted with water. She quickly righted it again, but the damage had been done. She was soaked. Soaked and stupid.

She'd done the worst thing she could think of doing to herself: she'd fallen for a guy who clearly was married or, at the very least, involved with someone. Maybe that's why they never had full-on sex. It wouldn't then feel like cheating?

She blinked and tried to clear her brain. *He's not like that.*

Wait. Maybe he was. Handsome, smart, skilled, generous, cool under pressure, with a monster truck. Of course, he was taken. Or at least playing the field because no one was that motherfucking perfect.

A gasp left her throat. His dad had called her the "giant cat in the wall *client*." Not girlfriend. Not date. Not… anything.

Persy had said someone had to save her from her sister's fate. She had to save herself from a growing disaster. She'd missed three classes this week to mother*fucking* feed him. She'd started to think how great he looked in her house, like how he belonged there.

Her pulse sped up. No. Lasagna. For. Him. The man did not deserve her home cooking. Like she'd help him feed that brunette?

She should dump the entire pan and its contents into the bed of his truck. No, she should leave it out for him like a message.

Maybe don't use the cooler and let the pan get rained on and be ruined.

Maybe she'd spell out *"Cheater"* with the lasagna noodles and let the red sauce drip down the stairs like blood from her heart. Her forehead grew tight, and raindrops had coated her lashes. She blinked away the wet. It was just the rain. She wasn't crying.

She should leave and never think about Brent again. That option would be the logical thing to do. *Stop. Think. Think. Think.*

Her brain delivered more options. Go knock on the door and talk to him. Confront him. Let him explain.

Except when he introduced her to the brunette it wouldn't be marinara on the steps—it really would be her heart. He was a good man. But a good man with someone else. Eve would turn into an instantly blubbery mess.

That was the moment when she first realized it. She'd fallen for him… hard. She wasn't in control of anything.

She released the thought and let it wash out with the rain. Her hand began to shake despite it being numb from gripping the umbrella.

She turned away, put the cooler in the passenger seat, rounded her car, and got into the driver's seat. Time to commandeer her life again.

She drew out her phone and shakily texted Brent.

**<<I'm going to have to lay off the renovations for a bit. I'll leave a check for you in a plastic baggie under my back door mat for you.>>**

Why did she give such details? Because she was a practical girl who had on her big-sensible-girl panties, pulled up to her belly button. Or rather, she had been that girl until the last week when she'd begun kissing a man, looking forward to seeing him, skipping classes, and *cooking* for him.

Worse, fantasizing about a life with him. The little Arts and Crafts house they'd share, fix up together.

She did exactly what she'd said she wouldn't. She'd turned into someone she wasn't. All because Brent could wield power tools while looking like a hero and kissing like one?

Sure, he was wonderful. Except he was someone else's wonderfulness.

She threw her phone to the passenger side, yanked her car into reverse, and got the hell out of there. Thor had the right reaction to interlopers all along: self-preservation at all costs.

# 24

"Dammit," she yelled at the cookie tray and dropped it with a thunk on the marble counter, which sent an echo through the empty coffee shop. She slipped her finger into her mouth to ease the burn. At least the sting made her more awake.

Who cared if she'd arrived hours before her shift formally got started? Greta could always use help with the morning baking, and she hadn't slept well last night. Her sister had snored so loudly all night she could hear it through the floorboards. Persy was still sawing wood when Eve left her a good-bye note by her pillow, whose pillowcase might have to be tossed given the amount of mascara smudging the fabric.

By now, her sister was probably retelling her whole sordid infidelity story to their mother, being as dramatic as possible. Persy had been right about one thing—Eve was smart and she'd right her life, pronto. She would not grieve a life that wasn't hers to begin with.

All the signs that adding a man to her life wouldn't work were there, from Thor's recent hiding to Brent showing up at all odd hours unannounced. She'd skipped too many classes and earned her first B on a paper she'd half-assed this week.

Instead, she'd changed her priorities for a guy. She'd even let him keep the key to her house.

*Shit.* How was she going to get that back?

"Careful there." Greta grasped her wrist and moved her to the sink, immediately running cold water on her burned finger.

The gesture was motherly and kind. Eve's throat tried to strangle her for the hundredth time since she found out about Brent's brunette. If only Scarlett had answered her phone last night when Eve was driving home, maybe she'd have rid herself of this incessant, wrenching ache inside her.

Scarlett was probably busy doing what Eve thought *she'd* be doing last night.

"Everything okay? School stressing you out?"

She pursed her lips and shook her head. She didn't trust her voice right now. It would come out like a pathetic, cracked cry. She was being ridiculous. She barely knew Brent.

She was more mad at herself than anyone.

Greta dried her hand off with a towel. "Eve?"

"I'm fine." At least her voice didn't crack. "A bad day, that's all."

She yanked her phone from the charger, happy to see it was recharged. She'd left it in her car overnight on purpose. She didn't want to be tempted to call him.

Scarlett, who finally arrived for her shift, came crashing through the swinging doors into the kitchen. "A few of those college cuties are back. Ya know, from Woodstone?" She stopped short. "What's up with you?"

"Later." She scooted by both Scarlett and Greta and went out to the counter and faced... Brent. His brows were pinched and his eyes fired.

He threw the envelope she'd left for him that morning on the counter. "What's going on, Eve?"

"Nothing. Black coffee? No sugar, right?"

He followed her march to the far end of the counter to the coffee machine. "I went by your house this morning to talk to you but you were already gone. Then I found this." He pointed over at the envelope with his name across it. "A check for eight thousand dollars? Are you crazy?"

She glanced around. The boys weren't paying any attention to her, but a couple sitting at the table closest to the counter stared at them.

"I'm paying you for your work," she said through gritted teeth. It also had emptied her savings and gifts from birthdays and Christmas from her dad she'd kept as an emergency fund. "I appreciate all you've done, but I might have bit off more than I can chew—"

"So you're giving me eight grand?"

"Who was that woman I saw last night?" The words tumbled out. Probably because they'd sat on her tongue all night and morning and now refused to be swallowed back anymore.

He straightened and lifted his chin. "Oh. I know what this is. Yeah, Meredith saw a woman through the window. Figured it was you by her description, but when I opened the door you were gone. Why didn't you come in? Or maybe look at your phone when I called?"

"I didn't get it. My phone was dead." She crossed her arms over her chest. "Who's Meredith?"

"My cousin. She's in town to see my dad. Showed up last night."

Eve's hand flew to her mouth. "Your cousin? But I thought..."

"You thought I was stepping out on you."

A wash of relief he wasn't cheating flowed through her like the Mississippi River. Big and wide and a tad muddy because, wow, she really did go to an awful place in her mind, didn't she?

She chewed on her lip. "Yeah."

His face stilled to stone.

Yeah, she was horrible.

She lifted one shoulder, slightly. "Good thing I didn't dump that lasagna I brought you in your truck." She tittered as if that would excuse her initial over-the-top reaction.

He took one step back and blinked. "You would have done that?"

"Sorry?" She bit her lip.

His face colored, and a muscle in his jaw tensed.

She clasped her hands together. "But I didn't."

"But you thought it." Those beautiful green eyes narrowed.

She stepped closer to him. "If it's any consolation, my sister would have done worse. Like hurled it through your front window."

He moved further away from her. "Is that supposed to make me feel better?"

She supposed not, and her sister was a bitch to him last night. Here she'd been the same.

The young guys started knocking on the glass counter as they grew impatient.

Greta said over her shoulder, "I need five black coffees, three cappuccinos."

Eve closed the distance between her and Brent and drew him further away from the counter space and all the listening ears. "I've got to get to work, but can we talk later? I can't—"

"No. A break sounds good to me." He gestured to the envelope in her fingers. "And I'm not taking that."

*A break? Oh, the renovations.* "I'm sorry. I didn't mean—"

"Mean what? Yeah, I get it, Eve. Think the worst of me.

Pay me off. You don't want to be anything like them, but you're as scared as they are."

Ow. Her chest cramped a little at his words, and the back of her neck bristled. "Excuse me? What did you expect? Seeing a woman—"

"I expected you to *ask* me about it. Not immediately think about revenge."

She could have asked him. But Persy showing up with her cheating story—her second time, to boot—colored her reaction. Couldn't he see that? "I'm sorry, it's just my sister and…" She turned away, her cheeks burning. She'd overreacted last night. She also had to get to work, and honestly, this whole thing had shown her she didn't know how to be with men. "Please. Can we talk later?"

"No, thanks." He spun and turned away.

Scarlett stared at her—hard.

"What?" She felt bad enough as it was without having Scarlett admonish with her eyes. "You don't understand."

"I overheard enough."

"And?"

"*Now* you're being stupid."

# 25

Thor growled under her comforter. "Yeah, two days of gray skies would put anyone in a grumpy mood." *Still talking to my cat, just great.*

She should be at work or class right now. Instead, she lay huddled in her bed like a crazy cat lady, comforting Thor with *Avengers: Endgame* showing on her laptop. They knew how to have each other's backs. She, however?

Backless, spineless, clueless.

But honestly, Brent was unforgiving, intolerant, and goddammit, still a great guy.

Another roll of thunder made the windows rattle, and Thor's tail twitched.

She should batten down the hatches or unplug devices. Instead, she turned up the volume on the movie.

Taking another night off wouldn't be the end of the world, she reminded herself. When was the last time she'd done that? *How about the whole last week?* Gah, she really was slipping.

Brent didn't answer her lone phone call or lone text. In both, she'd apologized again for thinking the worst about him and asked how his dad was doing. Still, no return message came.

She still fingered her phone, wanting to call again. Her dishwasher had stopped working and he could give her some advice. Except that excuse to reach out was slimy.

Her sister's advice rang in her ears. "One call and one text each is enough. I mean it."

The fact that she went to her sister again for advice showed how much she'd slipped in the be-your-own-woman department.

Listening to Persy? Good Lord. Within days of her waking up in Eve's guest bedroom hungover and makeup-less, she'd gone back to her husband, who'd promised the sun, moon, and stars for her return. Apparently, divorce would look bad to his company partners. According to their mother, he'd paid dearly for her sister's return—in Cartier, or Tiffany, or both. But Persy told her she really loved Kevin and "in the end, that's all that matters."

She punched her fists down on her comforter. Brent was being so unfair. He couldn't punish her for *thoughts*. "There," she said to Thor. "He isn't perfect."

The wind howled outside, this time far stronger. She startled when a loud gust crashed against her bedroom window. Thor complained loudly at being jostled, his paws scraping across her calves. "Ow, Thor. Watch it." She pulled her legs up to check the scratches. He usually didn't do that to her.

Another huge gust of wind hit the house and the walls creaked. *What the hell?*

"Looks like we're going to get one heck of a storm, buddy. Steel yourself." The air changed suddenly as if someone had sucked half the oxygen out of the room, lightening the space. The relief was short-lived. Howling wind suddenly engulfed the house like a tribe of banshees were invading.

She slapped her laptop shut and padded to the window.

Under lightning flashes, the huge trees up and down her street bent and swayed in a way she didn't think possible. Under the glow of streetlamps, a hazy mist was rolling toward them, too.

She jumped back into bed and Thor settled between her leg and body pillow. He was shaking all over as if he knew this storm would be bad. It sounded like the house was seconds from caving in.

"The house was built a long time ago, Thor. She'll hold." Her little bungalow had to have weathered many storms and wasn't made of the spit and glue of the McMansions on the other side of town. She still grabbed her phone to check the Weather Channel and see if there were any tornado warnings.

A loud crash came from the other side of the house. Wow, that sounded bad. She threw back the covers and jogged down the stairs to the kitchen. Metal tearing and banging were next.

She crept to the back door just in time to see the garage door flap in the wind like it was made of paper. The wind didn't look that strong. Her hands shook as she glanced at her phone. Still no warnings. If there was a tornado, wouldn't sirens be going off by now?

The largest limb of her apple tree cracked right off and landed in her backyard. She jogged backward, away from the window. "Shit." Could the glass shatter under such wind? She and Thor needed to get underground, but the cellar door was outside. Going outside would be stupid. Plus, Thor was still upstairs.

They'd hide in the pantry.

Calling his name, she took two stairs at a time to get back to her bedroom. She had to shout to be heard over the rattling of the old windows. Her breath was coming hard, yet she couldn't seem to make her feet move fast enough.

Where was he?

Another loud crash of metal. She peeked out the side window. A tree limb had fallen down on her car.

*Oh, my God. Oh, my God. Oh, my God.*

Her phone was still clutched in her palm. She'd call nine-one-one. She swiped at the screen, her fingers shaking. A weird tone sounded. Maybe she'd misdialed. Nope, the second call gave her the same response, a light honking tone.

She ran back downstairs and nearly slipped as she rounded the corner into the kitchen. She grabbed Thor's bag of treats from the pantry and began racing around the house, shaking it and yelling his name.

"Thor, baby, where are you? Mama's here. I'm here."

Starting to snivel like a baby, she dialed her mother, who didn't answer. She then tried her sister. No luck there, either. Those ungrateful family members. She was about to *die.*

Silence. The wind and rain dropped off—like it dropped off a cliff. The storm ended as quickly as it had come up.

The silence was broken only by a torrent of water outside, likely rolling off her roof and into the gutters—if they even had stayed on the house at all.

She crept to her back door. Water streamed over the gutter, now precariously hanging off the roof ledge over the back stoop. A few lightning bolts flashed in the distance, lighting up downed tree limbs. Wet leaves coated the slick concrete drive and backyard grass.

A small, ugly tree limb looking like a monster's arm lay on her car's hood, now dented, spider-web cracks across her windshield. The limb hadn't gone through the glass.

Thor howled. She spun. "Thor, it's okay." Where was he? "Thor?"

A long cry emitted from somewhere nearby. She stilled, the steady stream of water outside and metal twisting as it seemed to settle in its new position as the only sound.

She listened, hard. "Thor?"

A plaintiff mewl came from behind the cabinet next to her broken-down dishwasher. She'd yanked it out a few inches to see why it'd stopped working and decided to quit when it proved too heavy to pull out fully.

Thor had likely followed her downstairs and crawled into a space she couldn't get to. And he was probably stuck —again.

# 26

Eve didn't cry, so that was something good. Even when—in typical YouTube DIY disaster fashion—she'd tried to yank out her dishwasher to get to Thor, the sucker tipped toward her and a big metal piece underneath stabbed her big toe.

The stupid appliance could attempt to thwart her all it wanted. She would win this one. She pulled up every bit of anger she could muster and yanked that effing dishwasher out until it was almost fully removed from its cabinet space. Water splooshed everywhere across her new tile floor in a gush.

Her house was officially a renovation disaster, and she added *"attempt to remodel a house"* to her ever-growing list of things never to do again.

After opening a can of tuna fish to lure her wandering cat out, she forged through the puddles and mud to the basement and turned the house water off for the umpteenth time. When she returned, Thor hadn't budged from his hiding spot.

Then she made the call she didn't want to—to Flow 'n Go Guys. Her pride that she had to call at all wasn't an issue.

Rather, Brent might answer, and she knew herself. She'd hang up in humiliation, which was what a seventh grader did, not a grown woman.

He'd see on caller ID it was her, and think—again—what a schmuck she was.

He would call back—which meant she'd have to admit said schmuckiness. Again.

Or worse, he wouldn't call back, and then she'd have to face the truth. She *was* a shmuck. Worse, she was a shmucky coward.

The phone rang exactly six times—and a nice guy named Frank Bellows picked up the phone. Within minutes, he was on his way over to stop the leak. No Brent, the Thor-god-look-alike, was coming to her rescue, which was a flipping godsend. *Really.*

Stupid emotion still lodged itself in her throat like an unwanted house guest.

She had her hands full keeping the house habitable. She shouldn't have her hands full of Brent Shadwell.

Thor meowed behind the wall. "You're fine." Having been through this Thor-exploring-inside-walls thing, it was now officially old hat.

Frank arrived, a man in his mid-fifties with a paunch belly and black hair combed over his bald spot, and was able to patch her dishwasher, saying it was only a matter of time before the patch failed. At least he was honest. He also provided all the polite small talk about "hell of a storm" and "we'll get you fixed right up" platitudes.

However, he wasn't as deft as Brent in getting Thor out of his hiding place. It took opening yet another can of sardines to get him out. Her little beastie squeezed himself out and went for it. Frank could then place her dishwasher back to its rightful place.

She tore a check out of her checkbook. "Thanks for coming."

"No problem." Frank took the check from her outstretched hand. "Sorry your dishwasher isn't fully repairable. It'll run for a bit, but expect it to die again soon. It's old. But hey, I heard Home and Hearth is having a sale."

"Thanks. Appreciate it."

After Frank left, she went back to her kitchen to find Thor pushing the near-empty tin across the floor. The scent lingering in the air didn't even bother her. That was progress, she supposed.

She glanced around her house, a heaviness settling over her shoulders. 331 Magnolia Street had had a good run, but she was officially in over her head. It was time for her to bite the bullet and admit maybe her mother was right. Aren't they always?

Eve would sell this place and get an apartment somewhere closer to campus where she could walk, one that had absolutely no nooks and crannies or open walls for Thor to play hide and seek. Then maybe she'd go for a master's degree while working because school was one thing she knew how to do.

Relief mixed with a shame that she couldn't handle the house project, but smart girls knew when it was time to quit. And she was tired. Time to give home repairs a rest.

She made herself a cup of tea, wrapped herself in a fleece blanket, and sat out on the back stoop. Who cared if her butt was soaked through in less than two seconds?

The apple tree, once majestic in how it reached out with its limbs like big, inviting arms, didn't look as charming as it once had. An ugly gash marred one side where the largest limb had ripped off. The limb sat in a webbed puddle of mud and leaves, its impact having torn up the small patch of grass.

Once the world opened up later in the morning, she'd call

a tree guy—they had those, right?—and a car body shop in case her car was salvageable. Then it was time to talk to a realtor about what she could get for the place.

She gazed out over her backyard, now lit up with golden light from the budding sunrise. "Yep. Gave you a good run." She took a big swig of tea, now lukewarm. "Now it's time to grow up."

"What's the fun in that?"

She nearly slid down the concrete steps at the male voice. She peered over her shoulder toward her driveway.

Brent stood next to her car, holding a chainsaw. *Gretel.*

# 27

With one hand dangling the chainsaw, Brent scrubbed his hair with the other. He sent his gaze around the backyard. "Man, that was one heck of a derecho. When I woke up, I heard on the news it ripped through your part of town." He glanced around. "The tree limbs can be cut up, but your car…"

"Why are you here, Brent?" Even her voice sounded tired.

He cocked his head. "I knew you were probably alone and I heard it was bad on this street."

He'd worried about her, which was more than she could say for her family. Her mother and sister hadn't returned her two panicked calls as they obviously only needed her when parties needed to be planned or infidelity was afoot.

"I wasn't exactly alone."

He placed one foot on the concrete step and set the chainsaw body on his knee. "Thor much help last night?" He smirked. "Heard we got a call in the middle of the night about a cat behind a dishwasher. I took a guess."

"It got handled." She stood, and her stupid blanket slipped, having gotten caught in a crack between the step and where it affixed to the house. *See? Nothing in this place works.* A loud rip sounded when she yanked harder.

The noise was too much. The night had been too much. And now Brent was standing here like a knight with shining power tools even though she'd been a complete moron about him. Well, it was all *too much.*

A sob broke from her chest, and she turned away from him as if that might spare him from a humiliating female wail that she laughed about when she saw it in movies. The damsel in distress. The broken china doll. The sleeping princess awaiting her prince.

Brent's arms went around her, and she startled. It didn't deter him. His whole body pressed against her back. She shuddered and sputtered and made all the snorty sounds she hated because who cared anymore? She was done. *Done, done, done.*

At some point, he twisted her around and they were both engulfed inside the blanket.

She sniveled into his wet shirt. "You shouldn't have come."

"I can leave. If that's what you want." A tease lay under his words.

She grasped his shirt in her fist to keep him close. "You have your dad to help. And I was the bitch who wanted to throw lasagna in your truck."

"And pay me off." A slight smile stretched his lips. "It was a fight, Eve. It happens."

She mock-punched him. "I wasn't paying you off." Thor rubbed along her legs. "How did you get out, Thor?"

Brent pulled her into him again. "He'll be fine. And yes, you were. I won't be a kept man."

"And I won't be a kept woman." She pressed her fists into his chest. Or a kept-then-dumped one like Persy, even if she'd reconciled with Kevin.

"Then we're even." He inclined his head downward to their feet. "But Thor, you like being a kept man, don't you?"

She laughed into his chest. Brent could make her feel better faster than anyone she'd ever known. "You do know he's a cat, right? They're kind of born to be worshipped."

He pulled back a little. "I have to tell you something. About a past relationship of mine. It might explain my... aversion to having lasagna threats."

She snuffed up snot. "Did someone dump food in Hans?"

"No. But I had an ex who did a lot of things. Tools down the garbage disposal when I was late. She'd show up on job sites, accusing me of ignoring her. And when I broke up with her, she went a little nuts."

Her mouth dropped open.

"Called my employer and spread some rumors about me. It was over four years ago, but still..."

"I wouldn't do anything like that."

"I know. It's why I find you refreshing. Your comment about the lasagna took me off-guard. I know you're the opposite of that craziness."

Thank God he wasn't a mind reader, then. She often felt crazy. "Then I'm shocked my family didn't scare you off."

He smirked. "Don't leave me alone with Carolina? She scared me a little."

"I'll protect you. Better still, hold Thor. She's not getting near cat hair."

He chuckled. "So, we okay now?"

She nodded.

He leaned down and picked up Thor. "Come on, let's go inside. We have storm recovery as well as renovations to discuss."

She sniffed and drew her ripped blanket around her as she followed him inside. "No. I'm through with that." Once inside the kitchen, she spun to face him. "I mean it."

"I didn't take you for a quitter." He set her cat down.

Her spine went ramrod straight. "I'm not quitting. I'm reassessing, redirecting. It's what a non-crazy person does."

"Uh-huh." He stared down at her. "You know what my favorite quote is? *'I'm not going to tell you it's going to be easy. I'm telling you it's going to be worth it.'*"

Her chin lifted another inch. "It's not worth it."

"It will look better in the morning."

She sighed heavily. "It's already morning."

His chuff in reply should have annoyed her, but it didn't.

"Are we done with the pep talk now?"

"You can do this, Eve. I believe you can do anything."

She chewed on her lip, letting his words sink in. Her eyes stupidly stung. "Does everyone want to quit when renovating a house at some point?"

He placed his hands on her shoulders. "Everyone. All those beautiful houses you saw on Poplar, however? They didn't."

"I want a beautiful house like I saw on Poplar." It wasn't all she wanted, but this house had called to her for some odd reason. Sealing the deal with her father was so close, and the thought of having her degree, a home, and a new job all at once felt… complete. Her father had warned her about believing she could have it all.

Brent held her by the shoulders. "You want it? Then you shall have it."

The corners of his eyes crinkled. He believed it, and somehow, when he said it, her dream seemed possible again.

She snuggled back into him. "Thanks, Brent. I had a moment."

"Like I said, anyone who is renovating does. Now." He steered her toward the hallway. "Let's get you cleaned up."

She looked a mess she had to. "I need a shower."

"Want company?"

She paused. Pure intent shone from his eyes.

An image of being in the shower with him broke so freely in her mind. His green eyes cast down at her with such caring—and the fact that he worried about her at all—felt different than she thought it would. It was warmer somehow.

She swallowed. "We *were* interrupted the other night."

When he didn't move—seemed actually frozen at her answer—she rose on tiptoes and pecked him on the lips.

He arched an eyebrow. "Is that all I get?" He dropped his voice. "I brought most of my power tools with me. I mean, I don't bring out Gretel for just anyone—"

"Shut up." She jumped up, letting the blanket fall to the ground. He caught her by the ass, and she circled her legs around his waist.

"Had I known my chainsaw would elicit such a reaction, I'd have brought my log splitter over, too." His lips came down on hers and he placed her butt on the kitchen counter. Dishes clanged from the blanket falling on top of them. Her thin T-shirt and sleep shorts could have been made of air for all the barrier they provided against his hard body.

"Say more."

"Grinders and drill presses." His hands yanked her hips so her crotch met his. He ground his considerable hardness against her, and she lit up inside like the New Year's Eve ball in Times Square.

"You know exactly how to talk dirty to me, ya know?"

His lips came down on hers. "I want to take you upstairs," he said into her mouth.

She nodded, not wanting their lips to part.

He managed to navigate them to the stairway with her hanging on like a monkey in a tree.

"Wait," she said. "Thor."

"He's inside, remember? Door's closed. He won't be

getting out. I can't vouch for him getting into the wall again, however."

She smiled. "I know someone with a drywall saw who can get him out if he does."

"Yes, you do."

"But I also can do it now."

His chortle rumbled through her chest. "So competitive."

When they got to her bedroom, he laid her down on her comforter. He yanked his T-shirt over his head and lowered that wide chest on top of her again. His weight comforted her, making her insides turn all warm and mushy.

His hands roamed her body without an ounce of hesitation. When his fingers slipped inside her panties, she moaned aloud.

"Second best sound ever," he whispered in her ear.

"What's the first?"

He lifted himself off her a bit and grasped her chin. "I'll show you."

He then climbed down her body, taking her sleep shorts and panties with him. When his lips began kissing her between her legs so intently, she had to suck in air to deal with the sudden sensation. She clawed at her comforter until she was sure she'd left gashes in the fabric.

Within minutes, she was keening toward the ceiling. Let all of Magnolia Street hear her.

After her orgasm subsided, he climbed back up her body. "*That's* the best sound."

When he went back to kissing her mouth, she tasted her own saltiness, which aroused more desire in her. She hooked her legs around his waist again. "I want to hear you now."

His now-famous grin returned to his face and he scrambled up. He shucked his jeans. He made a show of it, too. First, the buttons. Levi's 501's. Nice. Then lowering them, taking his boxers with him.

Her lungs expanded of their own accord. He was beautiful. Every part of him was.

She nearly tore her T-shirt off her body trying to get it off.

At the sight of her bare breasts, he stilled. His gaze fixed on her nipples, and then he crawled back onto the bed. He dove for her breasts. His warm mouth moved from one and to the other until she was a panting beast again. Every time she tried to position her hips to capture him, he'd move away. He was such a tease.

"Hey, you said I could win your body?" she whined. She reached into her nightstand and grabbed a condom, praying it wasn't expired, and tossed it his way.

He caught it with one hand.

Finally, sheathed and stiff, he settled himself between her legs and thrust inside her. For long minutes, Brent moved inside her until she came again, this time crying into his mouth.

God, she'd forgotten how much she loved sex, and he was as spectacular at that as he was wielding power tools. So spectacular she nearly forgot her own name, let alone the fact that she had to be at work sometime that morning. It wasn't until she awoke with a start she remembered that not-too-little detail.

She sat upright. She guessed conking out after sex wasn't only for men.

Water rushed close by. *Not again.*

Her foot slipped on Brent's jeans and boxer briefs he'd left. She knew it. He *did* leave his underwear on the floor.

She stilled and caught her breath. He was in the shower. This was her moment, wasn't it? To *choose*—be on time for work or join him.

She then did that thing she'd seen in the movies. She slipped into the bathroom and eased the shower curtain back. She'd use the derecho as an excuse for being late. After all, her car was under a tree limb.

The old Eve wouldn't have used a non-functioning car as an excuse. But, right now, knowing how Brent was in the shower was more important.

He was great at shower shenanigans, she learned. The fact that he left a glob of toothpaste in the sink didn't bother her one bit.

# 28

Fifteen minutes later, they stood in her kitchen. He was shirtless and in jeans, which only gave her more ideas that involved him losing said jeans. "I'll take a look at your car later if you want," he said as he poured granola into a coffee cup.

A quick yank on her robe belt kept her focused—and clothed. "Sure. Thanks. I'll Uber to work." She really was late as hell.

"I can drop you."

"That's okay." She had to get a move on, and he still had *tools* to load up.

He crunched his granola while she placed a quick call to Scarlett for cover. A death storm had to be a good excuse.

"Is that what we're calling it now?" Scarlett asked. "Tell me you've finally gotten nailed."

She cupped her hand over the mouthpiece. "Yes, but don't squeal—"

A screech came through the phone. Brent grinned. She stuck her tongue out at him. He shook his head and knelt down in front of her dishwasher.

"Gotta go, Scarlett." She killed the call and stepped up to Brent. "The dishwasher is broken. Well, it's semi-fixed now. And don't say I should have called you the first time it broke."

"Why would I?" He rose to his full height. "I mean, it's not like you don't know a plumber." He pointed at his own chest.

"I do know a *particular* one." In the biblical sense, too.

He set his cup on the cupboard and beckoned her closer. Once wrapped up in his arms, he did his hair swipe move across her forehead again. "And I'd like to be the only one you know forever, Eve Chatham."

*Whoa. Forever.* The air crackled with something she couldn't name. Like maybe he meant his words. "Forever is a long time."

"Time is short. Trust me." His hands ran down her shoulders and her arms.

"You like to move fast, don't you?" She'd meant to sound teasing, but she was more than a little serious. He couldn't possibly be deciding forever *anything*. She certainly couldn't.

His dad must be on his mind. Time had to be different for someone who might lose a person they cared about.

He reached over to grab his T-shirt. "It's the only speed I got. About this weekend—"

"I have to work," she said quickly. "And you said you had to help your mom."

His lips twisted up on one side, which probably didn't mean anything. She didn't have time to figure it out because her doorbell rang.

She padded to the front door. Her mother stood on her front porch. Did her family forget how to use a telephone?

"Mom, what are you doing here?"

Her mother pushed her way inside in her wholly impractical suede heels on such a wet fall day. "You called me in a panic in the middle of the night, Evangeline. What happened?" She pointed toward the street. "Your car..."

"Who is it?" Brent's voice boomed from behind her.

Her mother's gaze lifted to Brent, who was coming down the hallway, pulling his T-shirt on over his still wet hair.

If that wasn't a signal they'd done the deed, nothing would be—at least where her mother was concerned.

Her mother showed not an ounce of propriety in her eyes as she drank in Brent, letting her gaze run up and down him. "My. What do we have here?" She pulled back the collar on Eve's robe and eyed her neck, a huge, smug smile in place. "Hmm?"

Oh, my God. Her mother was searching her for hickeys.

She should have never opened the door.

Her mother strode forward and held out her hand. "Why, Brent. I'm so happy to see you here."

He shook her hand. "Nice to see you, too, Mrs. Chatham."

"Katherine, please."

Eve tried to angle herself between Brent and her mother. "Brent came by to help me with cleanup. We had a derecho come through."

"A what?" She turned back to Brent. "I don't watch the news as much as I should."

"Mom, a derecho is a sudden storm surge. And, as you can see, I'm fine. How about I swing by later?"

"Later? When would you have time for that?" Her mother couldn't help but send her gaze back to Brent, could she? "This girl has had no time for anything but school and work. School and work." She cocked her head back and forth in a singsong gesture. "But I'm glad to see you're changing your tune a bit, Evangeline." Her eyes drifted down to her neck once more.

Brent put his arm around Eve "The storm did a lot of damage. Trees down, and we'll need to attend to her car. Got hit by a limb."

Her mother's hand flew to her chest. "Oh, my. I am so

glad you have some backup," her mother said to her. "Thank you, Brent. I don't know what she would have done without you."

Eve's forehead bunched. "I don't need—"

"Sweetheart." Her mother's voice steeled. "Before you say it, everyone needs backup, and you're smart to have someone skilled around." She turned her adoring eyes back to Brent. "She's smarter than me, you see. Always has been. And I'm proud of her." Her eyes misted.

Seriously? Eve quickly forced down a growing lump in her throat. Her mother hadn't ever said those words about her before. Then again, a real live man stood in Eve's house, which to her was akin to Eve winning the Pulitzer Prize.

Brent pointed to the kitchen. "Going to get my chainsaw and start hacking up that limb out back. I mean, if you're okay with that, Eve."

"Thanks." At least he asked—sort of. She didn't want to seem ungrateful, but he did have a way of taking over. Then again, *she'd* jumped *him* last night, and she wasn't sorry. She just had to figure out how to make it all work—starting with extra credit assignments to get her GPA back on track. One 'B' on a paper wouldn't kill her.

When Brent was out of earshot, she turned to her mother. "Mom, is everything all right?" Her mom was acting weird. First, she showed up to her house, which she openly hated, and then she made a "proud" comment.

"I have my hands full with your sister. She's decided to go back to school of all things." She spat the last few words.

*Oh, my God.* "That's fantastic."

"You would say that. I thought she and Kevin worked it out." Her mother's lips turned downward. "But this school business... Anyway, Kevin's affair wasn't true love after all. I told your sister forgiveness is a powerful thing, and they do love each other. Kevin is a good man." She straightened the shoulders on Eve's robe. "Like Brent. I like him."

"I like him, too. And he's nothing like Kevin. But it doesn't matter. I'm not getting seriously involved with anyone right now." One whiff of any other status would have her mom on a quest to find out everything about Brent. Her mom could have been a detective.

"Why not? And don't give me that line about being too busy." She sniffed. "I know all about your need to *not* be me. Yes, I know that look. But don't be stupid. I didn't raise a stupid daughter."

She put her hands on her hips. "I'm not stupid."

"Of course, you're not." Her mother's lips twisted. "Now, do you need a lift?"

The startup of Gretel sounded in her backyard. "Thanks, but I'll take an Uber. My schedule is tight the rest of the day." Plus, she could end this conversation. "I have class tonight, but I promise to come by this weekend. Okay?"

"Perfect. Saturday. I'll have Delores come in."

"I don't need a pedicure or a manicure."

"Oh, honey. Every woman needs a nail tech," she craned her neck toward the back of the house, "and a fine-looking man who can use a chainsaw."

## 29

As soon as her mother left, Eve walked to the back to give a hasty goodbye to Brent. He stood by her garage, huffing, holding Gretel. He even made that look sexy.

A long stack of cut-up wood pieces lined the side of the garage. He'd already freed her car of the tree limb.

She marched up to him. "Hey, thanks. You sure you have time for this right now?" She had to shout over the rumbling engine of the chainsaw.

He killed the engine. "It's no problem."

"Um, I have to get to work, and we can talk later?"

He scratched at his growing beard. "Need a ride to work?"

"Nah, Uber's on its way."

"So I can get started on the garage, cleaning it out…" He hitched a thumb toward her pitiful garage building. "I mean, now that you aren't selling." He chuffed like he knew all along she never would.

Her skin prickled. "Let's wait on that. When I can be here?" While punching a gift horse in the mouth wasn't smart, she had different priorities. She also wasn't used to having someone else create a schedule that she didn't control every second of the day. Maybe it was time to surrender some control when unexpected things arose.

"Sure, you can probably turn that garage into some serious storage." His eyes squinched in the sun as he gazed up at the second floor. "Without it, this house would be tight quarters with a family. But it could work." He looked down at her. "So, four kids or five?"

She stopped breathing, and her lips fell open.

"Your face..." Brent laughed. "Kidding."

Her diaphragm kicked in and forced a deep inhale. "It's just I... I..."

His head swiveled to face the street. "I think I hear your car."

"Great." She spun and jogged away without a goodbye. Four kids or five? Joking aside, was he out of his mind? Kids were so far off her radar screen they might as well live in another galaxy.

A Toyota Prius pulled up to the curb in a loud screech. She scrambled to get inside. "Peppermint Sweet. You know the place?"

The driver, a middle-aged guy wearing a beret, nodded. "Great pies."

"The best." She picked up her phone and called Persephone. She had to find out what was going on with her. It would be good to talk about someone else's life, and Persy's favorite topic was herself.

Plus, she could talk Eve out of overreacting about Brent's kids joke. If anyone understood manspeak, it was Persy.

"Eve?" Her sister sounded breathless.

"Where are you?" Her Uber driver took the turnoff down Magnolia so fast she had to grab on to the door handle. "Hey," she called. The guy raised his hand in a sorry.

"Treadmill. Where are you?"

She should have known by the foot-pounding in the background.

"I'm on my way to work. Listen, Mom came by—"

"Yeah, I heard your message. Storm over now?"

Gee, thanks, sister, for being worried. Then again, she had a lot on her plate reuniting with her husband. "It's fine. Some damage." Like her car, garage door, shed, and who knew what else that she had yet to discover. "Mom said you're going back to school?" It would be so much easier if Persy was in school, too. Maybe her mother would lay off judging Eve's choices if she saw both daughters carving their own way.

"Not anymore. I'm on to something else, something better."

Eve should have known it was a passing fancy. "That was fast."

Her sister's huff grew louder. "I got news. First..." She blew out more air. "Amanda has been transferred to California, which is still six states too close, but I can live with it."

Eve picked at her cuticle. "That's good, I guess."

"Kevin moved fast since I had *other* news to deliver. Guess who's having a baby?"

*Please don't tell me.* "A. Baby. Like a—"

"You're going to be an auntie!"

Eve had to pull the phone from her ear due to Persy's high-pitched squeal. "A..." She couldn't say the word again. Had the storm last night transported her to a parallel universe? First, Brent raises the subject of children, and now her sister was having an actual one. "Are you sure you're pregnant?"

"Yep. Took four pregnancy tests. All positive. I see Dr. Transom later today."

Thank God, because the woman had drunk so much vodka the other night, which couldn't have been good.

Persy's foot pounds on the tread continued. "Kevin is over the moon and he dumped that Amanda like a knockoff import." Her words were a little halted given the exertion she was under. "I'm talking less than twenty-four hours. He's running out to get a crib I picked out online. Can you believe it?"

She could. It was exactly how things would always go because redirecting men was the Chatham woman way.

A long string of beeps like Persy was decreasing her speed came over the line. "You're the first to know. I haven't even told Mom yet. Speaking of which, don't you dare tell her about the other night. I mean, *that* won't happen again."

Her mother would be thrilled with the baby news—or maybe not because that meant she'd be a grandmother. Of course, her mom would adopt a name like Gigi or even ask the baby to call her by her first name.

Persy squealed anew. "Isn't this the greatest news ever?"

"It is. Best news ever." Eve swallowed.

After ending the call, she closed her eyes and tuned into the car's vibrations under her like a meditation.

"Congratulations to the new mom," the Uber driver said. "Sorry. Couldn't help but overhear. Had my first one last year. It's the best thing in the world."

She fluttered open her eyes. "Sure. It's my sister. Best thing ever." And it was—for Persy.

"Don't worry. Your time will come."

"Excuse me?" She stared at his eyes in the rear-view mirror.

"Remember, God's delays are not God's denials."

Oh, my God. She *had* landed in a parallel world—one that resembled 1958. "I'm good. Really." Did she really want to argue with a car service driver? No, she did not.

She dialed her father. Of course, she got his voice mail, but that was fine. Hearing his voice was enough to get her back in touch with herself. Now she was going to class straight after work—and would not skip another one until she held a diploma in her hand. It was something that didn't wake you up at three a.m. and demand to suck on her boobs.

Great. Now she could only think about Brent and his mouth.

# 30

Professor Latham cleared his throat dramatically, and everyone in the packed lecture hall quieted.

"What's going on?" she whispered to the guy next to her—someone she had never seen before.

"You didn't get the news? He's bringing in guest lecturers and opened the whole class to anyone who can find a seat."

That was nice, she guessed. By the size of the crowd, she supposed a lot of people were into renovations.

Her professor then introduced a real-world general contractor who covered all the basics about putting up drywall. That was one thing she hadn't had to do yet and hoped never to.

While everyone around her either tapped on their laptops or jotted down notes the old-fashioned way on paper, she did neither. She couldn't keep her mind on her professor's words at all, instead replaying the conversation she'd had with her sister—and her Uber driver, of all people—like a mental loop. By the end of the night, she'd rather have had the Baby Shark song stuck in her ear for an eternity.

As it neared nine p.m., Professor Latham asked what

they'd like to learn next, and Eve blurted out without being called on, "Plumbing. Specifically, old house plumbing."

"Yes, those old houses require a delicate touch." He sounded like Brent, which immediately swung her mind to him. She blinked a few times to clear her head.

By the time she got home, she was dead on her feet. She wanted a hot bath and her pillow—and that was it. When she got dropped off by her driver, Brent's truck was still in her driveaway, parked behind her damaged car. *At this hour?*

"Hey." She dropped her purse in the hall chair. "Whatcha doing?"

Brent was screwing a lightbulb into the overhead light in the main hall. "I saw this was out."

"At ten p.m.? Didn't you have classes today?"

"Yep. Two this afternoon plus a few hours of study group. I swung by Martin's Hardware, got you some lightbulbs, and thought I'd pop this in."

"That's so out of your way."

"S'okay." He hopped down off the short ladder.

"Brent, I appreciate all this, but we need to talk..." Breathe. Just breathe. "About boundaries." She loved having him around, but if this was going to work, she needed a bit more structure.

He stared at her blank face. "It's a lightbulb, Eve."

"I know but..." He was wonderful, but he also kept showing up without warning. Sometimes a girl wanted her space—and to say when that happened. "It's just..."

"What?"

"We're still getting to know each other. We seem to be skipping over some steps." That was it, wasn't it? They went from meeting to business to sex and now he was letting himself in anytime he wanted. It was partly her fault, and she could fix it. "I mean, usually you date a while before..."

"Before, what? Getting to know my power tools?" He was

trying to make light of the situation. He sobered. "I know what's going on. First, your sister the other night. Then your mom came by today. It does have an effect on you." He pushed his ladder together. "They make you cranky."

She lifted her hand in a stop sign motion. "Let's not go there. No, this is me saying we need to be a bit more… measured. I need to get used to all this."

He put his elbow on one of the ladder rungs. "Measured."

"Yes. Can we slow things down a bit? Until I graduate? I've missed too many classes and…" She tried to smile but her cheeks weren't lifting.

He nodded. "You know, I take it back. I'd say this has nothing to do with your family."

"Oh?" Like he would know?

"This is what happens. You have a need or a breakdown. I come in and fix it. And then you push me away."

Now she *was* irritated. "Are you calling me a user?" Because that was *so* not her.

"No. Look." He scrubbed his hair. "I've been noticing a pattern, that's all."

"Don't analyze me, Brent," she gritted out. She'd spent all day doing that to herself.

"Don't like it when people point things out to you, huh?"

What the ever-lovin'… "Look, my life isn't like yours. You have your dad, and I have school, and we need to handle those things *first*."

"No kidding." He slipped his arm through a rung so it rested on his shoulder. "I'm going."

They were both overtired, and tonight wasn't a good time to have this conversation.

She stopped him at the door. "Brent. Look, I care about you. And I'll always need your… skills." She'd hoped he'd get the innuendo in her words.

His eyes glazed over like stone. "Glad my skills served you well."

"Brent, please."

He set the ladder against the door and took her hand. "Look. When I see something I want, I go for it. But I don't think you know what you want. You can't have me around only when it's convenient. I won't be one of your to-do list items."

"I hardly—"

"Are you sure? Don't have me in your life unless you really want me. Like I said, life is short." He dropped her hand and lifted the ladder back up on his shoulder.

The ladder banged against her front doorjamb as he strode out. She fought the urge to run after him or move to her front window to watch him leave. The truck door slamming shut told her everything she needed to know.

They really were on different pages—only she didn't know what was on his page.

# 31

She managed to get through most of the night without sending most of the texts she'd written and promptly deleted.

<<**I'm sorry. I *really* like you. Isn't that enough?**>> That one even offended her as she was typing it.

<<**Can't we keep seeing each other but not so intensely?**>> It was mature—and true. But maybe this wasn't intense to him?

<<**You're right. I can't see anyone right now. I wish you all the best.**>> Her fingers shook as she typed that one. Delete, delete, delete!

<<**Can you come over? Or can I come see you?**>>

Stupid, stinging tears filled her eyes on that one. She was begging.

Dammit, all she'd wanted to do was come home and have a bath alone. She threw her phone down.

None of her messages were right. She didn't know what she felt anymore. Her heart did funny things around him. She loved seeing him at her house, yet his constant presence got her hackles up at the same time.

Why?

She knew why.

She had a path carved by her own making. For the most part, the march to her future hadn't been interrupted in years. *Of course,* having a man jet into her life that she couldn't stop thinking about and lusting after would feel like squeezing into Spanx one size too small when she'd been fine hanging out in yoga pants.

Surely, they could work things out. Except he kept getting pissed and leaving without talking things through. Then her guilt would set in. But it wasn't her sole responsibility to fix things—they both had to.

She texted something simple. <<**Hey, are you busy tomorrow?**>>

His reply came back fast. <<**Yes.**>>

She didn't know what to say to that. Before she could think of a reply, another text came in.

<<**Got a plumbing problem? Can send Frank over.**>>

His answer crushed her like King Kong's fist might. He was mad—like really, really mad.

For several hours, she stared at her ceiling, sure she'd never sleep a wink.

His words pinged in her brain like raindrops against a tin roof. At which point she realized she needed to stop thinking about roofs because the Universe might get ideas to do something to hers.

She threw her covers back and got out of bed. She then went down to her kitchen and proceeded to scrub her oven with an old toothbrush. It was either that or consume a pint of Chunky Monkey.

She talked to Thor about what went down as she scrubbed.

"I'm not asking too much here, am I?" No, she was not.

Thor's tail twitched as he lay on the kitchen table, a place he wasn't allowed.

"He overreacted to me. He'll have to get over it."

Thor laid his head down and rolled to his side. His purring joined with her scrubbing.

"I'm not using him. He's just here all the time. And we love it, but we also like our space, don't we?"

Thor let off a meow.

"I knew you'd agree with me."

When the oven was so shiny she might see her own reflection, she dumped the now-ruined toothbrush into the sink and peeled off her rubber gloves. She should feel better now that she talked it out with Thor. She glanced at her phone. Still nothing from Brent. She fingered it and pursed her lips. Thor, the god, would never ice her out like this.

She peered down at Thor. "It'll all blow over, right?"

Thor jumped down from the table and moved to his food bowl. He pawed his bowl, making it clang.

Why couldn't Brent understand her as well as Thor? He always knew what to do. She moved to the freezer and pulled out a pint of Chunky Monkey ice cream.

She and Thor then sat together—she with the best ice cream known to man and he with another can of tuna fish—on her brand new, beautiful tile floor… laid by Brent.

# 32

Eve rolled over and a swath of sunshine attacked her face. She sat bolt upright and glanced at her clock. It was seven a.m.

Colors danced across her comforter. The stained-glass window Brent had gifted her was propped up against the windowsill. Twin rose-colored swatches of light landed across her legs, one from her window and one from his.

Thor meowed loudly from the end of the bed. He wanted breakfast.

"I'm coming." She stretched her neck. A sharp pain shot down her arm, probably from sleeping at an odd angle. She swung her legs off the bed. Her phone vibrated on her nightstand. Brent's face flashed in her mind. She answered the call without looking.

"Did you hear the news?" Her father's voice sang in her ear.

She fell back on the bed again. "Yep. You're going to be a grandpa."

"Apparently, I'm Paw-Paw and your mother is going to be Gigi."

"Of course, she is."

He chuckled. "She nabbed that one before Kevin's mother could. Hey, can my Eve-bee have lunch with me today? I haven't seen much of you lately."

She bolted upright. Perfect. "I'd love to, Daddy." Her father steadied her, and she could use a big dose of steady right now. "Let me see if I can get Scarlett to cover for me."

"You're not working too hard, are you?"

"Like father, like daughter."

"Meet me at the St. Regis at noon. We'll play hooky together—at least for an hour."

She called Scarlett, who agreed to cover during lunchtime but under conditions. "You cover for me next Tuesday," she said. "Mark wants me to go canoeing."

"You seeing him a lot?"

"Almost every day now. You really, really need to get going on Brent because we would have so much fun together!"

"Yeah, about that. I may or may not be seeing him again."

Scarlett groaned. "Is this the point where I tell you you're being stupid again?"

"No, this is the part where you're telling me I was right." She killed the call before Scarlett could argue. She needed a shower. She couldn't wait for her lunch with her father—the sensible one in the family. He'd tell her she was being wise. He'd remind her if a man couldn't accept her boundaries, then he wasn't right for her.

She then dialed the windshield repair people whose advertisements said they could replace a windshield in under an hour, hoping they were right. She had a schedule to keep.

~

Eve leaned around her dad and picked another tiny quiche off the silver tray. "One more."

Her father smiled and waved at a table across the St. Regis restaurant. He seemed to know everyone here—or they knew him.

She loved coming here with her dad, especially for lunch. They wheeled around a fancily scrolled cart filled with finger-sized cucumber sandwiches, tea cakes, tiny fruitcakes, shrimp and greens salads in martini glasses, and assorted skewers of chicken, veal, and beef, and roasted vegetables. The variety kept everyone happy—the ladies who lunch that are perpetually dieting and the men who could load up on meat.

Her dad took a swig of his iced tea. "You look tired, Eve. You sure you don't want to come back to work for me? We can find something for you before you graduate. Make it a bit easier on you."

Pitch herself back into Rumorsville? "No, thank you."

He chuckled. "My independent Eve-bee." The pride shining in his eyes soothed her soul like nothing else did.

"If I'm tired it's because house renovations are keeping me up. Plus, I had to get my windshield fixed early this morning from the storm." She took a bite of the quiche's cheesy goodness.

"Your mother filled me in. You could have called your old dad, here." He tapped a fingertip on the table.

"I know, Dad. But it's okay." She added a bright tone to her last words. The last thing she wanted to do was look like she couldn't handle her own life in front of him. "I'll be driving around with a dented hood for a while, but it's no big deal. The house is looking better these days."

He snapped his napkin into order on his knee. "Your mother tells me your young man there, Brent, is helping. He seems quite capable."

"He's not my young man." Her heart still panged at the thought of him and the fact that his face kept rising in her mind.

"I see." Her father leaned back and eyed her. "Anything you want to talk about?"

"No." Now that she sat before her father, talking to him about Brent felt… weird.

He took in a sudden breath and changed his tone. "So, happy you're going to be an aunt?"

"Yeah." She was. Somewhere between her house and the St. Regis, she'd made peace with the fact that her sister wasn't going to live a life like she was. Eve would make sure the baby had a huge library of books at his or her disposal, from *The Velveteen Rabbit* to *The Great Gatsby*.

Her father adjusted his suitcoat. "Speaking of changes, getting excited about graduating?"

"I am." She should sound happier, be bouncing up and down in her seat. "Too bad Persy isn't joining me. I'm sure Mom talked her out of going back to school, too?"

"No."

She snorted. "So, she'll go back to planning parties and decorating a baby's room."

Her father arched an eyebrow. "Do I detect a bit of jealousy? Your time will come, and—"

"Jealous?" Of ruining her feet in high heels? Of spending more time on the treadmill and in a salon chair than getting educated? Of worrying that if she ate a pint of Chunky Monkey her husband would leave her? Of picking out baby clothes… cute little overalls and dresses that made her insides soften thinking of them… "Why would I be *that*?"

"Your sister—"

"Has done little with her life." The second the words left her mouth, she wished she could take them back. Being a mother certainly was something—a big something.

Her father's face turned steely.

She lifted her hands. "I'm sorry. I'm sorry. I mean," she leaned forward. "don't you think Persy wishes she'd done more? More than just helping Kevin be successful and having nothing for herself? Like going back to school?"

"More? If she wants to go to school, she will. Like you, she can do anything she wants, and her life suits her." He leaned back and tapped the fingers of one hand on the white tablecloth. "Lord knows, your mother helped me be successful."

She twisted the fork on the table up then down and back again. "She does throw a mean party."

"She's done a helluva lot more than that," he spoke slowly.

Eve snorted. "Yeah, decorating your office."

"I'll have you know, miss, that's the least of your mother's talents." Her father's bark pitched her back in her seat. "She's been editing my contracts, my memos, my proposals for years. Your mother," he pointed his finger on the table, "is how we got the Emerson deal last year. She caught a major problem in the proposal."

He could not be talking about Katherine Chatham. "Seriously?" Why hadn't she known any of this before? "You never told me."

"You never asked. And honestly, I don't think she wants people to know. I mean, at first, *I* never asked, but I'd find these sticky notes—"

She burst out laughing. "Sticky notes?"

He grinned and lifted his iced tea. "I got in the habit of leaving things out on my desk when I got home from work, and the next morning, there they were. Underlines and sticky notes." He took a sip of his drink. "She's partial to shocking-pink highlighter, which took some explaining in the office, let me tell you." He laughed, his gaze going soft as if recalling it.

*Holy cow.* Her mother helped her father *in business.* This was stranger than her sister who was going to let her body grow large with a baby when she'd have run three miles if she gained a pound. Eve didn't know her family at all. They were like, from a different country. No, space aliens.

"I can't see Persy ever doing anything like that."

He chuckled under his breath but then sobered. "Your sister isn't quite as confident as you. In fact, I think Persy is a little jealous of you. You two always were competitive."

There was that word again. "I'm trying to be different." She sat straighter in her seat. "Like you said, don't be her, so I didn't."

His eyebrows squinched together. "I told you to be yourself. And honestly, I'm proud of both of my girls. Both accomplished in their own way, smart and beautiful. Like their mother."

She let out a puff of air. "But Persy dropped out of school."

He shook his head slightly. "She wasn't doing well at UNC. She barely got out of high school. All that boy-chasing over studying finally caught up with her."

"That certainly is where we diverged." Eve spent her school weekends studying and catching up on the latest Avenger movies. Persy spent her weekends hopping from frat party to frat party. Oh, and shopping for new outfits for each.

"And now?" he asked. "How is the boy thing doing?"

She flushed. "I've decided I don't have time for that. And please, don't tell me I'm running out of time. I get that enough from Mom."

"I don't think it's a matter of time, Eve. It's a matter of *will.*" He leaned forward. "And that, you have in spades. You have everything ahead of you. Just make sure what you're doing is what you *really* want. Don't avoid a relationship because it doesn't fit into your schedule. It rarely does. Trust me."

Was her father seriously giving her romantic advice? "Did Mom coach you?"

He slapped his chest. "Don't trust your dear old dad to give you good advice on his own?"

"But you always wanted me to—"

"I want you to be happy, Eve. I don't expect you to give that up in the process of becoming successful."

Her eyes stung. Her father seemed really concerned for her. Compassion for what Brent might be feeling about his own dad took hold. Losing someone you loved, who honestly cared for you, is terrible.

Her father's hand fell to hers. "I'm proud of you. You're focused."

She nodded vigorously and sniffed. "I am. Like you said, keep your eye on the ball because we can't have everything."

"Everything?" He seemed taken aback. "No one can. But something tells me you need to hear this, too." He waited a long second. "You're allowed to have more than one ball."

Her gaze shot up from studying their joined hands. "I thought I was."

"Are you? Of all people, *you* can handle a lot of balls." He leaned back once more, his hand slipping from hers. "The trick is knowing which ones you want."

She took one long second to breathe. "What if I don't know what I want?" She thought she knew: get her degree with no one's help and have her own house not tied to anyone else's bank account. But what if she could have all of that plus… more balls? She'd been critical of Persy because she seemed to have a one-dimensional life. But Eve had done the same, only in the opposite direction.

Her father eyed her. "Follow your gut. After that, your heart."

"What about my brain?"

"Always smart to use it. Just don't let it run amok without the other two. You have a life, not an assembly line. And I'd say it's time you start living."

"I've been doing that," she grumbled.

"Oh? There's more to life than to-do lists."

"That's what Brent said." And there went her heart again, banging against her ribs at the mere thought of him—being with him, losing him. It was beginning to feel the same, which was a mind fuck-cluster if there ever was one.

"I like him. Brent. He seems solid. He's one of your balls, isn't he?"

She nodded.

He leaned forward. "Only one problem. There is no ball large enough to contain love."

Who was this man sitting with her? Her legs squirmed with more than a little embarrassment. Love Brent? She'd known the man for *weeks*. It wasn't enough time to feel such a strong sentiment.

Her father, mercifully, didn't go on. He leaned back, gazed over her shoulder, and lifted his hand toward the waiter who was wheeling the dessert cart from table to table. "Now, ready for dessert?"

She was always ready for sugar. She lifted her iced tea to him in a toast. "I love you, Dad." Of that, she was certain.

"Love you, too, Eve-bee. Now. Crème brulee or flourless chocolate cake?"

"Yes, please."

He winked—like Brent might have. "There's my girl. Sometimes, it's better to have it all."

All. What a concept. And maybe Brent and her father had more in common than she'd ever believed. He was wrong about the love part, though. It was too soon.

# 33

The lecture hall for Professor Latham's renovation class was full. Eve plunked her butt down in one of the few empty seats she could find. She threw her backpack at her feet and drew out her phone and her laptop. Still, no message from Brent showed up on her screen. Brent hadn't answered her third—okay, fourth—text. Hang Persy's advice about only sending one.

It was for the best despite her father saying she could juggle balls and the whole love talk and whatever else he was trying to tell her. Her life wasn't a to-do list. It was a living, breathing monster out to get her.

A professor had emailed her asking if anything was wrong. He'd written, "I had no choice but to give you a 'C' on your latest paper. Something unexpected from you." It was on a paper for her qualitative market research class—not even her hardest class.

She also had several texts from professors she needed to return about doing some extra credit to get her GPA back up. She had an extra shift to pick up at Peppermint Sweet because she owed Scarlett from the last few weeks. And Thor had yakked all over her brand-new daisy rug in the bathroom while she was playing hooky with her father at lunch.

A quick call to the vet and the only advice she got was, "Watch him." *When*? They'd said so long as he wasn't constantly throwing up, he'd probably eaten something he shouldn't have and it was a good sign his body rid itself of the unwanted stuff. How about that furry lump covered in ick that she'd used ten paper towels to pick up?

She almost stayed home to crack open a bottle of wine after that to sit with Thor, but she had to get a handle on things.

Scarlett came over to watch Thor because throwing up wasn't even close to breaching her "ick" scale. Benefits of being raised on a farm, she supposed. The woman had veterinarians on speed dial.

Then Eve went to class to distract herself from the fact that Brent hadn't answered her damned texts.

The lecture hall crackled with voices. Not a single seat was left open. Her professor's idea of opening up the class to anyone in town must be working.

Professor Latham stood behind the podium to the left of the large table which usually was strewn with tools and other visual aids used to discuss modern-day renovation. A man with blond hair stood at the chalkboard, doodling something on the wall.

"I see word got out about tonight's guest lecturer. You're all welcome because I know how popular our Mr. Shadwell is."

The man turned in profile. *Brent?* Her chest bloomed in happiness at seeing him, and she rose taller in her seat.

How had she not recognized his shoulders and the way they tapered down to his trim waist? And that toss of blond hair? And the casual, cool way he stood as if nothing bothered him, which she knew was not true.

"Tonight, we're going to talk about something suggested by one of our students." Professor Latham pushed his glasses to the top of his head and looked down at his notes. "Evangeline Chatham. Miss Chatham?" He glanced around.

She'd suggested something? When? She tentatively raised her hand.

"Ah, Miss Chatham. I understand this is an elective for you but you wanted to know more about plumbing. Having a few issues at home, are we?"

A few snickers filtered through the room.

She cleared her throat. "You never know when a pipe might burst."

Brent finally turned around and looked up at her. "And never at a good hour." He'd been mic'd with a lavalier so his voice, deep and gravelly, boomed across the space and ran over her skin like his fingers.

More laughter filled the hall. She gave him a big smile, but he didn't return it. Giving her the cold shoulder, huh? They could fix their minor blip—if he'd only talk to her.

Professor Latham returned his glasses to his nose. "You'll be happy to hear Mr. Shadwell is an expert on such matters." He then lifted a piece of paper and recited Brent's credentials: A Bachelor of Arts in Architectural Studies from Virginia Tech, a Master of Architecture from Stanford University, and now, earning a second Master's in Architectural Engineering from A.U. He'd also worked for two archi tecture firms in Chicago in between those degrees.

And she thought her schedule had been busy.

"Houses." Brent's voice boomed across the hall. "They need love like everyone else."

The tittering stopped and everyone stilled. The man riveted everyone in the room with eight words. *Eight*. Then again, he really did have a commanding presence.

"But sometimes, it doesn't feel like they love you back—

especially anything to do with water." His statement earned more laughter as he moved his big frame around the room. Over one hundred sets of eyes followed his pacing, including her own.

Any fatigue she had vanished. Her fingers settled on her laptop keyboard, ready to take down every word he might speak. Brent knew his stuff—she'd seen that first-hand.

"But first," he said, "you have to know how important plumbing has been to every civilization before us."

He began to go into the ins and outs of plumbing, starting in ancient Rome and how it evolved. Copper piping appeared in Egypt as early as 2400 B.C., and galvanized iron was preferred in the US from the late 1800s to around 1960.

"But," he said, "if you're lucky, you'll discover copper pipes in some of the homes built after World War II during a lead poisoning scare." He let his gaze go soft. "And there is nothing like seeing that patina on an old copper pipe inside a wall."

Eve swore she heard at least a dozen of the female students sigh in response—*over pipes*. Her pulse quickened at how greedily their eyes ran over him. She was most definitely going to have to watch a few of them, like a beautiful blond a few rows down, in case they got any romantic ideas about him.

He talked for a few more minutes but then paused to show off some of the basic plumbing tools she recognized. The snake camera he'd used that first night she'd met him, pliers, wrenches, and a plunger that when he wielded it in the air, her mind superimposed a Thor hammer on top of it.

Brent went into the repairs one could easily make at home, and she was heartened to hear a leaky washer was on the list. Then there were repairs that required a professional, like a burst pipe deep inside a wall. She took copious notes even though, after this talk, she realized nothing she could do could compare to his knowledge base.

The man was intelligent—a level of practical smarts rarely gained through books. His enthusiasm and conviction also were mesmerizing. And the way he fingered the tools? The man made plumbing sound sexy. It didn't hurt he looked amazing in that suit coat, donned over a T-shirt and jeans. She'd not seen that look on him before.

He truly was the total female magnet package.

She ripped her gaze from him and glanced around. Yep, he'd mesmerized the females—and a few of the men, too. By the time he got to questions, half the room was in love with him. He was so passionate about the topic. His fervor reminded her of their one date where they'd walked on Poplar Avenue.

Had they only gone out once? Her birthday party did *not* count. And somehow, he was always around, helping, cracking jokes, letting her cry into his amazing pecs, turning her insides into mush—when he wasn't throwing around ridiculous assertions about her, storming out. She refused to take all the blame for their strange stand-off—for surely, that's what they were in.

A tall woman with long blond hair and naturally rosy lips raised her hand. "Mr. Shadwell—"

He moved up the aisle to get closer to her. "Brent, please."

"What's been your hardest job?" Her lashes blinked at him.

"Anything involving an animal." His beautiful green eyes cast down on the blond.

She shuddered. "Like a mouse?"

The class laughed.

"No, like a dog down a drain. Or, in my case, an entire litter of puppies."

Gasps sounded all around her.

He looked around. "I haven't lost one yet. We got them all out."

The amount of "awwing" was ridiculous, but Eve had to admit visualizing Brent lifting roly-poly puppies from a drain was superhero material. By the way the woman looked at him, she was one second away from sewing the man a cape. Eve understood the sentiment because he was superhero material, wasn't he? He had more than skills. He cared about people—and puppies.

"And cats." He looked directly at Eve. "I've pulled a lot of cats from walls."

A man howled. "Sounds like a stupid cat."

"They're not stupid," Eve said under her breath but kept her eyes on Brent. With any luck, he'd see the plea in her eyes. *Talk to me.*

Brent broke his gaze from her and peered over at the man. "They're adventurers. Sometimes more than their owners."

He looked back at her, still unsmiling. His expression was flat like he saw right through her. Her nerves grew jittery.

She lifted her chin toward him and tried to shake some emotion from his eyes. "I'd say taking on any home renovation is quite adventurous. Especially if you have the right help." She added a smile to her lips at the end. Still, no response.

Brent moved up the aisleway and stopped at her row. "It is. Provided you don't quit too soon." He turned back to the crowd. Seats creaked as everyone shifted so they could watch him.

The blond girl rested her hand on her chin in pure adoration.

When he was finally done with all the questions, he clasped his hands together. "So, class, what did we learn today?" He was trying to be funny, mocking a teacher.

"Don't have a cat?" the cat-hating guy called out.

Brent finally looked straight at Eve. "Expect the unexpected."

And there was her weak spot—rubbed in her face. Maybe he had been right—a little. Right then, she couldn't fathom why him showing up to fix a stupid lightbulb had been such a big deal.

When he was done with his lecture, a dozen students swarmed him—mostly women, of course. Brent didn't seem to be hating all the attention as they sang, "*Oh, Mr. Shadwell* this," and, "*Oh, Mr. Shadwell* that." The women fingered his power tools like they were pashminas on sale—or Brent was.

Eve moved down to wait her turn in line. For the next twenty minutes, he unwound the crowd like a seasoned politician, giving each one a few minutes of his time, answering questions and nodding.

Once he was freed of a short brunette who'd bolted on to his forearm the whole time she'd been yakking at him, he turned to her and smiled. "Miss Chatham."

"Hi. Nice talk."

"Learn anything?"

She tucked hair behind her ear. "That I have a long way to go when it comes to some things." And more. "Um, do you have a second to talk?"

Brent took her by the elbow and led her to the corner of the room. Of course, blondie followed. As if he might be getting away?

She lowered her voice. "I think we need to clear up—"

"Your renovations?" He bent closer to her, bringing his wonderful scent closer.

She shifted on her feet. "Sure, that and—"

With a long inhale, he straightened his spine. "No. I'm afraid I won't be able to. I'm all booked up now."

Her chest caved in a bit. "Booked up?"

"I am."

He was so formal and stiff, her stomach sank to her knees. He couldn't possibly mean… She drew her lips between her teeth and released them. "Can we talk? Please?"

"Sorry." He turned to Professor Latham, who had sidled up to him.

"Thank you, Brent." He offered a handshake. "I can't thank you enough. I want to introduce you to my niece, Jennifer."

The blond with the pouty pink lips smiled wide and took his hand even though Brent hadn't offered it. She started to talk but Eve couldn't hear her words. Her ears filled with the white noise of her blood rushing through her veins.

Eve turned away. Her own words had dried up, and her throat had closed shut.

She hadn't failed at much in her life. Keeping herself at the top of her class since seventh grade, negotiating her house purchase, navigating two jobs to the point she'd never been denied a requested raise when needed—they all came easily to her when she really thought about it.

Until recently. Before Brent, if she'd wanted to accomplish something, she did. Now, she couldn't figure out how to get Brent to listen to her. The thought of him being gone from her life was…

She couldn't think. She rubbed her forehead as if that would erase the fact that he was *all booked up*. All because she needed to draw some boundaries—that was it. What was the big deal? He was being so unfair.

"Brent…" She spun to face him, but he was already walking away, and Jennifer had her arm hooked in his. She probably had a lightbulb that needed fixing, and God forbid her manicure be ruined if she tried to do it herself. Eve, on the other hand, could do anything. She should feel great about that fact. Instead, her bones nearly crumpled as she made her way to her car—alone.

That's when her father's words made sense. Love didn't fit into a ball. It didn't fit into anything. It just was. That was the moment when she thought it. She loved him, and it was terrifying… and dangerous.

Jennifer had her hand on Brent's arm. They looked good together. But then, Brent would look good with anyone he stood next to. Better still, he'd make them happy. He'd done that for her for a little while. Now, it seemed, he was moving on.

She could get a clue. He didn't want her anymore, and it was okay. It would have to be.

# 34

Somewhere between the lecture hall and her car, her ire rose. In fact, by the time she reached her car, flames might have been coming out of her ears. Brent had dropped her like a hot brick.

"That unforgiving, fickle..." She rounded her car and stopped short then blinked a few times. Her front driver's side tire looked a little low on air.

How about no air at all?

Scarlett was right. Accidents followed her. Maybe she was cursed.

It was no problem. None at all. She went to her trunk, popped it open, and rummaged around until she found her can of Fix-A-Flat. She slammed down the lid.

Brent stood there, and she nearly jumped out of her skin.

His hands were stuffed in his jeans, the flaps of his jacket splayed out on either side like wings. He glanced at her Fix-A-Flat. "I wouldn't use that."

She sent her free hand to her hip. "Oh?"

"No. It won't work."

He thought he knew everything. "We'll see." She crossed

to her driver's side door and shooed him backward with her fingers. He had the nerve to snigger. At least he backed up.

Behind him, about twenty feet away, Jennifer stood, her eyes wide like she didn't know if she should interrupt. *News flash, girlfriend. You shouldn't. Get too close and you might get a smudge on your tight white jeans.*

Eve studied the back of the can.

Brent pointed down at her tire. "The valve stem is broken."

"So what?" She spat hair out of her face.

He heaved a sigh and moved to go to her trunk. "You've got a spare back here."

"What are you doing?" she gritted out.

"What works. Changing your tire."

"Stop. Stop right there." She moved to him and jabbed him in the chest with her finger. "Don't. I got it." He didn't want to be used only for problems? She wouldn't present any.

He looked down at her fingers, then back up at her face and arched an eyebrow.

"Go back to your..." she waved her arm toward Jennifer, who blinked like she didn't understand what was going on, "harem."

"Ohhh," he let out the word with a laugh. He then crossed his arms, and she'd never wanted to punch a smug smile off someone so badly. "I see what's going on here." He leaned down. "Jealous."

He tossed his head back toward Jennifer and... now, a second girl had joined them. They stared like they wanted to approach him as if he was a celebrity and they questioned how to move closer, beg for a selfie with him, an autograph, a chance to slip their phone number down his jeans pocket.

She mirrored the arrogant bastard's stance. "Ooooo." She

blinked her eyelashes rapidly. "How noble. Flex your big, manly muscles in front of your entourage."

He snorted. A sliver of satisfaction arose that she wasn't the only one who nose-honked her way through their time together. *Together*. They weren't together. Tonight, he'd made that abundantly clear.

She crouched and examined her valve stem. It was bent at an odd angle.

Her trunk popped open. She shot to standing again. "What the hell are you doing?"

The rustle of fabric was followed by a snap. "I'm flexing my manly muscles." A clang she could only guess was the jack and lug wrench to change the tire was next. "Followed by basking in the admiration of doing the simplest thing in the world." The sound of metal spinning, and then he had the spare tire out of the back and bounced it down on the pavement in fifteen seconds. "Helping a stubborn-as-shit woman change a tire."

The gall. The nerve. The… so *Brent Shadwell.* "Listen, you—"

"Still doing it, Eve." He rolled the tire closer and leaned it against her car door.

"Do you ever listen?" she shouted.

"Do you?" He dusted his hands. "Don't cut off your nose to spite your face."

In her periphery, she watched Jennifer's friend urge her away. Thank *God.* No need to have witnesses to a long-time-coming conversation.

Had he been smoking something? "That's rich given you didn't answer me all day."

"You're not the only one who needs space sometimes, especially when someone freaks out over a lightbulb."

"I did not freak." Her teeth began to ache from clenching them so hard. He was the one who'd strode out, banging his ladder down her front steps in anger because she wanted a heads up before he showed up at her house. "And it was *my* lightbulb to change."

He spun and picked up the jack. Held it up to her. "God forbid someone enter your sphere without written permission." He crouched down, stuck the jack under the car frame, and grunted a little as he tried to position it. "In fact, you should issue your own entry documents, have passport control at your front door."

So funny. "Your passport is revoked. I mean, you made it clear tonight—to everyone."

"Back there?" He hitched his thumb back toward the school building. "I didn't want anyone to know I was hireable. I have my hands full with one pain-in-the-ass girlfriend."

"Excuse me? I'm..." She stopped, unwilling to identify herself as the said girlfriend, and who was wholly unfairly labeled as a pain in the ass to boot. And how could he expect his brush-off to be anything but exactly that? *Use your words much, big guy?*

"But..." He twisted the winch. "You can count on the fact that from now on I'll just be the hired help, stick to your renovation list." Man, he was fast. The car lifted quickly. "Or, if you want, you can find someone else to take over."

Her anger had cooled as fast as it rose. Having someone else in her house, touching her baseboards, her floors? And she was no longer the girlfriend? NASA computers didn't work as fast as this guy's mind.

He twisted to look up at her and balanced his forearm on his leg. "In fact, I think you should."

Her heart dropped to her feet like an elevator that had its cable snap. She looked down at her laced fingers and bit her top lip. "You're free to do what you want."

"And you'll be free, too. Since that's what you want. Your freedom." He nearly spat out the words.

"I want my independence, a little space. That's not the same thing."

He stilled and stared at the side of the car. "No one can take that from you but you."

"Oh, yes, someone can. A baby," she blurted out and instantly spun away. She couldn't face him. She herself didn't know those words would escape her brain and through her mouth. She fought to keep the tears from rising in her eyes.

She was happy for Persy. But Eve knew how her sister's life would unfold. She'd have a nanny, maid service, all the help she needed. But she'd be alone in it. In the end, despite her husband's decree he wanted them to stay together, they would rarely *be* together. Kevin prized his work and his reputation over all else.

Was Eve any better?

Brent's body was behind her, so close his shadow thrown from the parking lot streetlight engulfed hers. "Eve. My God, are you..."

"No." She turned to face him. He stood so close, she had to crane her neck to look up at him.

She held up her hands. "I couldn't possibly be—"

"Pregnant?" His eyes glanced down at her belly and his arms reached out.

She pushed his arms away. One touch and she'd crack. "My sister is pregnant." She wrapped her arms around herself. "You know, the one who lives and dies by her size four wardrobe?"

"Oh. Congratulations."

"Yeah. It got me thinking if that ever happened to me..." Why was she trying to explain this to him? He didn't understand her—not really.

His brows furrowed. "If you did, I'd take care of you." His voice was so serious, she stilled.

But she could see him as a father. He'd throw kids in the air until they squealed. He'd get up in the middle of the night to warm up bottles—if they even did that anymore. He'd build treehouses and swing sets by his own hands.

He and Jennifer Latham would have beautiful babies—all blond curly hair and blue or green eyes. Maybe that was for the best. Despite her father saying sometimes it was better to have it all, she couldn't see how. They were too different.

"I know you would." She shuddered. "But now's not the time for me to have my choices taken from me."

He peered down at her and nodded slowly. "You know what? I take back everything I've ever said." He pointed at her forehead. "Your mind is a bigger prison than anything ever will be. You think up all kinds of things that haven't even happened yet."

*How dare he?* "I do not." Okay, she did sometimes. "I certainly didn't make up tonight."

"Like I said, wasn't trying to drum up business."

"You certainly drummed up a lot of other interest. You had to have noticed. Then you dismissed me so thoroughly in front of all those women. And I can tell you, that blond? *Jennifer—*"

"Latham's niece?"

"Yeah, her." A honk ripped from her nose. "She'd love to make babies with you. Crawl right into Hansel's back seat and…"

He laughed—heartily. "It's *Hans*. She just wants to land someone—unlike you, who is terrified of any landing at all."

Her face flushed. "I. Am. Not. And don't talk about her like that." She tilted her chin. "I'm sure she's a lovely person."

He sighed. "She is. Sorry, I…" he waved his hand, "violated the sister code or whatever is among you women. But seriously, Eve? How I could possibly be interested in Jennifer Latham when all I do is think about you."

Her breath caught. "Me."

"Of course, *you*. You think I change lightbulbs at ten p.m. for someone I don't care about? *Jesus*." His hands moved through his hair, sending the ends into a tousled mess. It made her want to run her fingers through it. "Stop thinking I'm waiting for the moment to take something away from you. I'm trying to *give* to you."

She waggled her finger at him and spun. "Don't. Do not do this."

"Do what?"

His face grew wavy in her sight. "Don't make me fall for you."

"You already have." His large hand wrapped around her bicep. "I love you, too."

Her heart did that prancing thing inside her rib cage and her stomach fluttered—like a teenager. But had she ever felt like this when she was sixteen? Or seventeen?

Or ever?

*No.*

"I can't be in—" Oh, fuck her. Yes, she was. She was one hundred percent in fucking love with him.

"And before you get back in your head about how I'm going to take over your life or whatever else it is you think men do, I won't."

"I didn't say you would." With words anyway.

"So, what's the problem then?"

They did that staring thing at each other again, like who would cave first, or maybe they didn't know how to move forward from here. If love was all it took, then so many couples would still be together.

Truth was, she hadn't a clue what kept people together or how they made things work. Not nailing Amanda on your desk was one thing, but other than that? "I'll bite. I don't know how to be with a guy and still be independent. I don't know how to do it *all*." There. She'd said it aloud.

He sighed. "Is there a way to be?"

She screwed her face into a frown. "There must be. I think." But then, she thought she'd known the women in her family, too. And the fact that her father wanted her to have her eye on the ball—singular.

*You're allowed more than one ball.* His words slipped into her brain so easily. *There is no ball large enough to contain love.*

Brent slung his arm over her shoulder and pulled her close like two buddies about to have a conversation. "You know what I've learned from renovating houses? The unexpected finds are the most fun. If everything goes to plan, it's actually unlucky for the house."

"You made that up."

"Yeah, I did. But I believe it." He lifted his chin a little and peered down at her with his beautiful eyes. "What if we turned out better than you could have imagined? Would it be worth it then? Because that's what I found in you. When I first met you, I had no idea what lay underneath that pretty face. You have a beautiful brain."

Her breath stalled. "You think?" she squeaked.

He nodded slowly. "So, Eve Chatham, you're smart. Why can't we have something no one has never seen before?"

Man, he was good at this. He was confusing her, however. "What do you mean? Exactly." Clearly, a more detailed roadmap to this strange, romantic country was required.

"I mean create something that's unique to us. You tell me what you need for things to work. I'll do the same."

She squared herself to him. "Okay. Don't surprise me, and don't rush me. I'm a planner." Before he could lean back in protest—because she could see it coming—she continued, "You move at warp speed. Like… like Thor's hammer. And it freaks me out. I really do need some boundaries. And then don't get all grumpy and ice me out when I exercise them."

"That's two things. Maybe three." One side of his mouth slowly—glacial-speed slowly—arched up in a smirk. "And I knew Thor was your favorite."

"Yeah? What gave you that idea?" She was blushing like a Victorian virginal bride. She quickly raised her hand. "He deserves it. Thor is loyal and strong and..."

He grasped her wrist and brought her hand to his lips. "I'll work on my boundaries and stop thinking it means something more than it does."

"What else would it mean?"

"That you don't want me around at all."

Her belly somersaulted. He honestly thought anyone wouldn't want him around? She almost said something to that effect then thought better of it. That Jennifer chick could be listening. "I like it when you're around." She raised a finger. "And not just because you come bearing power tools."

"Thought they turned you on."

"You turn me on." She couldn't believe she'd said it, but some honesty dam had broken. "One more thing. I need you to know I have never tried to pay you off. Just pay you an honest wage. I'm not a user. Not even a very good user of power tools."

"I know that. But I disagree on the tools. You're amazing at it, Eve."

She bumped him with her shoulder. "Flatterer." She slapped her sides with her hands. "So, I guess I'm not too independent to try to figure things out, and share..." She couldn't even say the words *"my life."*

"Thor?" he asked, an eyebrow raised.

An easy chuckle released from her throat. "Yes, Thor."

"Good. Now, can I finish changing your tire?"

Brent didn't wait for her answer because he kissed her

long and hard until she breathed into his mouth. Finally, he broke the kiss.

"Only if you show me how, too." God, she panted.

"My stubborn woman."

"Quicksilver."

"I'd rather be Iron Man."

"Deal."

He shucked off his jacket and rolled up his sleeves, and she let him change her tire. So, progress on her part? Forget power tools, working the handheld ones did fantastic things to the muscles in his arms.

He asked her to spend the night at his house that night, and she really, really wanted to.

A quick call to Scarlett sealed the deal. Thor turned out to be fine and her friend, who didn't own a TV set at home, was more than happy to binge her Avengers collection while Eve *"finally was giving in to the inevitable,"* as Scarlett had declared.

After he got her old tire in her trunk, she followed his taillights all the way to his house. When she pulled in behind him in his drive, she glanced down at her phone to once more read what Scarlet had sent as inspiration, written in her latest book draft. It was a love letter from her hero to her heroine. Eve shook her head, still in disbelief over what she'd sent.

*Will there be no end to discovering new things in you?*

*Like how the inside of your thighs grow hot when I'm between them.*

*How you say my name when I kiss you between your legs, like licking honey off the wings of a butterfly.*

*How you moan as I enter you that first time. Soft and powerful.*

*And tonight, when your back is burned from the rug because, yes, I took you on that god-awful rope rug in front of the fireplace,*

*I will learn even more. Then I will kiss the bruises and tell you you're beautiful. Because you are. And you are mine.*

Eve had never read anything of Scarlett's before. The woman had some depth and a very dirty mind. Eve only hoped she hadn't wet her car seat.

Brent rounded the front of her car and cracked open the car door. "Everything okay?" He glanced down at the phone in her hand. "Thor get stuck again?"

She tittered a little. "No. Everything's great." She took his hand and he helped her out. "You don't have a rope rug in front of your fireplace, do you?"

His brows pinched together. "No, why?"

"Oh, no reason."

They didn't collapse in lust before his large, beautiful fireplace. Instead, he took her straight into his bedroom. Maybe loving someone made you do things you never thought you would. She let him place her in the middle of his California king in the most amazing bedroom. Not a single thought of doing anything else crossed her mind.

Panes of stained glass were propped up in every window. She didn't pay much attention to them. His green eyes were all she needed to see. She'd study the panes in the morning because she most definitely would be there when dawn broke.

Maybe Scarlett's words were magic.

*Nah.* Brent was.

# 35

She laced her fingers through Brent's and swung his arm high so she could pirouette underneath it. For the last six weeks, they'd been taking their Friday night stroll up Poplar Avenue after gorging themselves with crabs and beer—their new weekend ritual after a week of classes, renovations, and work.

They saw each other when they could, and when they didn't, well, it was okay. She managed to inch her GPA back up, making the 4.0 she wanted—by a tenth of a point. Brent even got in the action, drilling her on a Winston Churchill speech she had to memorize and recite to her history professor.

His dad was feeling better but still needed him around, mostly just to hang with him. Eve loved that about Brent, how he brought such peace to people.

Her family certainly had adopted him wholeheartedly, including him in every single party invitation and family gathering, though he and Eve limited their time at them. Her mother couldn't help herself, dropping hints about marriage and family every five seconds. Persy, too.

Brent had even taken her father truck shopping, which floored Eve. Her dad and trucks didn't mix.

She and Brent had developed a comforting routine, however—nothing too fast, nothing too slow. It was exactly the right speed.

He had added at least a dozen more projects to her renovation list, and he spent two nights at her house during the week. Thor would curl up between them, and they often woke up staring across his furry body at one another. Thor refused to sleep at the end of the bed now that he had two bed warmers at his disposal.

On the weekends? She spent a lot of Saturday evenings at Brent's amazing house with him and Homer, studying for her final exams. She loved his old house with its rich wood smells and oversized furniture to lounge on.

He had a shed in his backyard chock full of power tools that he was showing her how to use. It was fun—putting on her gloves and safety goggles and chopping and cutting stuff for the heck of it. She especially loved Gretel, though she was one heavy girl. It was oddly satisfying to hear the wood finally split down the middle, the two halves of the limbs she'd been practicing on baring their creamy white center.

Thor was getting used to Homer's smell on her clothes, too. At first, he hid under the bed when she returned home on Sunday afternoons, but now, he seemed to barely notice some of her clothes carried *eau du golden lab*. He'd curl up to her for extra cuddles, which she gave him in spades for his generosity in sharing her and being alone for a whole twenty-four hours.

Brent twirled her in the street. "Dad says *'hi.'* I think he might have a crush on you."

She laughed. "I might have a crush on your mom." She was the really handy one. They'd been visiting with them whenever they could. His mom seemed super interested in the home renovation lessons she was learning from Brent.

"Oh." Eve reached into her back pocket. "That reminds me. I have a gift for your dad. To use after his last chemo treatment next week." She pulled it out of her jeans.

"Is that…" He blinked at her offering—her last Thor bandage.

"I was saving him for something special, so… your dad is pretty special."

He cleared his throat and stared at the small thing for so long, she had to lift his hand and place it in his palm.

"But it's your last one," he said.

"Like your dad's chemo. I have high hopes it's the last one he'll ever have," she clarified. "Maybe it'll bring him luck." God, she hoped so. She really loved the Shadwells—all of them.

He engulfed her in a hug. She felt him swallow against her forehead. "Now you can tell me. It really is all about the long flowing hair, isn't it?"

She laughed into his shirt. "It's his big, manly muscles." She playfully bit into his pec.

When he released her, his eyes were wet. They only made his lashes look ever glossier. "I have a surprise for you. I'm telling you in advance. It's happening in about ten more steps. Ready?"

He was getting really good at giving her a heads up on things. And sticking around to talk things out if they disagreed.

"Come on." He tugged her along until they stopped in front of one of their favorite homes, a little Arts and Crafts bungalow in cheery yellow with brown trim. A "For Sale" sign had been stuck in the ground sometime over the week. "I know what I'm going to do moving forward."

"What's that?"

"Renovate houses. Flip them. Like this one." That's when she noticed the sign had a big "SOLD" banner across it.

"You might be too late on this one." She rested her hand on its adorable white picket fence. "Plus, it's a risky business. Listen to the business major here, and someone who's blown through her entire reno budget in less than three months."

"Ah, but you have an 'in' with a—what did you call me?"

"A renovation specialist."

"See, you're already a business branding genius."

"But Brent, are you serious? About flipping houses?"

"I am. That's something you've done for me, Eve. You are so focused, it showed me I could be a bit more, too. So…" He pushed open the gate of the house.

"Brent," she whispered loudly. "What are you doing?"

"Focusing." He yanked up the "For Sale" sign from the ground. "I bought it this morning. No time like the present."

"You already decided." His patience thing had a big learning curve yet to master.

He smirked toward her. "I'm independent like that."

God, he was adorable—and hot. She'd never grow tired of that boyish grin that soaked her panties and made her feel all was right with the world for once. "Are you sure?"

"Never been more sure in my life. Except for you being my girlfriend."

She pinked—like she did every time she heard that term. She would have thought she'd have gotten used to it by now.

"Need a business development manager? I mean, for Shadwell Enterprises?"

He pointed at her. "See? I knew you'd be good at this. Tell you what." He set the sign against the fence and swung the gate open for her to enter. "Once you earn your degree, I'll grant you an interview."

"How generous of you." She slapped her hand over her sternum.

He shrugged. "Eh. I'm tight with the owner. A big, fat cat named Thor."

Her mind slipped through the next few years like an old-fashioned rolodex on a wheel. She could see it. Getting her degree in a few weeks. Graduating. Working with her father or Brent. Maybe even walking down an aisle in white. Or blue because it was a better color for her.

She looked at Brent. "How much does it pay? Because my dad is offering health insurance, too. And a parking space."

"That's it?"

"I know, it's so beneath my skills. I mean, I know how to work a *chainsaw* now." She pointed at her bicep.

"Much call for that in mergers and acquisitions?"

"You wouldn't believe it."

"Well, given I bought this one today," he pointed up at a beautiful green and burgundy-colored stained-glass window, "I can pay, uh, nothing? But I'll let you fondle my sander."

"Ooo, tough one. And the drywall saw? Because Thor most definitely has not learned his lesson." Together, they'd had to get him out from a forgotten crawl space opening in her closet, giving him access to the internal rafters. "Or," she sidled closer to him, "let me drive Hans."

"Now you're pushing it. I got something better. How about a fifty-fifty partnership after you get your degree, Miss Chatham? And whenever you feel like starting?"

A partnership? When she felt like it? And he wanted her to be a college graduate. In fact, he sounded insistent. This man truly was too good to be true.

"On one condition. You be my boyfriend, too." She hadn't used that term yet, though he was free with the girlfriend moniker.

"A boyfriend." He measured the words.

"Yes. Boyfriends and girlfriends can be in business together." She thought about her mother and father around that one. Her father had told her she'd have a job with him, but only if she wanted it and to make up her own mind.

"Yes, I believe they can. There's just one thing." He brushed a finger across his jaw. "Who's going to break the news to Thor? I mean, that you may be spending even more time with another man your life."

She wrapped her arms around his waist and tipped her head back. "Homer?"

He laughed. "He's not getting near those paws again."

"We might have to try a second reunion. I mean, since we're going to be paw-tners."

"Partners and paw-tners. I like it."

And then he kissed her until her knees gave out. She didn't mind one bit when he held her up because her mother was right. Everyone needs backup. She'd be Brent's, and he would be hers.

(Thor, however, could be up to anything in the future.)

Thank you for reading
***It Was All The Cat's Fault.***

If you loved this story, you'll love the next story in the Meet Cute series, ***It Was All the Daisy's Fault.*** Request it at your favorite bookstore or library. Or find it on Amazon and Barnes and Noble.

Writing is Scarlett's destiny, her purpose in life. *If* she could finish her novel. She just keeps getting interrupted by all the people in need—and animals and trees and flowers.

Like Cole. He splats face-first before her feet like it was fate. Kismet. A *sign*. He is just the inspiration she needs for her book. Tall, dark hair, glittering eyes. A surgeon sporting a super-hot, disapproving stern face. Surely, a smile lived inside him somewhere.

But Cole has no plans to get involved with anyone. Certainly not with a sassy, hippie who thinks flowers have *feelings*. Still, somehow he keeps tripping into her, even when he tries his hardest to stay away.

That incredible urge to back her up against a wall and do *things* to her? That chemistry couldn't be real. It just couldn't be.

**A meet cute, opposites attract, can't-help-yourself, steamy romantic comedy.**

## ALSO BY ELIZABETH SAFLEUR

*Sexy rom-coms:*

The Sassy Nanny Dilemma

It Was All The Pie's Fault

It Was All the Cat's Fault

It Was All the Daisy's Fault

*Short story collections:*

Finally, Yours

Finally, His

Finally, Mine

*Steamy Contemporary romance:*

Tough Road

Tough Luck

Tough Break

Tough Love

*Erotic romance with BDSM:*

Elite

Holiday Ties

Untouchable

Perfect

Riptide

Lucky

Fearless

Invincible

*Femme Domme:*

The White House Gets A Spanking

Spanking the Senator

# ABOUT THE AUTHOR

Elizabeth SaFleur writes award-winning, luscious romance from 28 wildlife-filled acres, hikes in her spare time and is a certifiable tea snob.

Find out more about Elizabeth on her web site at www.ElizabethSaFleur or join her private Facebook group, Elizabeth's Playroom.

Follow her on TikTok (@ElizabethSaFleurAuthor) and Instagram (@ElizabethLoveStory), too.

Printed in Great Britain
by Amazon